− 2 DEC 2009		

DEADLY QUARREL

DEADLY QUARREL

An Anne Cartier Mystery

Charles O'Brien

This first world edition published 2009
in Great Britain and in the USA by
SEVERN HOUSE PUBLISHERS LTD of
9–15 High Street, Sutton, Surrey, England, SM1 1DF.
Trade paperback edition published
in Great Britain and the USA 2009 by
SEVERN HOUSE PUBLISHERS LTD

British Library Cataloguing in Publication Data

O'Brien, Charles, 1927-
  Deadly quarrel
  1. Attempted murder - Fiction 2. Inheritance and succession
  - Fiction 3. Great Britain - Social life and customs - 18th
  century - Fiction 4. Detective and mystery stories
  I. Title
  813.5'4[F]

ISBN-13: 978-0-7278-6740-7   (cased)
ISBN-13: 978-1-84751-130-0   (trade paper)

All Severn House titles are printed on acid-free paper.

Typeset by Palimpsest Book Production Ltd.,
Grangemouth, Stirlingshire, Scotland.
Printed and bound in Great Britain by
MPG Books Ltd., Bodmin, Cornwall.

ACKNOWLEDGEMENTS

I wish to thank Andy Sheldon for the use of his computer skills. I am also grateful to Gudveig Baarli for assisting with the maps, to Jennifer Nelson of Gallaudet University for helpful advice on issues pertaining to deafness, and to the professionals at Severn House who produced this book. My agent Evan Marshall and Fronia Simpson read drafts of the novel and contributed much to its improvement. Finally, my wife Elvy, art historian, deserves special mention for her editorial eye and her support without which the novel would not have been written.

LIST OF MAIN CHARACTERS

IN ORDER OF FIRST APPEARANCE

Anne Cartier: *teacher of deaf children, former music hall entertainer, and wife of Colonel Paul de Saint-Martin*

Sir Abraham Parker: *baronet, patriarch of the Parker family*

Beverly Parker: *Thomas Parker's estranged wife, Anne Cartier's cousin*

Seth Judd: *sea captain, illegitimate eldest son of Abraham Parker, half-brother of Oliver and Thomas Parker*

Catherine Judd: *Seth's mother and Abraham Parker's former mistress*

Oliver Parker: *Abraham Parker's oldest legitimate son and heir to his fortune*

Martha Parker: *Oliver's wife*

Janice Parker: *Oliver and Martha Parker's daughter*

Thomas Parker: *Abraham Parker's youngest son, Beverly Parker's husband and Janice's guardian*

Amelia Swan: *Thomas Parker's mistress*

Paul de Saint-Martin: *Anne Cartier's husband, provost of the French Royal Highway Patrol*

André Cartier: *Anne's paternal grandfather and wealthy gunsmith*

Jacob Woodhouse: *son of David Woodhouse, Quaker printer and abolitionist in Bath*

Harriet Ware: *Anne Cartier's friend; prominent soprano and actress at the Bath Royal Theatre*

Peter Cartier: *André's nephew and Anne's cousin; a widower and justice of the peace in London*

Dick Burton: *retired Bow Street London officer*

Nate Taylor: *Seth Judd's assistant for smuggling; also a waiter at the Upper Assembly Rooms in Bath*

William Williams: *retired Admiralty judge*

Isaac Grimes: *young seaman from the Parker estate*

Agnes Grimes: *widow, former servant on the Parker estate, Isaac's mother*

BRITAIN AND FRANCE
1789

SCOTLAND

NORTH SEA

Edinburgh

IRELAND

ENGLAND

Waterford

WALES

Bristol
Bath
Morland Court

London

Bristol Channel

Calais

Channel

N

Paris

FRANCE

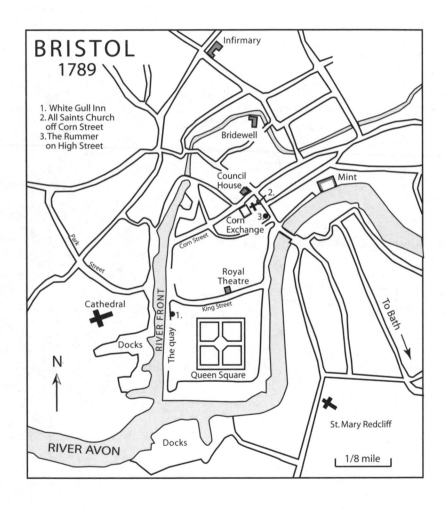

BRISTOL
1789

1. White Gull Inn
2. All Saints Church off Corn Street
3. The Rummer on High Street

Infirmary

Bridewell

Council House

Mint

2.

3.

Corn Exchange

Park Street

Corn Street

Royal Theatre

King Street

RIVER FRONT

The quay

1.

Cathedral

Docks

Queen Square

N

To Bath

St. Mary Redcliff

RIVER AVON

Docks

1/8 mile

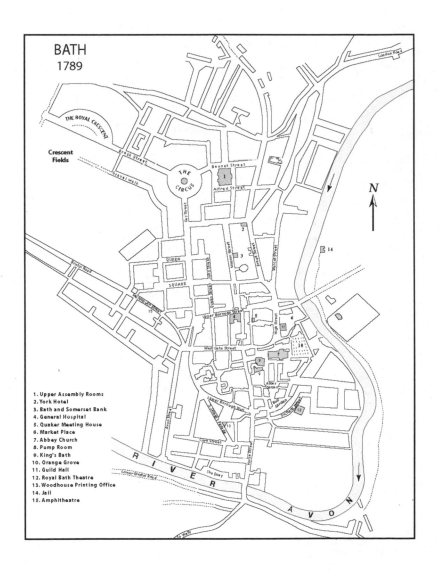

BATH
1789

THE ROYAL CRESCENT

Crescent
Fields

Brock Street

Gravel Walk

THE CIRCUS

Bennet Street

Alfred Street

Royal Road

Bristol Road

QUEEN

SQUARE

N

1. Upper Assembly Rooms
2. York Hotel
3. Bath and Somerset Bank
4. General Hospital
5. Quaker Meeting House
6. Market Place
7. Abbey Church
8. Pump Room
9. King's Bath
10. Orange Grove
11. Guild Hall
12. Royal Bath Theatre
13. Woodhouse Printing Office
14. Jail
15. Amphitheatre

West Gate Street

Corn Street

RIVER

The Quay

AVON

London Road

To Wells

Lower Bristol Road

A WARNING

Morland Court, the Parker estate, near Bristol,
Tuesday, 1 June 1773

E arly in the afternoon, a liveried servant led young Annie
Cartier into the old baronet's room. Often during his
health's decline, when he was mostly confined to his bed,
he had asked her to sing and dance for him. She did this
gladly for the pleasure that it gave him. Only fifteen, she was
unaccustomed to witnessing the slow approach of death. As many
times as she saw Sir Abraham Parker, she continued to be shocked.
He looked like a barely living skeleton. This might be the last
time that he would hear her sing.

Propped up with pillows, he smiled kindly when he saw
her. She was touched. His smiles were rare – and usually
ironic. Her ballads and airs seemed to take him back to his
childhood, a much less stressful time in his life, before he
grew absorbed in the business of gaining wealth. He once
mentioned that she reminded him of a nanny he loved who
used to sing for him.

Annie asked how he felt.

'I'm weak, but still able to enjoy your sweet voice. What
will it be?'

'An Irish air, this time, a simple lullaby.' As she sang, he
closed his eyes. The gentle melody calmed his laboured
breathing, washed lines of care from his pallid face. At the
end, his eyes remained closed for a few moments. He seemed
to savour the melody. His lips moved slightly, as if he were
humming. Then he gazed at her fondly and thanked her.

'What will you do this summer?' he asked.

'My parents and I shall spend a month entertaining a noble
French family at their estate, Beaumont, a few miles south of
Paris. I'll sing French as well as English ballads and play
Puck in Shakespeare's *A Midsummer Night's Dream*. This is
my last day at Morland Court.'

'I'm sorry to lose you,' he said. 'You have some of Puck's

spirit, especially the playfulness. I wish my sons had it. I envy the French family.'

She thanked him and bid him goodbye.

For a moment she stood in the open doorway and looked back. He said, 'I'll remember you, Annie. One of the many regrets of my life is that you aren't my daughter. I'm unhappy with my sons.' He sighed. 'Enough of them! I want your song to linger in my mind after you're gone. Farewell.'

She closed the door gently and breathed a prayer for the old man.

At the head of the stairs, she met her cousin, Beverly, who had recently married into the Parker family. Her husband was Thomas, the youngest of the baronet's three sons, the most handsome and amiable – and a bit of a fop.

'How did Old Parker look?' she asked. He was only called Old Parker behind his back.

'Poorly,' Annie replied.

'He's writing his will, isn't he?'

'Not while I was with him.' Annie thought her cousin showed too much interest in money and the fine things it could buy.

Beverly glanced over her shoulder. 'The family thinks he'll die any day now.'

Annie shook her head. 'They're like vultures hanging over his body. He's a most tenacious man and may live for months.' She started down the stairs.

But Beverly had more on her mind. 'Let's talk outside where we can be alone.'

'At the Observatory,' Annie suggested. 'Nobody ever goes there at this hour. They're napping or playing at cards.'

Under a blue, sun-soaked sky, the cousins walked up the hill to the west of the manor house. On its highest point they reached a whitewashed octagonal building, crowned by a balustrade. Sir Abraham had added a platform to the building's flat roof and mounted a telescope. He used to watch ships sailing to and from the port of Bristol, many of them carrying his goods. He wasn't much interested in the stars.

The two women entered the building and climbed up a narrow iron stairway to the platform. A stout canvas covered the telescope, so they let it be. A gentle westerly wind billowed their skirts as they looked out over a sheep pasture stretching for half a mile to the Bristol Channel. A dozen ships rocked calmly in the channel, sails furled, waiting for high tide to carry them into the city's harbour. The Welsh coast lay in the distance.

Beverly turned to Annie. 'As your older and wiser cousin, I want to warn you about Seth Judd.'

'I know him, Sir Abraham's illegitimate son, the oldest of his boys. Has he threatened me?'

'Your blooming beauty seems to fascinate him. He has been talking about you in the company of his lusty male friends. And because you're a young singer and an actress, he thinks it shouldn't be too difficult to . . .' Beverly paused. 'How shall I say this? Well, I'll use his words. He intends "to bed you". He's pressed for time since he'll soon sail for Jamaica on one of his father's ships.'

Annie felt her cheeks flush hot. 'Presumptuous man! Handsome and strong, to be sure, but he's a cruel brute. When he rides, he lashes the horse more than he needs to. He smiles as his spurs dig into the horse's side. I've heard that he treats kitchen maids and Bristol prostitutes in much the same way.'

The two women came down from the roof and started back to the manor house. 'Thank you for the warning, Beverly. I'll watch out for him.'

Annie went to her room in the upper floor of the manor house to pack her trunk. She asked her maid, a young country girl, 'Please fetch my undergarments that have dried outside in the laundry shed.' A few minutes after the maid left, Annie happened to glance out the window. The maid was walking towards the shed. Annie was about to return to the trunk when she noticed a man hiding in the shed's shadow, spying on the maid.

Annie retrieved her opera glass, studied the man and gasped. It was Seth Judd. He emerged furtively and slipped into the shed. The maid had earlier complained that Judd followed her and taunted her with lewd remarks. In an instant Annie realized that he intended to harm the maid and had to be stopped.

She rushed to the door, down the stairs, and out to the shed.
For a moment she listened to muffled voices. Then she heard
the maid cry out, 'No!'

Annie tried the door. It was latched. She hammered on the
door with both fists and shouted, 'Open up, Seth, or I'll call
my friend, the groom, and every man in sight. We'll break down
the door.' For a few moments, there was dead silence inside.
Then the latch was pulled and Judd slipped out, shutting the
door behind him.

'You crazy bitch, what do you think you're doing?' A tall,
muscular man, he leaned over her, jaw thrust out, eyes blazing.

She stepped back, stared at his groin and said calmly, 'Button
your breeches, Seth. You look foolish.'

He glanced down, confused and embarrassed, then fumbled
with his buttons. Finally, he sputtered, 'What I do with the
maid is none of your business.' His words took on a whining
tone. 'She agreed to this meeting.'

'She did not!' Annie retorted. 'I sent her here, saw you
sneak into the shed, heard her scream.' Annie sneered at him.
'Now leave her alone or I'll report you to Sir Abraham. He's
still the master at Morland Court.'

Men working nearby had become curious and moved towards
the shed. The groom stepped out of the stable, frowning. Judd
glanced at the men, then stared at Annie, his eyes burning with
impotent malice. He hissed, 'You'll pay for this, someday, I
promise.' He squared his shoulders and marched off.

Annie ignored him and entered the shed. The maid was
crouched in a corner, sobbing, her clothes in disarray. Annie
raised her up and brought her back to the room. 'Rest here,
I'll finish the packing. Sleep with me tonight. The rogue will
soon be thousands of miles away. Good riddance! When I'm
gone, the housekeeper will look after you.'

A few moments later, as Annie laid a gown in the trunk,
her hands began to tremble and her knees wobbled. Then
her whole body shook. She leaned against the wall, gulping
air. The fright passed and her nerves returned nearly to
normal. But she was certain that Seth Judd had not finished
with her.

A DYING MAN'S WILL

Morland Court, Wednesday, 17 November 1773

I t was a cold, damp evening. Seth Judd burst into the kitchen where his mother, Catherine, was stirring a pot of stew. He had only recently returned to Bristol from Jamaica with a rich cargo of sugar and rum. 'My father is close to dying!' he cried.

He pulled off his boots and hung up his coat. 'The steward has called the estate's staff to the great hall an hour from now for the reading of father's will. The old man wants them all to hear it before he dies.'

Catherine whacked the kitchen counter with her spoon. 'I suppose the steward made it clear where we should stand – among the servants.'

'Yes, Oliver is gathering the family. They'll enter the hall in rank and order – Oliver in the lead, of course.'

Catherine threw down the spoon, seized her son by the shoulders. 'Seth, don't expect your father to finally recognize you as his son. He should but he won't. His wife has gained too much influence over him. You are the oldest of his sons – and by far the most able, but you are illegitimate and must yield to her Oliver.'

She returned to stirring and added under her breath, 'Yes, Oliver must lead, though he's a weak, undeserving man, more like a bank clerk than a man soon to become a baronet and lord of the manor.'

Seth's anger flared up, stoked by his mother's. For years Catherine Judd had been Parker's wife in everything but name. But when he found a rich woman who would have him, he married her and moved his faithful mistress and their son from the manor house to a cottage nearby and reduced her to a domestic's rank.

Several years later, he longed again for Catherine's sexual favours. To enhance his frequent visits, he enlarged and embellished her cottage. His shrewish wife never objected. Seth believed she tacitly encouraged her husband's infidelity, once she had produced two sons. She cared only that he should be discreet and not bring shame upon her.

'For now, mother, I'll play the humble, grateful servant, but not forever. Later, we'll have a conversation and I'll reveal to you the drift of my thinking.'

As Seth and his mother entered the hall, the steward met them with a list in his hand. He checked off their names, and then waved them to the back of the room, where many servants were already standing. Again Seth felt a sharp pang of resentment. His mother gave him a cautionary glance, and he held his tongue.

He found a tall stool for his mother from which she could watch the proceedings. Then he joined a few other bold servants who edged their way from the back of the hall to one side for a better view.

Seth looked about him with awe. A galaxy of lighted sconces and chandeliers threw off a lively golden light, even up to the lofty wooden hammer beam ceiling. This was the main room of the manor house, dating from the reign of Elizabeth, and now used for major festivals and solemn occasions. Abraham Parker loved to preside here, his family and servants gathered like sheep before him.

Over the entrance hung large oil portraits of him and his wife at the time of their marriage. He was in his vigorous prime with jutting jaw and crafty eyes. She was a small, thin-lipped, sallow-faced woman with a shifty, calculating gaze. At their marriage she had added vast fertile lands to his estate. Thanks to her energetic and vigilant oversight, it had prospered. Meanwhile, her husband tended to his thriving commerce in slaves and sugar and grew prominent in nearby Bristol's civic life.

Tonight, acting the baronet, he sat on a dais in an ancient, ornate chair. But, with a blanket on his lap and a woollen cap on his head, he was an emaciated, pale spectre of himself. Still, his rheumy eyes surveyed the crowd, gauging each of them in his feverish mind, as if he would strike from his will anyone showing him insufficient respect.

The family appeared at the door and were led by the steward to the row of chairs below the dais. Dull-witted Oliver and his wife, Martha, came first. She was a thoughtful, kindly woman, Seth admitted, and she had given Oliver an infant daughter, Janice, but no son.

The next person to arrive was charming, handsome, irresolute Thomas, preening like a peacock. His beautiful wife, Beverly, followed gracefully a few steps behind. From this parade Seth concluded that the Parker women of this generation were much superior to their men.

Seth's eyes had often lingered on Beverly's thick, wavy brown hair, clear, creamy complexion, golden brown eyes, and shapely figure. He had boldly tried to draw a smiling glance from her, but she ignored him as if he were a country lout. Following her was her cousin, Miss Anne Cartier, a frequent visitor to the estate. Tall, slender, blonde, and blue-eyed – she had an engaging, forward look and an easy manner.

The steward – a scandal monger – had told Seth in a hushed voice that she sang and danced with her stepfather in London music halls and could ride a horse and shoot like a cavalryman. She soothed Old Parker with ballads and airs and would receive the promise of a stipend today. A clever woman and only fifteen.

But Seth had a score to settle with her. Back in June she had butted into his affair with a maid, shamed him publicly, and claimed she'd report him to Old Parker.

'A fetching morsel, nonetheless,' Seth murmured to himself. Barmaids and servant girls never fully satisfied him. Even before his voyage to Jamaica, he had lusted for her. Now he wanted her more than ever. Yesterday, he had followed her into the stable, hoping to engage her in conversation and pretend to make amends. From a distance she noticed him, then studied him with a critical eye. When he approached her, she frowned and walked away, probably afraid of him. He would wait for a better opportunity.

The last person to enter the hall was Madame Parker, a shrunken, bird-like figure. She shuffled to her place on the bench without a glance at her husband or her family, preoccupied apparently with the portion of his fortune that he was about to leave to her.

On the bench behind the family sat the senior members of the staff: the steward, the housekeeper, the cook, the groom, the chaplain, and the butler. Fearful of the old man's whims and his tenacious recall of past missteps, they tried in vain to appear composed. But their facial twitches and hand wringing betrayed their fears.

When everyone was in place, Sir Abraham raised a hand.

A nervous silence came over the room. He beckoned his solicitor who was standing stiffly to one side. He came forward,
pulled papers from a portfolio, and began to read.

In a loud, clear voice he announced that Mr Oliver Parker
would inherit the family estate and a trust fund comprising most
of his father's wealth in banknotes and other financial papers.
Mr Thomas Parker would receive a modest annual allowance
from the trust fund's income. Much of the art, furniture, and
other moveable property, plus an allowance from the trust fund,
would go to old Mrs Parker. The senior servants would each be
given small stipends and the promise of pensions. Seth and his
mother would retain the use of their cottage. They, and the rest
of the servants, would receive lesser benefits. Small gifts were
to go to Miss Cartier and other acquaintances, as well as to a
variety of local charities.

None of this surprised Seth. By Common Law and custom
the bulk of the estate was supposed to pass virtually intact to
the eldest son. But Seth objected that *he* was in fact the eldest,
as well as the most deserving. He felt cheated and very angry.

On a cue from Oliver, the assembly politely clapped. He
announced that the family invited everyone to a reception in
the hall in honour of Sir Abraham. He bowed to the old man.
The crowd added a subdued murmur of appreciation. Sir
Abraham gave a signal. Servants appeared and carried him
from the room. Food and drinks soon arrived, together with
a more festive atmosphere.

Pale, trembling with rage, Catherine turned to Seth. 'We
must leave. I feel ill.'

Seth closed the cottage door behind him and shut out the
November chill. Then he helped his mother into a chair by
the hearth and wrapped her in a blanket. He stirred the glowing
embers and laid on wood. In a few minutes a fire blazed and
soon heated the room. Meanwhile he poured glasses of hot
buttered rum and served his mother and himself. By the time
he joined her at the fire and they raised their glasses, her rage
had subsided.

'Son,' she began, 'you said you had a plan.'

'Yes,' he replied and thoughtfully sipped from his glass. 'During
the past few years, I've learned to show deference to persons of
high rank, to flatter them and to make them trust me.'

'Yes, son, I've noticed how you speak to your brother, Oliver, as if you genuinely respect him.' Her voice carried a hint of reproach.

Seth shook his head. 'Oliver is greedy and not very clever. In our conversations recently I proposed sheathing the hull of his newest ship with copper. By increasing its speed during the Atlantic crossing, I would lose fewer slaves. The copper would also reduce maintenance costs. He liked the prospect of greater profits and will hire me as the ship's captain in the spring.'

Catherine seemed confused. 'He accepted what appears to be an excellent proposal. Is he not clever?'

Seth replied with a sneer. 'When he put me in charge, he hadn't figured out that I'm his mortal enemy. In the coming years I'm going to master the shipping business and ingratiate myself with its principal personages. I'll make myself indispensable to Oliver – that is, until I find an opportunity to destroy him. It may take me twenty years, but somehow I'll seize his place at the manor and sit in Old Parker's chair in the great hall.'

She stared at him for a long moment. 'Contrary to common sense, I believe you can do it, but not peacefully or without a bloody struggle. Don't underestimate Oliver. He may not be as easy to fool, as you seem to think. He might sense your intention and oppose you. If you were to kill him, you would still face his brother, Thomas, and perhaps other obstacles that you can't even imagine now.'

He nodded. 'That doesn't matter, mother. I intend to claim my birthright, come what may.'

His mother raised her hand in a blessing. 'If I'm still alive twenty years from now, and see you sitting in that ancient chair, I'll go to my grave content.'

DEATH AT SEA

The Bristol Channel, Thursday, 21 June 1782

On a dark, cloudy night, the ship *Mercury* from Ireland sailed towards Bristol. A strong southwesterly wind filled the sails. The small sloop sliced through the waves like a hot blade through butter. After a few hours on deck, Oliver Parker and his wife, Martha, retired to their tight little cabin and lit a lamp.

'Something's afoot,' said Martha, uneasily. 'Since we left Waterford, the captain's mood has changed. He's preoccupied. I smell fear or anxiety on him. That's not typical. He's such a bold man, a privateer, so used to danger at sea. Perhaps he senses danger. We're still at war with the French and the Americans. These waters aren't safe. The American captain John Paul Jones has taken many prizes here. We don't have a single cannon to defend ourselves.'

'The danger is all in your imagination, my dear Martha. This sloop is light and fast, rigged for two seamen, and can outrun every ship afloat.'

'Still, I wish you hadn't brought that gold on board. It's very tempting to the common sort of seamen, like Grimes and Taylor, or even our Captain Seth. It might also entice French privateers who operate out of Ireland and have spies there.'

'Rest easy. I've kept our treasure hidden from everyone. This is the best way to bring it to England and take it past customs undetected. They will think this was merely a pleasure trip to our properties in Ireland.'

'Yes,' she remarked wryly. 'That's why I had to accompany you and throw a cloak of respectability over your criminal scheme. I'd much rather have stayed home with our sickly little Janice. I feel badly having left her.'

'Don't fret,' he chided her. 'I couldn't very well rent a thirty-gun frigate with a crew of seventy, plus royal marines, and sail into Bristol. Someone might wonder what I had hidden aboard.' He checked his pistol, hid it under the bed next to the chest of gold, and slipped under the covers next to his wife.

After saying her prayers, Martha opened the locket that she wore around her neck. For a moment she gazed tenderly at the portrait of her bright, lovely daughter Janice. They were the best of friends. Then she extinguished the lamp.

But anxiety kept sleep at bay; fear crept into her mind. This voyage would end in disaster. What would then happen to Janice? Oliver had provided well for her financial future, but he had designated his brother, Thomas, to act as her guardian. Martha shuddered at the thought and began to weep. Thomas was selfish, irresponsible, and utterly devoid of sympathy for Janice. For what seemed like hours, Martha lay on her back, tortured by irrational fears for her daughter and herself. Finally, the rocking motion of the ship lulled her to sleep.

Suddenly, the couple were awakened and sat up. The captain stood before them. He hung his lantern on a hook and patted the long knife on his belt. 'Give me the gold, Brother Parker. We'll divide it. You cheated me once; I want my fair share now. Don't threaten me with the law. You hid the gold from the Admiralty's Prize Court, so this is a reckoning between thieves.'

'Have you lost your mind, Seth?' asked Oliver, a mixture of fear and anger in his voice. 'You can't possibly think you can get away with this.'

'Of course I can. Over the years, I've gathered enough evidence of fraud in your business practices to put you in prison for life. From now on you will do as I say. In the past, you've treated me like a servant. I took most of the risks while you received most of the profits. Now I'm going to be your senior partner with an appropriate voice in our affairs. We'll split the profits, fifty-fifty.'

'You bastard! This is an outrage! I'll have you hanged before I'll be your partner.'

The captain's eyes narrowed, his jaw grew rigid. He drew a pistol from his pocket and cocked it. 'That insult was uncalled for, Oliver. I've changed my mind. I'll take all the gold. Now! Be quick about it.'

Martha tried to calm the trembling in her voice. 'Do as he says, Oliver.'

He stared at her, dazed, as if struggling to comprehend her. Finally, shaking his head, he reached under the bed and seized his pistol . . .

A SUSPICIOUS ACCIDENT

London, Tuesday, 13 October 1789

It was early afternoon, a fog had settled upon London, bringing a premature twilight to the city. Janice Parker glanced out the carriage window into a familiar cobbled alley off Old Bond Street. To the left and right were rows of three-storey brick buildings. At the moment many shops were closed for dinner – others for vacation. The alley was free of carts and tradesmen. Halfway down the alley, a scaffold stood above the milliner's shop, but the workers were not in sight.

Janice's older companion, Amelia Swan, leaned out the other window and called to the coachman. Janice, who was deaf, couldn't see Amelia's lips. But she must be telling him to stop here and wait for them. The alley was too narrow for the carriage. Sometimes Janice would stretch out her arms and touch the opposite walls.

The two women set off at a brisk pace, Amelia carrying a basket filled with strips of silk cloth. At the shop, Amelia faced Janice and spoke slowly and distinctly. 'I'll visit with the milliner for a few minutes. She promised to show me her latest hats and ribbons. They must be spectacular. Her silk is of the highest quality. Are you sure that you want to wait outside?'

'Yes,' Janice said. She had lost her hearing five years ago as a twelve-year-old child, so she could still speak, though she preferred to sign. She now recalled her first visit to the milliner, two months ago, together with Amelia. The hats on display were large, silly structures of fabric and feathers. A small model warship with sails and rigging crowned one of them.

While Janice had stood off to the side and observed, Amelia and the milliner talked about the latest, most fashionable hats – and Amelia bought one. They went on to discuss various silk cloths and compare Amelia's strips with the milliner's fabrics. Amelia seemed to know the various qualities of silk, where it came from and its price. In fact, the two women appeared to be bargaining though no money exchanged hands.

Later, Janice had asked Amelia if she had once been a milliner herself.

'For a short while,' she had replied, appearing to resent the question. So Janice hadn't probed farther into what looked like a murky past. The servants claimed that Amelia had been a courtesan. Janice wasn't sure what that meant exactly: probably a whore who could sing and dance and offer men more than just her body. Amelia had those talents and was unusually beautiful. She had an uncanny ability to beguile a silly man like Thomas Parker, Janice's uncle and guardian.

That first visit to the milliner's shop had been an unpleasant experience. Janice had felt left out, a silent observer of others' pleasures and preoccupations. Neither Amelia nor the milliner had paid attention to her. She couldn't read the milliner's lips, anyway. She spoke too fast.

Janice hadn't concealed her disinterest in her older companion's discussion of hats and ribbons, silk and feathers, or, for that matter, her taste in anything else. In fact, she didn't like Amelia. Granted, she was a clever woman and articulated well – Janice could read her lips. But she was far too sly and self-absorbed. Janice wondered why Amelia insisted on her company.

To tell the truth, Janice accompanied Amelia chiefly to enjoy the antics of a ginger cat and her kittens in the bow window of the shoemaker's shop across the alley. The kittens jumped and skipped about, climbed up on their patient mother's back, playfully batted and wrestled each other. At this time of day the shop was always closed for dinner.

Janice admitted to herself that the kittens weren't the only reason for following Amelia. Afterwards they would go to an elegant teashop nearby for hot chocolate and candied fruit. Still, she would have much preferred to spend the day with her friend, Charlie Rogers, walking a slack rope, playing chess, or hiking in the countryside around Hackney, a few miles north of London.

Today's visit started out like earlier ones. But after a few minutes in the alley, Janice began to wheeze. Something in the air – a fine dust – set off her asthma. Annoyed, she turned her mind back to last year's vacation on the Mediterranean coast of Nice: its orchards and olive groves, its snow-capped mountains in the distance, its blue skies, mild, clean air, and endless sea. She could breathe so much better than in damp, smoky, stinking London. She closed her eyes and savoured her memories.

Suddenly, bits of stone fell on her shoulder and called her back into the present. She brushed herself off, sensed a movement above her, and instinctively glanced up. At that moment, something hit her from the side, knocked her off balance. She staggered and fell. Her head struck the pavement with a painful crack. She lost consciousness.

Slowly, Janice began to feel pain in her head. A hand touched her and she awoke. She opened her eyes.

'How are you, Janice?' Amelia was looking down at her. 'I'm so worried about you.'

Janice felt with her hand and found a bump on the back of her head. The pain was throbbing now. She glanced at her fingers – they were bloody. She asked Amelia, 'What happened?'

'A large stone block fell from the scaffold above you. Fortunately, a young man passing by pushed you out of the way.'

Janice tried to rise. She had been carried inside the milliner's shop and was lying on the floor. 'I want to thank him.'

'Rest a while. I've given him a coin. He has gone about his business.'

'Did you learn his name?'

'No, he's only an artisan. I had *you* on my mind.' She turned away and started for the door. 'I'll hail our coachman to take us home.'

Several minutes later, Janice felt well enough to rise. Outside the shoemaker's shop the fallen masonry lay in the alley. Janice stopped to study it, even though her head hurt. What had been a large single block of limestone was scattered in pieces over the cobbles. Dazed, she struggled to figure out how this could have happened.

The milliner, who had joined them on the street, looked up, a puzzled expression on her face. She said something in her rapid way. Amelia explained, 'Masons have been working on the building's cornice and are half-finished. They're not here today. No one is up there.'

Janice followed the milliner's gaze and saw that a few blocks of limestone were piled neatly on the scaffold beneath the cornice. She addressed the milliner, then Amelia. 'So how could the stone have fallen?'

'Careless dolts!' exclaimed Amelia. 'They must have left one of the blocks teetering on the edge of the scaffold.' She addressed the milliner. 'You must talk to the master mason about it.'

'I certainly shall! For weeks the masons have dropped dust and debris in front of my shop. I've complained in vain.' Then she turned to Janice who was about to walk to the coach at the end of the alley.

'Young lady,' she said in a low, urgent voice. This time she spoke slowly and clearly. 'If the artisan had not pushed you out of the way, the stone would surely have killed you.'

Janice was now fully awake and frightened. 'This might not have been an accident,' she said to the woman. 'Could someone have tried to kill me?'

The milliner frowned. 'Well, I don't think so. Still, I'd better call the constable.'

A DESPERATE JOURNEY

Paris, Tuesday, 20 October

After breakfast in her garden on a fair morning, Anne Cartier was reading through a stack of recent letters from England. Her husband, Paul, was pruning his rose bushes nearby. A letter from Harriet Ware, a dear friend from Sadler's Wells, and now a popular singer and actress in Bath, urged Anne and Paul to visit her. The apartment above hers on Queen Square would be at their disposal.

Another invitation came from Mr Braidwood at his school in Hackney, where Anne first learned the art of communicating with the deaf. He reported that her friend, Janice Parker, who helped tutor the younger students, would enjoy seeing her again. Braidwood added that he would like to receive her impressions of the Parisian Institute for the Deaf where she worked with its founder and director, the Abbé Charles-Michel de l'Épée.

A letter from Hampstead particularly concerned Anne. Her beloved paternal grandfather, André Cartier, reported the unexpected death of his widowed sister, Adelaide. The letter had a melancholy tone. Only a few years ago, André had lost his wife. His sister moved in to keep him company. Now he was alone again at home. Still, his health was good, so he didn't complain. He had the gun business to occupy his mind and the companionship of the men working in his shop.

Paul left the rose bushes and sat down beside Anne. She asked him to read the letters.

When he had finished, she asked, 'What do you think, Paul?

Should I travel to England and visit these people? Could you go with me?'

He returned the letters and replied, 'I'm sorry, Anne, I can't go. Paris and its countryside are still in crisis. Yesterday, brigands attacked a convoy of grain carts near Villejuif. The Royal Highway Patrol is stretched to its limit and can't afford to lose anyone, not even its provost. But I think you should go, especially for your grandfather's sake. He's dear to you, and you could cheer him up. After all, he's seventy-four years old and has outlived all his closest relatives but you. It's been more than two years since you last saw him.'

'It's not fair to leave you here alone. I should help you.'

'You could indeed be useful. But this is the time to give a month to your family and friends. I'll manage here. Rent a coach and travel with Beverly.'

Anne's cousin, Beverly Parker, was in Paris on her way to London from the County of Nice on the Mediterranean coast. She had arrived late last night, too tired and indisposed for conversation. After a good night's rest, she would explain the reasons for her trip. They were complicated and emotionally draining.

In the winter of 1788, Anne and Paul had spent several months as her guest in a villa near Nice, leased by her husband, Thomas Parker. Shortly after they arrived, Thomas left Nice and returned to his mistress in London, leaving his ward, Janice, and his wife behind. Soon afterwards, his wife fell in love with Jack Grimshaw, an amateur archaeologist in Roman antiquities and the villa's steward. They continued to live together in the villa, even while her husband still held the lease – a curious arrangement, to say the least.

A servant stepped into the garden to announce that Madame Parker was dressed and on her way to the garden. Breakfast would soon be served. Beverly appeared shortly afterward in a pink silk dressing gown, looking refreshed. At thirty-nine, her hair still showed no trace of grey; her complexion was free of lines or wrinkles; and her eyes had kept their luster.

Breakfast arrived. A servant poured coffee and left. Beverly began to speak about mutual acquaintances among the several hundred British winter visitors in Nice. They formed a separate, cozy community on the western edge of the small Italian port city.

At a lull in the conversation Anne asked, 'What's your situation in Nice?'

Beverly appeared to expect the question but hesitated to reply. 'My husband has changed his attitude towards Jack and me. At first, while you were still in Nice, he didn't seem to care about us. Perhaps he was preoccupied with his mistress. But a few weeks after you left, he wrote that he had given up the lease to the villa.'

'How do you and Jack manage?'

'The owner has hired us to work there. The villa is now an inn for wealthy, cultivated winter visitors, including the occasional duke and duchess. We are the innkeepers.'

Doubt flashed through Anne's mind. She hoped it didn't show on her face. She bit into a piece of bread to disguise her feeling. Her cousin had always been a pampered, privileged lady. It was hard to imagine her in a servile role.

Beverly gave her a sardonic smile. 'I *can* manage a household, Anne. Now I get paid for doing it. I have in fact enjoyed our visitors.'

'And Jack?'

'For the time being, he remains in charge of the villa. The owner also encourages him to continue to dig in the adjacent Roman ruins in the hope that he might stumble upon a buried treasure.'

'What has become of Janice Parker?' When Anne arrived in Nice, relations between Beverly and the young woman were strained. At age ten, her parents died in a shipwreck and Janice became the ward of her uncle, Thomas Parker. But her care fell mainly to Beverly. Two years later, a severe illness deprived the girl of her hearing and nearly her life. She came to believe that her foster parents, especially Beverly, were negligent in caring for her and contributed to the loss of her hearing.

Beverly resented the burden of raising Janice, who could be rude and surly. The two women also communicated poorly: Beverly couldn't sign and refused to learn.

Anne was genuinely interested in Janice, communicated with her in signs and gestures, and won her over to a more civil attitude, even towards Beverly.

Beverly frowned at the question. 'As you may remember, my husband wanted me to return to England with Janice. I refused to leave Jack, but eventually I sent her back in the company of winter visitors returning to England.'

'So what's drawing you to London now?'

'Recently, a friend wrote a letter advising me to return to England to deal with Parker on certain important property issues. At that point, Jack and I decided I should go to London and engage a dependable solicitor.'

'What would you hope to obtain?' Paul asked evenly.

'A legal separation of persons and property,' Beverly replied. Her voice had become strident. 'It would release me from Parker's control and protect my property. He would no longer be my heir.'

'What's he likely to want from you?' Anne asked. She knew Parker personally and could guess the answer.

'My money. That's clear. I don't know what else might be on his mind.'

'A divorce?' Paul asked, taking care not to provoke her to an outburst. Her hatred of Parker was almost palpable.

'Possibly,' she replied, visibly struggling to control her temper. 'But divorce involves a long, expensive, and uncertain procedure in Parliament. It was much easier for our notorious Henry VIII, who divorced two wives and beheaded two more. Parker might hesitate to seek a divorce. It would expose his own infidelity – he lives openly with his mistress. His own financial advantage might be better served by maintaining our marriage and his rights as my heir. Travellers from England tell me that he's having severe financial difficulties.'

She finished her coffee, her hand shaking as she held the cup. 'There isn't much that Jack could do for me in London. I'll rely on Solicitor Edward Barnstaple on Jermyn Street. He looks after your affairs too, doesn't he, Anne?'

'Yes, he's capable and trustworthy.' Two years earlier, he had won the dismissal of a false assault charge against Anne.

Beverly nodded. 'And yet I'm worried. Parker's mistress is a cunning, malicious woman. I don't know her intentions towards me. I fear that they are not kind.'

Fair weather blessed the three-day trip from Paris to Calais. Beverly seemed to shed her bitterness in the rocking motion of the coach. As she gazed at the soft yellows and browns of the autumnal landscape, and at peasant women and children tranquilly gleaning the fields, she began to smile.

Anne also enjoyed these bucolic moments but she was relieved to see heavily armed troopers of the royal highway patrol guarding the road. They were badly needed. Evidence of the chaos sweeping the country appeared in many of the villages and towns. Placards denouncing aristocrats were pasted on the walls of shops around the market squares. People in the streets and in the inns appeared irritable, discontented, or angry. The women had prudently chosen a simple coach and common clothes for the trip, so as to avoid being taken for aristocrats fleeing the country.

To pass the time, Beverly and Anne talked about their mutual acquaintances in Nice. Anne inquired about Jack Grimshaw's discoveries among the Roman ruins by the villa.

'Mostly jewelry of no great value,' Beverly replied, 'as well as cups, vases, and other small household items. Jack dutifully adds them to the owner's collection of Roman antiquities.'

'Is it housed in the villa?' Anne asked.

'Yes. The owner is trying to sell it in France, but his price is too high. The current unrest in the country has depressed the market. Many wealthy aristocratic collectors have left the country.'

As their coach approached the port of Calais, Anne ventured to ask, 'Has living with Jack been as rewarding as you had hoped?'

'More so, if possible. He helps with the innkeeping but allows me to take the lead. I direct the servants, plan the meals, deal with the guests, and so on. He looks after the vineyards and orchards in addition to the excavations. He's kind and considerate, attentive to my needs, receives affection gratefully, and gives it generously.' She hesitated, and then said with a shake of her head, 'He's as different from Parker as day from night.'

'Do the British winter visitors object to your relationship?' Anne recalled that they were generally wealthy, respectable, and middle-aged or older. They came chiefly for the dry, mild winter weather by the sea. Some of them were clergy who might raise moral objections.

'Frankly,' Beverly replied, 'I feared at first that we might be ostracized. That hasn't happened. The winter visitors greet us respectfully, invite us to balls and other social events, and give us many marks of kindness and appreciation.'

Anne must have appeared surprised, for Beverly quickly

added, 'I thank Dr Douglas McKenzie for our favourable situation. He speaks well of us and has introduced us into the visitors' society.'

The Scottish physician had retired to Nice and had won the respect of the winter visitors and many prominent citizens of the city. Anne held him in high regard. He had also befriended Paul's cousin, the Comtesse Louise de Joinville, though she was reputed to be a dissipated woman and suspected of murdering her partner.

On second thoughts, Anne realized that British visitors in Nice, even the clergy, could afford to be more tolerant of unconventional behaviour than in London. The distance and obscurity of the remote Italian city hid the visitors from prying eyes back home. Association with women of tainted reputations, like Beverly and the countess, wasn't so compromising as it otherwise would have been.

Crossing the Channel from Calais to Dover took the better part of a day. The sky was overcast; the wind from the west was brisk. The ship pitched and rolled, sending most passengers into the cabin. Beverly and Anne stood on deck, braving the weather, adjusting their balance to the ship's movement.

Anne fell into a pensive mood. This voyage reminded her of the one she took three years ago in the opposite direction. A handsome French colonel, Paul de Saint-Martin, was at her side. He had come to England to inform her that her stepfather had murdered his mistress and killed himself. Anne doubted the truth of the accusation and set out with the colonel for France to disprove it.

During that crossing, Anne had begun to realize the enormity of the challenge facing her. A small army of rigid French magistrates would oppose her at every turn with arcane language and procedures. Moreover, two persons had died violently, so danger lay ahead. The future looked like sailing in a small ship across a deep sea, prone to dangerous, unpredictable, contrary winds. A sense of powerlessness and futility had almost overcome her. But the calm presence of the French colonel had reassured her.

'May I ask what you are thinking?' Beverly searched Anne's eyes without prying, and smiled expectantly. In the course of this trip the two cousins had grown closer.

Anne related her story. 'I'm glad I took the risk. My life with

Paul has been a wonderful adventure. With his support I've learned ways to bring justice and comfort to some of the poorest and most vulnerable of our fellow human beings, particularly those who are deaf.'

'I'm happy for you, Anne. My life with Parker was dull and unrewarding. Unfortunately, it promises to become more challenging than I would like.' A grim expression settled upon her face.

They disembarked in Dover late in the afternoon and spent the night in an inn. The next day they journeyed to London in a rented coach, arriving at dusk. Anne accompanied Beverly to her home on Berkeley Square. They were uncertain of the reception she would receive. She had heard that her husband was usually to be found at the apartment he leased for his mistress rather than at home.

'Anne, I'm afraid,' said Beverly, her voice trembling. 'Mr Parker might be at home after all. I'd hate to face him. At the very least, he might have turned the servants against me, poisoned their minds with tales of my wickedness.'

Anne took her firmly under the arm. 'Let's not expect the worst,' she said, and urged her towards the entrance. An elderly male servant opened the door, gazed at Beverly with surprise, and broke into a wide smile of welcome. Anne released her grip and breathed a silent sigh of relief.

In the entrance hall, the servant informed Beverly and Anne that Mr Parker had left London for Bath twelve days ago. He said he would spend the season there. The servant didn't know whether Janice went with him. She was living at Braidwood's school in Hackney.

'You won't need me now,' Anne said to her cousin. 'I'll ride on to my grandfather's house in Hampstead. You can reach me there if you need help.' The two women embraced and Anne left.

Night had fallen when Anne's coach reached Hampstead. Lighted lanterns along the drive showed the way to the house. André knew she was coming but not exactly when, given the vagaries of travel. A pair of noisy terriers announced her arrival.

Servants welcomed her at the door and led her to André's study. He was at his writing table, pen in hand, a pair of eyeglasses near the tip of his nose.

He jumped to his feet and they embraced. 'You look happy, Anne, more self-assured than when you left England three years ago, and just as lovely. Colonel Saint-Martin has been good to you, true to his word to respect your wishes. Are you tired?'

'Not really. We found decent lodging along the way and slept well. The journey passed without mishap. I left Beverly at her home in London and came directly here. I was so anxious to see you.'

A few logs were burning in the fireplace. They sat at a table near the fire. Servants came with hot cider, bread, and cheese.

Anne glanced sideways at the letter on the writing table. 'Have I interrupted something important?'

'I'm instructing the new manager of my shop on what needs to be done tomorrow. He's learning the business. When he's ready to take over, I'll retire.' André spoke in a matter-of-fact way, with just a hint of regret. For over fifty years, the shop had been a large part of his life. Anne looked more closely at him now. He was still vigorous but thinner, his breathing slightly wheezy.

Yet his spirit was positive. As they spoke to each other, he smiled easily. He seemed resigned to the infirmities of old age, to the end of work, and to the loss of his wife and his sister and other persons close to him.

For another hour they talked about the trip to Bath that they had planned in their letters. They would stay for a week or two, depending on how much pleasure they were having. André looked forward to the mineral water and the baths; Anne, to the music and the theatre.

'I'll lodge with my friend, Harriet Ware, on Queen Square,' Anne said, taking a sip of her cider.

'And I'll stay with my nephew, Peter Cartier, your cousin, in his apartment on Gay Street, a few minutes' walk away. You'll have an opportunity to renew your acquaintance with him. He's a Justice of the Peace and a fine man, still a bit saddened by the death of his wife.'

'I remember him, of course. We played together as children and later drifted apart. I've heard that she left him with two small children. How has he coped?' Anne brought him up from her memory: a fair-complexioned, smiling face, with

blue eyes beneath a mop of curly blond hair. In his youth he
was thickset and muscular. She recalled that he played foot-
ball with passionate intensity. Later, he studied law, entered
his father's business in London, and probably became rich.
His parents, especially his mother, had disapproved of Anne's
stepfather, a music hall entertainer. So the families ended
contact with each other, and Anne lost sight of her cousin.
She didn't know where he lived. Somewhere in the London
area, she supposed.

She stared into her glass, beginning to feel apprehensive.
Had Peter shared his mother's contempt for actors and
actresses? Anne couldn't recall. What would he think of his
cousin, Anne, a former music hall entertainer and married to
a French colonel? Would he welcome her when they met in
Bath?

André seemed unaware of Anne's concerns. He continued, 'An
aunt cares for the children. I believe Peter would like to marry
again but has only begun to leave off grieving and re-enter society.
This season in Bath is his first step in that direction.'

As the clock struck eleven, Anne noticed that her grandfather was tiring. 'It's bedtime, André. We'll have a busy day
tomorrow.'

André gave her a weary nod and moved to dampen the fire.
'My groom is working on the coach. It's nearly ready. We'll
leave on Thursday.'

'Good. I'll be prepared.' Anne rose from her chair.
'Tomorrow morning, I'll saddle Mignon and ride over to
Thomas Braidwood's Institute for the Deaf in Hackney.'

André looked up, curious.

'Yes, I'm concerned about a rich, young, deaf woman there,
Miss Janice Parker. I befriended her in Nice last year. Her
uncle, guardian, and heir, Thomas Parker, covets her money.
His estranged wife, my cousin Beverly, finds Janice unpleasant
and troublesome. I'll have more to say about her after I've
visited the school. She might have left for Bath with her uncle.'

In her room Anne got ready for bed. A maid had unpacked
her luggage and laid out her nightdress. While brushing her
hair, Anne reflected on being in this house again. In her
youth she had often come here. André had taught her to
shoot and to ride on his spacious lands and had encouraged

her independence. From the beginning, her relationship with her grandfather was always close. Later as a mature woman, she realized that he saw in her something of his only son, Henri, her father, who died in a hunting accident when she was an infant.

She laid down the brush and picked up a pen, and started a letter to Paul. She missed him. They had been apart for a week, one of the longer separations since they married two and a half years ago. He would be relieved to learn that she had passed through northern France without incident. She didn't mention that other travellers had reported a breakdown in law and order along their route. On the main highway bandits looted grain wagons, stopped coaches, and robbed their passengers.

Paul had enough of such news. Instead, she recorded her impressions of her grandfather. He seemed to be coping well with the problems of aging and was eagerly looking forward to his vacation in Bath.

She considered how to express her concern for Beverly. Though Parker appeared to be a genial man, his character seemed weak and self-indulgent. His relationship to his mistress was nearly servile. But he had also earned a reputation for ruthless business practices. Much of his wealth came from the slave trade. Anne suspected that his soul harboured erratic, dangerous passions. How would he react to his wife's challenge?

Suddenly fatigue set in. She could hardly hold the pen. She put the letter aside, changed into her nightdress, and slid beneath the bedcovers. In a minute she was fast asleep.

AN ATTEMPT AT MURDER?

England, Hackney and London, Tuesday, 27 October–Wednesday, 28 October

Early the next day over breakfast, Anne and her grandfather chatted about recent events in France. 'Are you safe there?' he asked, a worried look in his eyes. 'Since July, Paris has become a dangerous place.'

'It's true,' she admitted. 'Paul and I have been living in the midst of violence.' She described the fall of the Bastille, the assassination of royal officials, and the chaos that followed. She explained that the crops had failed, bread was in short supply, and the people of Paris feared starvation.

'Nonetheless,' she admitted, 'the mob's savage violence towards the city's royal intendant shocked us. He was a good man doing his best under very difficult circumstances. Later, we discovered that agents of the Duc d'Orléans had incited them.'

'Has the king really lost control of the country?' André asked, a sceptical expression on his face. He had a visceral distrust of the French monarchy. As a child, he and his Protestant parents had fled from France to escape royal persecution. He had never been back, though he followed French news in the London newspapers.

Anne buttered a piece of bread and bit into it. 'He may not have lost all of his power, but he must share what's left of it with an elected assembly. Paris now governs itself. The Marquis de Lafayette has organized a national guard to replace the former royal police. No one knows what will happen next.'

'The kings of France have brought this trouble upon themselves. It's too bad that the country must pay the price.'

They finished their coffee and walked to the stable to visit Anne's mare, Mignon. She stroked the fine-boned black thoroughbred's gleaming neck. The horse whinnied with pleasure and nuzzled her.

At midmorning Anne rode Mignon to Braidwood's school. For several months prior to moving to Paris, she had worked there and learned his methods of signing and oral expression.

Now they met in his office. 'May I visit with Miss Janice Parker?' Anne asked. 'We became friends in Nice on the Mediterranean during the winter and spring of 1787–1788.'

'Unfortunately, Madame Cartier, you've missed her. Two weeks ago, her uncle and guardian, Thomas Parker, took her to Bath for the season. He claimed that she needed the city's medicinal waters and mild climate. Her health had deteriorated in the foul air of London, and she was wheezing too much.'

'That might be true,' Anne remarked. 'A change of air could improve her breathing. Bath is sunnier and its air cleaner than London's.'

'No doubt,' Mr Braidwood conceded. 'But I could have told Parker that her asthma is due, at least in part, to the strain of living with him and his lady friend, Miss Swan. Now I couldn't tell him that, could I?'

'No, you would surely have provoked him and wasted your breath. He doesn't accept criticism.'

'I suppose you got to know him well at his villa in Nice,' Braidwood said, and then went on, 'I imagine that Janice complied with her uncle under protest. She would much rather stay here and tutor the younger students. They respond enthusiastically to her. She's an excellent teacher. Unfortunately, her uncle shows more interest in her wealth than in her talents.'

'I'm aware of her situation, sir, and will do what I can to help her. In a few days, my grandfather and I shall leave for Bath. I hope to meet her there. By the way, who *are* her friends? I'd like to visit with them and gather messages to carry to Janice.'

Braidwood led Anne through the building, introducing her to a half-dozen young people. She prompted them to write and put their messages in her bag.

'Last but not least there's Charlie Rogers,' Braidwood remarked as they stepped into the garden behind the house. Charlie sat on a bench reading. 'He and Janice have become like brother and sister and confide in each other. Both of them have thrived here.'

Anne was amazed by the boy's transformation since she had last seen him two and a half years ago. He had grown tall and robust, and self-assured, though he was not quite thirteen. He recognized her immediately, laid his book aside, and rose with a broad smile to greet her. He had his mother's grace and his father's good looks.

Anne hoped he had a better character than either of them. His mother, Lady Margaret, née Pakenham, had conceived Charlie in a secret marriage with Captain Fitzroy, an Irish adventurer in French service. She soon entered into a bigamous marriage with Sir Harry Rogers, a wealthy Bristol slave trader. Her duplicity had catastrophic consequences for both men.

It left a mark on Charlie, who grew old beyond his years. In addition, Lady Margaret resented her son's deafness and largely neglected him, as did his natural and his putative fathers. A kind nanny raised him.

After Braidwood left, Anne and Charlie walked together on a garden path. She faced him and spoke in a careful, normal voice. 'Are you in contact with your mother?'

He shrugged. 'She moved back to her family's estate in Ireland and is looking for another husband. The first two were poor choices.' He grimaced at his own cynical remark. 'I should think more kindly of her. She loves me in her own way and writes occasionally. Her lawyer administers the trust fund that pays for my schooling.'

'Tell me about Janice Parker. Is she happy here?'

'You asked if she's happy?' Charlie strained to read Anne's lips.

Anne repeated the question more carefully, signing also.

The boy brightened. 'She's my tutor and my best friend. Most of us are younger than she, but we get along well.' He frowned. 'She hates the days when her uncle Thomas and his friend, Miss Swan, come for her.'

The boy hesitated to go on. Anne gave him an encouraging smile, and he continued. 'Well, two weeks ago, just before going to Bath, Miss Swan took Janice shopping in London. Someone tried to kill her.'

'What?' Anne exclaimed.

Charlie nodded. 'That's exactly what she told me, and she wasn't pretending. She really looked scared and showed me the bump on her head.' He went on to relate the girl's story about a stone block almost falling on her. 'She took me to the place and signed to me what had happened.'

Anne listened with increasing distress. 'Charlie,' she said, 'you must take me there tomorrow.'

The next day, Anne and Charlie left Hackney by coach for the city. On the way to the milliner's alley, they called on Beverly at her home on Berkeley Square. Anne had forewarned her cousin of the visit, briefly described the attempt on Janice's life, and had asked a favour. So, at midmorning, Anne and Charlie were shown into a parlour and treated to hot chocolate – Charlie's choice. Beverly had promised to invite a person who could answer certain intriguing questions. A stout middle-aged woman wearing a servant's apron and a

belt of keys appeared at the door and was invited to sit at the
table with them.

'This is Mrs Dawson, my housekeeper,' Beverly began.
'She's a trustworthy person with an excellent knowledge of
millinery shops. I've shared your message with her. The attack
on Janice has upset both of us. She has agreed to take your
questions.'

Anne asked, 'Madame, are you familiar with the milliner's
shop in the alley off Old Bond Street?'

Mrs Dawson studied the chocolate in her cup for a moment
and added a spoonful of whipped cream. Then she spoke carefully. 'I've seldom been in her shop. But I've learned that she
sells high-quality French silk at the lowest price in the city.
Her customers come from all over and have made her rich. I
can't tell you with certainty how she does it.'

Anne could easily guess: the silk was contraband and thus
escaped the government's high excise tax. When engaged in
that kind of business, it was wise to hide one's shop in an alley.

Mrs Dawson came with an afterthought. 'I should add
that in the last year or two, I've heard of a decline in her
business.'

'Why?'

'The excise officers have become more effective, made
many seizures and arrests, and reduced smuggling generally
in London. The cost of smuggling silk, like everything else,
has gone up.'

'I have another question,' Anne went on. 'Are you acquainted
with Miss Amelia Swan?'

'A remarkable woman.' Dawson's reply had an ironic edge.
She continued with carefully measured words, obviously
aware that Amelia was Beverly's rival for the affection of
Thomas Parker. 'I know her well. She resided here on Berkeley
Square for a few months while *Madame Parker* was away in
Nice.' She cast a sidelong glance at Beverly whose back had
stiffened.

Beverly remarked, 'Mrs Dawson kindly kept me informed
of the sordid affair so that I wouldn't look like a complete
fool.'

The housekeeper nodded vigorously. 'If wives are ignorant
of their husbands' misdeeds, they are too easily cheated of
their honour and their property.' She drank her chocolate, dried

her lips, and resumed her story. 'Later, Miss Swan persuaded Mr Parker to establish her in a separate residence.'

'What kind of woman is this Miss Swan?' Anne asked. 'Has she no shame?'

'None whatsoever!' Beverly interjected.

With a sympathetic nod to her mistress, Mrs Dawson continued, 'I've learned that she's the only daughter of a bankrupt London silk merchant who killed himself in a debtor's prison. She has received a typical young lady's upbringing in manners and proper speech. Sings and dances better than most. Travels in France and speaks the language. But her father left her penniless and alone. For a short while, she eked out a wretched living in a milliner's shop. Then, one day, a ship's captain fancied her and eventually introduced her into an elegant bordello.'

'That's where my Thomas met her,' exclaimed Beverly in a voice heavy with sarcasm.

Anne could see a tirade coming and steered the conversation away. 'Mrs Dawson, you mentioned Miss Swan's connections to the silk trade. What do you make of her visits to the shop off Old Bond Street?'

'They fit a pattern,' the housekeeper replied. 'She visits other millinery shops as well. You could say that she has an extraordinary interest in French silk.'

'I thank you, Mrs Dawson, for this information. I'm sure it will prove useful.'

Mrs Dawson drank the last of her chocolate, rose from her chair, and bowed to Anne and Charlie. 'You realize, Madame Cartier, that the kind of commerce we are so delicately discussing carries serious risks to all concerned. I wasn't entirely surprised when Madame Parker told me of the attempt on the life of Janice Parker. You will understand therefore that I must remain anonymous. Beverly has assured me that you are discreet as well as brave. Good luck.'

Early in the afternoon, Anne and Charlie set off for the alley off Old Bond Street. On the way, she signed to him a summary of Mrs Dawson's remarks.

He reflected for a moment, a puzzled expression on his face. Then he signed, 'I think the lady said that the milliner and Miss Swan are in the business of smuggling. But is that such a bad thing?'

His question took Anne by surprise. She had to reflect for
a moment before answering. Like most people she had taken
smuggling for granted.

Finally, she explained, 'It's like cheating in sports or at
school. The smugglers gain an unfair advantage over merchants
who play by the rules. To make up for the lost revenue,
the government increases excise taxes for the rest of us.'

Charlie gave her a non-committal nod, meaning that he
would ponder her remarks.

In the alley many shops were closed for dinner. But the
milliner was open for business. And there was activity on
the scaffolding above.

'Show me what happened,' Anne signed to Charlie. He led
her through the incident, Anne playing the part of Janice. At
the climax, Charlie acted as the young artisan who had saved
Janice. At a signal from Anne, he gave her a vigorous shove.
She staggered but kept her balance and looked up. Masons at
work on the scaffold were watching her. To judge from the
grim expression on their faces, the milliner must have reported
the incident to them in scathing terms.

Anne wanted to question the master mason but thought it
best to wait until he came down from the scaffolding. In the
meantime she began looking for the helpful young artisan. He
most likely worked nearby.

She found him, an apprentice in a printer's shop at the end
of the alley. His master was reluctant to free him from his
bench, even after Anne explained that the young man had
saved her friend's life.

'I would like him to show me what he did. He has a good
character and deserves a reward.'

Anne's allusion to money persuaded the master to relent.
'He may go with you, but bring him back in ten minutes.'

Out in the alley the young artisan explained that on the
13th of October he had been on an errand for his master.
When he entered the alley, he noticed the young woman
standing in front of the shoemaker's shop. As he drew near,
a movement in the scaffolding caught his eye. A large stone
block was teetering on the edge of the boards above her. 'I
yelled but she didn't hear me, so I pushed her out of the way
just as the stone fell. It hit the pavement inches from my
foot.'

'You're a brave man,' Anne said. 'Did you see anyone push the stone?'

'I've often asked myself that question.' He pointed up to the scaffolding. 'As you can see, it's partially enclosed. The day was foggy and the light in the alley was poor. I can't say that I saw anyone.'

Anne thanked the young man and offered him a shilling. The young man hesitated to take it. She insisted, 'You've earned it.'

He thanked her, then politely asked, 'How is the young woman?'

'She's well,' Anne replied, unsure whether to encourage the young man's interest in Janice. She took a step away, intending to end this conversation and speak to the milliner.

'She's visiting Bath,' Charlie volunteered, his enunciation a bit halting. 'She'll breathe better there.'

The young man gave him a big smile and signed, 'Thank you, sir. My home is in Bath. I'll return there in a few days when my apprenticeship ends.'

Intrigued by this turn in the conversation, Anne came back and signed, 'What's your name, young man?'

'Jacob Woodhouse,' he replied in sign. 'My father's a printer in Bath. He sent me here to learn London's new printing tricks and bring them home.'

'I know your father from my last visit to Bath. He helped me save a black man from deportation to slavery in Jamaica. Where did you learn to sign?'

'From my mother. She's deaf.'

Charlie waved a hand to catch Woodhouse's attention. 'You must meet my friend Janice. She wanted to thank you but didn't even know your name.' Charlie turned to Anne with an expectant gaze.

She got the hint but hesitated a moment while she studied Woodhouse. She couldn't detect any guile in his handsome if rather grimy face. 'I think a meeting with Janice could be arranged. Contact me when you arrive home.' She gave him her address. In the back of her mind she wondered whether the slave trader, Thomas Parker, would approve of his ward meeting the son of a prominent abolitionist. She smiled at the prospect.

'I look forward to seeing you again,' said Woodhouse. 'Now

my master expects me.' He bowed politely and hastened back
to the printing shop.

The milliner, a sharp-eyed, vigorous, middle-aged woman,
glanced hopefully at Anne and Charlie as they entered the
shop. There were no customers. A young female assistant
worked at a table, cutting silk cloth. Anne addressed the milliner
directly and introduced herself and Charlie Rogers as friends
of Miss Janice Parker.

'We would like to speak to you about her nearly fatal
accident outside your shop.'

The milliner appeared slightly disappointed that they hadn't
come to spend money. But Janice must have still been on her
mind.

'Gladly,' she said. 'Give me a few minutes and we'll have
tea in my parlour behind the shop.' She told her assistant to
wait on customers.

While the milliner was away preparing the tea, Anne
surveyed the shop. Bolts of silk cloth filled shelves from floor
to ceiling. Anne inspected a few bolts, fingering the cloth for
its texture.

'They're French from Lyons,' said the assistant proudly,
'and of the highest quality. Other milliners often come here
to buy them.'

Further conversation with the assistant confirmed Anne's
earlier impressions that the milliner had only a small retail
clientele. But those few customers purchased large quantities.
So, the milliner was in fact a wholesale dealer in French silk
– most likely imported without a license. Who supplied her
shop? Anne asked herself. Smugglers on the coast sold goods
to a network of distributors. In turn they filled orders from
Miss Swan and dealers like her. That was how the system
seemed to work.

The milliner reappeared and beckoned the two visitors into
her parlour. The richness of her furnishings took Anne by
surprise. The tea table, chairs, and sideboard – all in Thomas
Sheraton's currently fashionable style – lent an appearance of
restrained elegance to the room. And the tea service was porcelain of the highest quality. A young maid came with the tea
and sweetmeats, served, and withdrew.

The milliner had obviously prospered in smuggled goods

and wasn't shy about it. And why should she be? Anne asked herself. It seemed like almost everyone in Britain was involved one way or another in smuggling.

For centuries, efforts to curb this illicit trade had been futile. The profits greatly exceeded the risks. But recently Mr Pitt and his government had cut the smuggling of tea by lowering the customs duties, reducing official corruption, and commissioning more revenue cutters. The traffic in contraband silk also declined. But it still seemed safe and profitable – to judge from this milliner.

Anne sipped her tea, wondering if it were contraband, but she didn't ask. Instead, she turned the conversation to Janice Parker's 'accident'.

'Tell us, Madame, what you saw that day. I'll translate for my young deaf friend when necessary.'

The milliner sighed. 'I haven't forgotten what happened. I dream about it every night. That stone could have crushed your young friend. I was watching her through the window – such a pretty girl.' The milliner shuddered and fell silent for a moment. Finally, she described the young man pushing the girl, the stone falling, the crash, and the cloud of dust. 'I just can't understand how it happened.'

During the milliner's tale, Charlie grew pale and clutched his hands, living the incident in his imagination.

To distract the boy, Anne shifted the conversation to a less stressful topic. 'Madame, tell us how the masons reach their work place?' Anne had learned that the milliner also managed the building.

'They take the stairs to the top floor and go out through the window of an empty street-side room. The stairs are next door to my shop.'

'Who lives up there?'

'I rent the top-floor furnished room on the back side of the building to a ship's officer. He moved in a few months ago. Pays regularly and in advance. He has his own key and comes and goes as he wishes.'

'What's his name?'

'Captain S. Jakes.' The milliner paused, frowning. 'Come to think of it, I haven't seen him for a couple of weeks.'

'Could we look at his room?'

'Come with me,' replied the milliner and set off for the stairs.

The room appeared empty, except for its furniture and some trash scattered on the floor. 'That's odd,' the milliner said. 'He must have moved out. Didn't tell me. But he's paid up to date.'

In vain Anne and Charlie inspected an armoire. He then sifted through the trash without result. Meanwhile, Anne searched under the bed and found a crumpled receipt from the York House in Bath. Mr Wilson, presumably a desk clerk, had signed it, the seventeenth of August 1789, for Captain S. Judd.

Stunned, Anne murmured, 'Captain Judd?' This ship's officer might be the same Seth Judd that she knew many years ago at the Parker manor. Why would he rent this room under a false name? She tucked the paper into her bodice. It could be a clue to pursue in Bath.

She asked the milliner, 'Could you describe this captain for me?'

'He's a big, muscular, weather-beaten man, about forty-five years old. Brusque in his manner.'

That description was general enough to fit many ship's officers. But with the receipt it identified the Seth Judd of Morland Court, Sir Abraham Parker's illegitimate son. What was he doing here? Janice was his niece. Why would he try to kill her? The attack on Janice was becoming more difficult to understand.

As they descended the stairs to the floor below, the milliner pointed to a door. 'Two of the masons working upstairs rent this apartment. Their families live in villages outside London.'

Anne wondered if they could have dropped the stone on Janice. But why would they? Perhaps someone paid them to do it.

At that moment, the sound of heavy boots came from the stairs above them. The milliner called out. The master mason replied and joined her and her visitors on the landing.

He explained to Anne that he and his masons were working at Saint Paul's Cathedral on the day of the accident. 'I can account for all my men that day.'

'Including the two masons living on the floor below?' Anne asked.

'Of course,' he replied testily. 'They were with me.'

'Then how could one of your stones fall into the street?'

The milliner had previously complained to him, so now he stiffened, his face pink with anger. 'We pile our stones carefully on the scaffold. They're expensive. We can't afford to lose them.' He beckoned Anne and Charlie. 'Come with me and I'll show you.'

They followed him back up the stairs and into the empty room. Leaning out the window, Anne had a clear view of the platform of boards that the masons were working on. Its surface was covered with a thick layer of dust and bits of stones.

The master mason joined her and pointed to a neat, low stack of stones in the middle of the platform. 'See, they can't fall off. We cut them in our workshop, bring up as many as we need for the day, and trim them here. On the thirteenth of October, only a couple of stones remained on the platform from the previous day, and they were in the middle.'

They withdrew into the room. The master mason confronted Anne. 'So, none of us dropped that stone. Perhaps that girl has an enemy, or the stone was meant for the milliner. Who knows?'

Anne smiled apologetically and thanked the man for his opinion. Like the mason and the milliner, Anne believed that this wasn't an accident. Who would benefit from Janice's death?

She rejoined the milliner and gave her a description of Thomas Parker, Janice's heir, a man in need of money. He had shown little genuine concern about this 'accident'.

'No,' said the milliner. 'I've never seen him here.'

But, Anne thought, Thomas Parker, like Seth Judd, could have hired someone to sneak on to the scaffold and heave the stone. By this time, of course, he might be at sea, bound for Jamaica or India. Anne hoped to find out more when she reached Bath.

A final question came to her mind. 'Have you spoken to the police?'

'Yes, I contacted the local parish constable, and he looked over the scene. When he learned that no one was observed with the stone and no one was seriously hurt, he declared it was an accident. He warned the masons to be more careful.'

Anne looked askance. 'He made it easy for himself.'

At the door, the milliner said to Anne, 'I see, Madame, that you believe someone was out to kill that girl. Well, I agree with you. You should certainly look after her. The villain might try again.'

'We'll do our best to stop him,' Anne said, and signed to Charlie that it was time to leave.

Outside, in the alley, he seemed preoccupied and asked to see the receipt Anne had found upstairs.

'S. Judd,' he signed. 'He's sort of Janice's uncle. She doesn't like him. He's also Miss Swan's friend.' The boy's eyes began to glisten with tears. He signed, 'Is Janice really in danger?'

Anne put her hand on his shoulder. 'If Seth Judd and Miss Swan are friends, they might have cooperated in this attempt on her life. In Bath they most likely continue to be close to her.' Anne's voice wavered. 'Yes, I fear that she's in mortal danger.'

A DISTRESSED YOUNG WOMAN

Bath, Thursday, 29 October–Saturday, 31 October

The next day, after breakfast, Anne and her grandfather climbed into his coach for a leisurely two-day ride to Bath. They would stop overnight at an inn halfway. His groom sat in the coachman's seat and a man from his shop rode as guard. When Anne raised an eyebrow at the guard's musket, André remarked, 'The main highway between London and Bath is unsafe even during the day.'

Anne reflected that the alleys and streets of Bath might be just as dangerous, at least for Janice Parker. Last night, Anne had told her grandfather of her investigation in the alley off Old Bond Street and her suspicion of a plot against the young woman.

He had listened with a grave expression. 'I hadn't thought of Bath as a dangerous place,' he had said. 'But now I know better and must pack accordingly.'

Today, as the coach left Hampstead, André carried two canes. Anne asked why.

'One of them is for you,' he replied and handed her a slender dark-brown stick, with delicate gilded classical ornamentation. His voice had a mischievous tone. 'It's the fashion in Bath to walk about with a cane, the more original the better. You will like this one. I made it for a lady, several years ago. When she died, her husband sold it back to me. It's yours now.'

The cane felt heavier than she had anticipated. Then she smiled, released a latch, and drew out a rapier. 'Thank you, André, it's beautiful.' She ran a finger over the weapon's cool steel blade.

'And this is also for you.' He opened a highly polished brown mahogany box containing two small pistols and gave her one. 'It will fit in your bag, and you just might need it. Sometimes I wish that England would hire your Colonel Paul and his Royal Highway Patrol. He would make our highways safe.' Anne checked the pistol's grip and its balance, and studied its mechanism. Then, as the coach was passing a tavern, The Red Devil, she took aim at a grinning devil in the sign over the entrance. Finally, she held the weapon in the palm of her hand and gazed at it.

'It's beautifully made, André. I must practice with it, as well as with the rapier. They will be useful, if I am to defend poor Janice.'

She exchanged knowing glances with her grandfather.

'You might be right,' he granted. 'From the little I've learned already about Amelia Swan and Seth Judd, I'd say it's best to be armed when you deal with them.'

Fortunately, the coach met no bandits on the highway. The hours passed in easy, often nostalgic conversation and in contemplation of the lovely English countryside in its autumn glory. In one of those reflective moments Anne gazed at her cane and admired its excellent proportions, the stick's smooth surface and rich finish, and the graceful design on its gilded brass fittings. She wondered how a gentle, peace-loving man, such as her grandfather, could devote his remarkable creative talents for a lifetime to making beautiful objects that were so sinister and lethal.

Late on Friday afternoon, Anne and her grandfather arrived in Bath, grateful for an uneventful trip. She went directly to her furnished rooms above Harriet Ware's apartment on Queen Square. André moved into his nephew's apartment on Gay

Street only a two-minute walk away. When they had each settled in, they joined Harriet for tea in her parlour.

She had changed since Anne last saw her two and a half years ago at a trying time in her young life. She was then nervously beginning a career in Bath as a concert singer. She now looked more self-assured, thanks to the public's appreciation of her music.

She greeted her guests warmly and seated them at a tea table. A maid served and then withdrew. In the following conversation, Anne learned that the Parkers had rented a house nearby in the Circus, a circle of fashionable three-storey buildings with uniform facades at the north end of Gay Street. Parker and his mistress had inserted themselves into the city's social life, as if they belonged there and money was of no concern.

Herself an acclaimed soprano, Harriet acknowledged that Amelia Swan had an excellent soprano voice, wore the finest silk gowns and carried herself gracefully. 'She likes to shine and is already much sought after for house concerts. Mr Parker appears to be an amiable man, mixes easily in good company, enjoys playing the host at his dinner table, and drinks more French wine than is good for him. Tipsy or sober, he's an accomplished dancer, perhaps the best in Bath. His relationship with Amelia creates hardly a ripple of scandal.'

'What can you tell me about Janice Parker, the niece and ward of Mr Parker?' Anne asked.

'I've seen her at the Pump Room,' Harriet replied. 'She's a pretty girl but deaf, unable to take part in society's silly chatter. Seems restless and unhappy, as you might imagine.'

Anne inclined her head, met her friend's eye. 'Someone recently tried to kill her in London outside a milliner's shop.' She described the incident, without speculating on possible culprits.

Harriet gasped in disbelief. 'That's troubling, Anne. Nothing is said about it in Bath. Why should she be in danger here?'

'We don't know her enemies. That's the problem.'

'Enemies?'

'Yes, I believe there's more than one. She might have left them behind in London. Or, they could have come with her to Bath.'

'I'm appalled, Anne. You can't possibly suspect her guardian, Mr Parker, or his mistress.'

'He stands to gain by the death of his niece, that's all I know now. But that's enough to justify keeping a sharp eye on him. To move that large stone he might have used an accomplice.'

She added more sugar to her tea and took a sip, then went on. 'Have you ever heard of Captain Seth Judd?' Anne described the man. 'I'd like to know where he was on the thirteenth of October.'

'No, I can't recall him. I live alone and lack a gentleman to bring me into Bath's society. Actually, as you can understand, I haven't wanted a man ever since Harry died. But that limits me to a rather small circle of musical and theatrical acquaintances.' Painful memories were reflected in her large brown eyes.

Anne did understand. Two years ago, her friend had an intimate relationship with Harry Rogers, Charlie's father, which came to a tragic end. Once bitten, twice wary, Anne thought.

'Judd's of interest to me,' Anne continued. 'Recently, he rented a room in London above the milliner's shop where Janice was attacked. He has left London and may now lodge at the York House.'

'I haven't been to the York in over a year, nor have I noticed the man you've described. Now that I know what he looks like, I'll keep my eyes open for him.'

Anne finished her tea. As she rose to leave, she remarked, 'Amelia could have been an accomplice, placing Janice in position for the kill. I can't imagine what her motive might be. Then again, Janice's enemy might be someone entirely unknown to us.'

André went with Anne to her rooms and examined the furniture with a sharp eye. It was, he concluded, in good condition. They sat by the window overlooking Queen Square. He had been silently attentive during the conversation with Harriet. Now he asked Anne, 'Would you like me to inquire about Captain Judd at the York House this evening? Mainly single men lodge there. I might draw less attention to myself than a female stranger would. I'll report my findings to you tomorrow.'

'I'm grateful for that suggestion, André. You're right, the less public attention drawn to us in this matter, the better.'

'I have more suggestions,' he said. 'A ship's officer might also frequent Bath's gambling dens. My nephew, Peter, and I could explore them and might gather information about Judd. Moreover, if he's not in Bath, or at sea, he might be in Bristol. Peter also knows that city and could help ferret him out.'

'You've encouraged me, André. We must begin this investigation somewhere. Captain Judd appears to be a reasonable place to start. I wonder if he has changed since I last saw him? He threatened me then.'

André raised an eyebrow. 'Why, may I ask?'

'Years ago at Morland Court, I prevented him from assaulting my maid and, for good measure, shamed him in front of other men. He said he would make me pay. I doubt that he has forgotten.'

'Our visit to Bath promises to be much less light-hearted than I expected. But I welcome the challenge.' André rose and put on his hat. 'Now, I'll excuse myself and go for a walk with Peter. We'll stop at the York on the way, perhaps have a bite to eat.' He left the room with a bounce in his step, shoulders squared for the chase.

The next morning, Anne and André met at her apartment and set out for Bath's famous Pump Room near the King's Bath. A visitor's social life was supposed to begin there with a glass of warm mineral water. Its medicinal properties and its taste were disputed. But it served as one of the city's chief opportunities for presenting oneself, meeting newcomers, and exchanging gossip.

'Seth Judd is known at the York and under that name,' André reported as they walked down Barton Street. 'He has had a room there since the fourteenth of October, but he comes and goes. He was out when Peter and I inquired. We also visited a gambling den on Alfred Street where he's highly regarded. He plays for large stakes and wins more often than not. We'll discreetly gather more information about him, as opportunities arise.'

As they crossed the square in front of the Abbey Church, Anne asked, 'Where was Judd between the twelfth and the fourteenth of the month when the attack on Janice took place? That would be crucial to his alibi.'

André nodded thoughtfully. 'If he's as clever as I think he

is, he will have a ticket and witnesses for one of the stage-coaches from London to Bath at that time.'

'Yes, he's clever as well as ruthless. He could have paid a shilling to a desperate seaman who would gladly push a large stone on to a young woman standing below.'

In the Pump Room a band of musicians were playing English airs. They could barely be heard above the clamour of the crowd. Visitors of all ages and social conditions milled about the room seeking out familiar faces or gawking at strange ones. A few decrepit patrons arrived in wheelchairs or on crutches. Servants at the pump dispensed glasses of the mineral water to a long line of customers.

Anne saw the Parkers before they could see her, so she hid for a few minutes behind her grandfather and observed them. Parker was as she remembered him from Nice: tall, handsome, well groomed, and amiable. He had an English gentleman's fine manners and effortless grace, and he smiled and conversed easily with a wide circle of acquaintances in the room.

His mistress, Amelia Swan, was likewise suited to succeed in this frivolous society. Her glossy, raven-black hair, clear, light-brown skin, and ruby lips led Anne to wonder if she or her parents might have come from one of Britain's colonies.

These physical attributes, as well as a full, rounded figure, appeared to bewitch Thomas Parker. But he was also prey to her wit and charm. From time to time, like a skilful courtesan, she turned her large, beguiling green eyes on him, clasped his hand, and whispered a compliment or a sweet fatuous word into his ear. He nearly glowed with pleasure.

Janice, in contrast, looked ill at ease. Men noticed her pretty face but shied away once they learned that she was deaf. Neither her uncle nor his mistress tried to involve her in conversation. With a glass of water in her hand she drifted out of the crowd to the window overlooking the King's Bath.

She had placed her glass on the windowsill and was gazing at the bathers below when Anne came up to her.

'Have you tried the bath yet?' Anne signed.

Surprised, Janice momentarily frowned, then brightened when she recognized Anne. 'Madame Cartier!' she exclaimed, then recalled that they had agreed in Nice to use their Christian names. 'Anne,' she said and embraced her. 'I'm so glad to see you.' She paused. 'No, I don't intend to bathe. The water looks filthy.'

'Shall we sign?' Anne asked. 'I'd like to discuss matters that others shouldn't hear.'

'Gladly,' Janice signed, looking intrigued. 'There are benches in the Orange Grove behind the Abbey Church. At this time of day we can be mostly by ourselves.'

'Shouldn't you excuse yourself to Mr Parker?' Anne asked.

Janice shook her head. 'He won't miss me. I often slip out of the crowd. In fair weather I take a long walk into Crescent Fields to enjoy the view over the city. When it's raining I sit in a tea room and read.'

As Janice predicted, the Orange Grove was nearly deserted. The sky was overcast. The westerly breeze was chilly. The two women wrapped themselves in their capes. Anne explained that she had come to Bath with her grandfather on vacation. However, she had serious concerns on her mind. 'Did you know that Mr Parker's wife, Beverly, has arrived in England?'

'No, Parker hasn't told me. Does he know?'

'If not, he soon shall. I'm sure he has spies in London. Beverly is speaking to her solicitor. She wants to persuade or force Parker to agree to a fair, legàl separation. A divorce seems unrealistic – an expensive, lengthy procedure in Parliament with an uncertain, perhaps harmful outcome for an adulterous wife like Beverly.'

Janice grew thoughtful. 'You saw Parker in the Pump Room. In public he's a man without a care in the world, giving everyone a smile or a handshake. But in private he's moody, short-tempered, and often angry. His business is failing and he doesn't know what to do about it. I think we came here to avoid his creditors in London. I try to stay out of his way. If Beverly hunts him down and confronts him here, she will face his wrath.'

During the last few minutes, people began to enter the Orange Grove, some to walk about, others to sit on the benches. A pale, thin man with a book in his hand sat near Anne and Janice.

'Don't look now,' Anne signed, 'but the man who just sat next to us was close to you in the Pump Room and has followed us here. Use this device to examine him.' Anne opened a silver case with a mirror inside and handed it to Janice. She studied the man discreetly.

'Have you seen him before?' Anne asked.

'Yes,' she replied, 'now that you've pointed him out. I've seen him once with Parker when they didn't know that I was watching. So he's working for him.'

Anne winked. 'I think we should go shopping on Milsom Street. I know where we can converse without the spy leaning over our shoulders.'

Ten minutes later, they entered the millinery shop of Madame Francine Gagnon, an acquaintance from Anne's visit to Bath two years ago. A French woman, long resident in Bath, she supplied the French government with useful, often intimate and embarrassing information about military, political, and other prominent visitors to the city. This morning, she was inspecting rolls of ribbons while an assistant dealt with a customer. Madame looked up, brow furrowed. She apparently sensed that Anne and Janice had a problem unrelated to ribbons. She asked evenly, 'Good morning, Madame Cartier. How may I help you?'

Anne drew near, presented Janice, and whispered, 'We're being followed by a nasty little man. May we escape from him by your back door?'

Gagnon nodded. 'He'll probably wait across the street. But if he comes in here, I'll know how to handle him.'

Anne and Janice passed through the back room and out the door into narrow passageways to Harriet's house on Queen Square.

Once inside, Anne let out a deep breath and signed, 'We'll continue our conversation in my apartment upstairs, free from prying eyes and ears.'

In the parlour they relaxed at a table with hot chocolate and sweet biscuits. Anne signed, 'Unfortunately, that little spy isn't the only one who might be working for Parker.' She described Seth Judd, the ship's officer. 'I have good reason to suspect that Captain Judd is probably the man who arranged the attempt to kill you outside the milliner's shop in London. He's now in Bath and has a room at the York Hotel. We must watch out for him. Have you seen him yet?'

'No,' she signed, mouth agape. Staring at Anne, she struggled to control her feelings. 'I know Judd – he's Thomas Parker's half-brother. I dislike him and try to avoid him. He fancies himself a Lothario.'

'How close are they?'

'Judd visits Parker's home on Berkeley Square and meets Parker in his study. According to the maid who serves them tea, they usually talk about ships and silk and excise officers. To my knowledge he has never been invited to dinner.'

'If my suspicions are correct, Amelia may have brought you to the milliner's shop to give Judd's accomplice an opportunity to kill you. How are Amelia and Judd related?'

'I don't often observe them together, but I can see that they are friends from the way they look at each other. I wonder sometimes if Parker notices.'

'Do you sense that Parker might ask them to cause your death? Parker would then inherit from you.'

Janice replied, 'I find it hard to believe that Parker is conspiring with anyone to kill me. True, he's in financial distress and covets my money. He's also self-indulgent and morally weak. His mistress has gained too much influence over him and could lead him astray. Nonetheless, I want to think that he wouldn't be part of a scheme to harm me. When I'm with him, I feel neglected and angry but not threatened.' She paused, working her lips, trying to suppress her feelings. 'After all, he's my uncle and guardian.'

For a long moment Anne gazed at the young woman, deeply touched with pity. Then she left the table and walked to the window overlooking Queen Square. 'As I suspected, the pale, thin man knew where to go when we disappeared in Madame Gagnon's shop. He's across the street reading his book.' She returned to the table. 'My friend Georges Charpentier claims that any man will kill another man, if given sufficient motive. From what you've just said, I conclude that Parker has not yet reached that point and maybe never will.'

'So why has he engaged that spy?' signed Janice.

'I think we should find out. I'll invite him to join us.' She sat at her writing table, composed a message, and carried it downstairs to the concierge. Her young son took it across the street. Anne and Janice watched from the window with Harriet's opera glass. The man read the message more than once, a perplexed expression on his face. For a moment he seemed paralyzed, then he glanced nervously left and right and followed the boy to the house.

'I'm apparently rather incompetent,' complained the spy, as

he tasted one of the sweet buns. He stole an embarrassed glance at Janice.

'I'm sure you will improve with practice,' said Anne. She learned that Parker had hired the man upon arriving in Bath. A recent, unemployed graduate from Oxford, a vicar's son, he agreed to follow Janice about the city for the length of the season. Parker also hired his sister. They were supposed to detect any dangers or threats to Janice. She had narrowly escaped death in a suspicious accident in London. As a deaf woman in a strange city, she was more vulnerable than most people. Parker had insisted that he would not and could not be her constant companion.

Anne understood that Parker's mistress would simply refuse to be Janice's guardian. 'Why didn't you and your sister openly accompany Janice whenever she left the house? Why be secretive?' Anne asked.

'Mr Parker thought Janice would object to having a constant guardian or chaperon and would refuse to cooperate.' He glanced again at Janice. 'Mr Parker said that you are very contrary and stubborn, nearly impossible to control.'

Janice grimaced at his assessment of her, both irritated and amused. She addressed the spy with carefully measured words. 'You report to Parker everything I do, whom I meet, where I go, don't you?'

He nodded sheepishly. 'That's what he pays us for.'

Janice turned to Anne and signed, 'You see, Parker mainly wants to keep track of me and control me without troubling himself too much. The dangers to me that he talks about are less important. Maybe, after all, he's conspiring to kill me, watching for an opportunity when he won't incriminate himself.'

Anne wondered what to do. She could wash her hands of the whole affair and allow Janice to face her fate alone. She might then defy her uncle and try to escape from his spies. She would also reject any chaperon she didn't like or respect and couldn't communicate with her. A killer would easily find her, vulnerable like a child in a jungle.

'I suggest,' Anne signed to Janice, 'that at least for now we let Parker's spies carry on.' She gave a smile to the thin scholar drinking tea at that moment. 'They mean you no harm and could even prove helpful in an emergency.'

She addressed the spy. 'In the future, would you please be

less obvious in carrying out your duty? Someone intending to attack Janice might also harm you.'

He appeared taken aback. He hadn't thought that he or his sister could be in danger.

Janice shook her head and signed to Anne with unmistakable vehemence, 'I don't want spies following me, even if they learn to be more discreet.'

Anne added a frown of reproach to her signing. 'I understand, Janice. You feel like you're on a leash, like a pet. Unfortunately, the law regards you as a minor and allows Parker to govern your behaviour. As your legal guardian, he's responsible for you. If you challenge him, he could confine you to the house. Or, he might force a constant companion upon you, even someone you wouldn't like.'

The spy had put down his cup and gazed at the women nervously. He couldn't understand what Anne was signing, but he knew that the conversation had taken a serious, contentious turn.

'Sir,' Anne said to him, 'you may leave now. I believe that we understand each other.'

He bowed and scurried from the room. His steps echoed in the stairway. The entrance door slammed behind him.

Janice appeared close to tears. Her breathing began to strain. 'I want to escape and hide in London.'

Anne leaned forward and signed gently. 'Is there anyone in Parker's household who seems sympathetic to you?'

The young woman reflected for a moment. 'Parker and Amelia each have a personal servant from London. I don't trust either of them. The rest of the household was hired here. They ignore me, except for one of the maids, Gracie White. She's friendly and helpful and one of the few servants who can read and write. We exchange notes.'

'That's promising,' Anne remarked.

Janice shook her head. 'Her duties tie her down. She has little time left for me.'

There must be a way out of this impasse, Anne thought. After a few moments of reflection, she decided to take a bold step. 'I'm willing to speak to Parker and offer to be your companion. Would you agree? We know each other from the months together in Nice. We like and respect each other. Together we could enjoy the air, the water, and the sights and pleasures of this city. Parker might continue to spy on us. But that wouldn't matter.'

Janice glanced at Anne with a flicker of hope in her eyes. 'I would like that,' she signed.

Later on that Saturday afternoon, Anne observed Parker walking alone through the Circus towards his house. She intercepted him before he could reach the door.

'Madame Cartier,' he said with surprise. 'What brings you here?'

'Do you have a few minutes, sir? I'd like to speak to you about Janice.'

He searched her face. 'This seems to be a serious matter, Madame Cartier. Shall we discuss it in my garden? It's sheltered from the cool breeze and warmed by the sun.'

Anne agreed. Parker led her through the house and out the back door. The sun cast long shadows into the wedge-shaped formal garden, enclosed by trellised, vine-covered walls. On the central axis were three flower beds in a terrace of fine gravel.

Anne and Parker walked past apple and plum trees heavy with fruit. At the far end where the garden widened, they sat facing the house.

Anne complimented Parker on the beauty, rich variety, and expert care of the flowers and bushes. 'Do you tend to them yourself?'

He smiled. 'Only a little, for pleasure and exercise. A gardener came with the house. That's one of the reasons why I've rented it. We enjoy tea here when the weather allows.'

A servant arrived with tea, poured, and left. For a few minutes Anne and Parker reminisced about their time together in Nice. Parker recalled the picturesque view from the villa over the Roman ruins with the blue sea in the background.

'The news from France this summer was very disturbing,' Parker remarked. 'I thought of you and the colonel when I read about the fall of the Bastille and the atrocities that followed. As a provost of the Royal Highway Patrol, he must have been in the thick of it.'

'He was indeed, and his life was threatened. The situation is still unpredictable, but some order has been restored. At this moment, England appears much more peaceful than France. But one can encounter dangers even here.' She paused, inclining her head in a gesture of disbelief. 'I've heard that Janice had a nearly fatal experience in London a few weeks ago.'

'That's true,' he said. 'A stone accidentally fell near her. Fortunately, she wasn't seriously hurt.'

Anne began a tentative explanation. 'I visited the site and spoke to witnesses. Still certain aspects of that accident are difficult for me to understand.' She pretended to hesitate, as if reluctant to continue. 'Are you aware, sir, that your half-brother, Seth Judd, rented a room near the scaffold from which the stone fell?'

Parker reared back in his chair. Lines of disbelief mixed with annoyance creased his brow. 'Are you suggesting, Madame, that Captain Judd may have tried to kill Janice? That's preposterous.'

'But it's a remarkable coincidence, don't you think?'

'You have a lively imagination, Madame Cartier, I'll grant you that. But you should leave this incident to the police. A constable has declared it accidental.'

Anne pressed on. 'I have no idea why Captain Judd might want to do such a thing. Nonetheless, the facts suggest that a man he hired may have cast the block of stone.' She met Parker's eye. 'Were you concerned for her safety when you engaged the Oxford scholar and his sister to keep watch on her?'

'The accident did arouse my concern,' Parker admitted. 'Simple prudence demanded that I guard her without arousing undue fear or resentment.'

During this exchange Parker's expression had become enigmatic. Still, Anne detected a hint of anxiety in his eyes.

'True,' Anne granted. 'Janice needs protection but she also craves respect. I've had a serious conversation with her. She's very restless and unhappy. Much of her distress comes from her deafness. Society in Bath treats her as an outsider and shuns her. So she wanders off by herself.'

Parker added, 'That could be dangerous for a young deaf woman in a strange city. As you may recall, her behaviour in Nice was similar.'

'I agree,' Anne granted. 'She is often imprudent. I can imagine that you might find her troublesome to deal with, but spying on her will only make matters worse.' Anne described her experience with the spy in the Orange Grove, on Milsom Street, and in Queen Square. 'Janice feels like a prisoner in chains.'

Anne paused for Parker's response. His eyes evaded Anne's gaze. He probably didn't like what he was hearing, but he made a gesture for Anne to continue.

'Janice needs guidance and companionship. I'm willing to offer both. During our time in Nice, I grew fond of her and have overcome the barrier of her deafness. If you were to entrust her to me, you would free yourself from much unnecessary concern and anxiety. Janice favours the arrangement.'

Parker took a few moments to reflect. Then he conceded that Janice was a problem for him. 'I brought her to Bath not only for her health and her own protection but also because she should experience the world, learn to live in it. But it's true; she's very unhappy here and doesn't suffer patiently. After two difficult weeks, I'm willing to suspend my experiment. I considered sending her back to Braidwood. But he insists that she has learned what he has to teach. She's helpful with younger students, but it's time for her to become independent.'

Anne nodded. 'That's my opinion as well.'

Parker smiled. 'I'm encouraged that you won Janice's confidence in Nice. Because you communicate with deaf people and understand them, you're a suitable chaperon for her. Shall we experiment for a week?'

'Yes,' Anne said. 'I'm willing.'

'Then Janice can move in with you. I'll cover her expenses. She's upstairs in her room. I'll call her down.'

A few minutes later, a servant showed Janice into the garden. She agreed gladly to the new arrangement. When Parker left and the two women were alone in the garden, Janice signed, 'What a relief to be away from Parker – and from Amelia. Her perfume sets off my asthma.' Anne recalled that the woman used a strong, exotic perfume.

'What else has that effect on you?' Anne would remove from her apartment anything that Janice couldn't tolerate.

'My uncle's pipe tobacco. His clothes reek of it.'

'I noticed. You won't find either perfume or tobacco in my apartment, nor in Harriet's either.'

Janice went back into the house to pack her things, and Anne set off for Queen Square to prepare a room. She trembled at the responsibility she had taken on, guiding a troubled young woman, the target of a murder attempt. On the way, she stopped at the house on Gay Street to speak to her grandfather. He was alone, resting after a tiring day. His nephew was expected within an hour.

'Would you have time to observe Mr Parker?' she asked. 'I suggested to him that his half-brother, Seth Judd, may have attempted to have Janice killed. Parker will probably try to reach Judd sometime this evening, perhaps at the York Hotel. I'm curious how they react to each other.'

André rubbed his hands with zest. 'Peter and I would enjoy a little adventure and be of help to your friend Janice. We'll develop a cautious strategy. These two men cannot be taken for granted. They might resent being spied upon and lash out at us.'

THE BOW STREET OFFICER

Bath, Sunday, 1 November – Monday, 2 November

The next morning, Anne and Janice inaugurated the new living arrangement with a hike on Gravel Walk into Crescent Fields. Crystal beads of dew sparkled on the thick grass to the left and right of the path. High up on the slope, the sun cast a golden light on the wide arc of elegant terrace houses known as the Royal Crescent. Down below, a thin mist hung over the peaceful city nestled in the Avon Valley.

But a cold wind blew from the west. The two women were thankful for their woolen capes. Still, they had to stop several times for Janice to catch her breath.

When the young woman began to wheeze, Anne grew concerned. 'This exertion in the cold air aggravates your asthma. Should we turn back?'

'No, we'll stay here. I'm enjoying the view over Bath.' She hesitated for a moment and then signed firmly. 'I also relish my new freedom from my uncle. It was so kind of you to take me in.'

A short while later they came to a sheltered bench that offered an unobstructed view of the valley. For a few minutes, they rested quietly until Janice's breathing returned to normal. Then Anne mentioned tomorrow's dress ball at the Assembly Rooms, the large, elegant center of Bath's social life, a short walk east of the Circus. Janice seemed intrigued.

'Would you like to go to the ball with us, even if you can't hear the music?'

'I'd love to go. Before my deafness, I enjoyed country-dances. Though I can't hear the music any more, I remember it well and enjoy it in my head. I also sense the rhythm, especially in lively country-dances where I can follow the movements of my partners and feel the stamping of their feet on the floor.'

'Good, we are glad to have you,' Anne signed. 'Now we must begin to prepare. My friend, Harriet Ware, is organizing a party in her apartment for this afternoon. You are herewith invited. I'll ask Harriet to include a country-dance in the program; it's good practice for the ball. She should also include a guest who can sign.'

Returning on Gravel Walk, they passed the rear entrance to Parker's garden where Anne had met him yesterday. That prompted her to ask Janice, 'How well do Parker and his mistress get along in private?' Janice had lived with them long enough to notice.

She stared at the house, as if peering into its secrets.

'I've learned from the maid, Gracie White, that Amelia and Parker talk a lot about money. They never seem to have enough. Sometimes they quarrel. On one occasion he said he couldn't afford to pay for some of her purchases. She claimed that he had more money than he let on. He was hiding it from her.'

'Were they ever violent?'

'Not when I was present, though they looked angry and shouted at each other.'

'Did they ever mention Beverly, Parker's estranged wife?'

'Yes. According to the maid, Beverly's lawyer recently proposed a settlement that Parker didn't like. The maid didn't know the details. Parker then wrote a new will that cut Beverly out.'

'Really? How could you know?'

'He left it on his writing table. Gracie sneaked into the room and read it when he was away.'

'Who is his new heir?'

'Amelia.'

Hmm, murmured Anne to herself. What could Amelia hope to gain by that new will? Parker was deep in debt. Were he to die, his creditors would take everything he left behind. But of course if he had inherited Janice's fortune, quite a bit would still remain in his estate.

Later that afternoon, Anne and Janice walked down to Harriet's apartment. She had cleared furniture from her spacious parlour to serve as a ballroom and had also set up a buffet table in an adjacent room. This party was designed to mimic tomorrow's entertainment at the Assembly Rooms.

A gifted comic actress as well as a singer, Harriet played the role of Master of Ceremonies in black silk coat, vest and breeches, powdered wig, and cane. She strutted about the room, greeting her guests with exaggerated bows and flourishes.

Among them was Anne's cousin, Peter. She had been in Bath almost two days and had not yet met him. He always seemed to be busy or engaged. Anne was beginning to feel that he was avoiding her. Now he walked into the room and recognized her, a polite smile on his face. Anne suspected that André had obliged him to come. Otherwise he would have insulted her and made matters worse between them.

'It's been a long time,' he said as they met. He bowed slightly, but his voice lacked warmth or enthusiasm. His eyes briefly scanned her. He seemed both curious and embarrassed.

'Too long,' she replied, mustering a friendly smile. Then she introduced Janice.

He faced her and spoke slowly and clearly. 'André has told me about you. I'll do all that I can to make you feel safe in Bath.' She gave him a sweet smile and a few words of greeting in her best voice.

It was soon time for the music. Harriet had invited a friend, a violinist, and charged him with playing tunes for the country-dances that Janice knew. A group formed consisting of André and Anne, Peter and Harriet. Peter was still reserved towards Anne. The old family tensions lingered. A second group included a young married couple, Janice, and her partner, a genial older man from the theatre who could sign.

They danced a few sets, followed by an intermission and a few more sets. With a little help from her partner, Janice performed well. Her eyes glistened with pleasure, her body moved with an easy grace. Anne was reminded of Janice dancing at the Carnival ball in Nice almost two years ago.

When the music ended, the dancers paused for a moment, then turned to Janice and applauded her. She bowed to her partner and signed her appreciation. The party shifted to the buffet for food and drink. Anne brought Janice into the guests' friendly conversation and games, translating for her when she couldn't read lips.

Late in the evening, as the party ended and Anne and Janice were leaving Harriet's apartment, the young woman signed to Anne, 'This has been my happiest day in Bath. Thank you.'

The next evening, Anne entered the Assembly Rooms, confident in her protégée's readiness for the dress ball. Janice was hesitant and shy, but her escort this evening was André, and his gentle manner and friendly smile reassured her. Anne took her cousin Peter's arm, determined to win him over. At first, he was stiff, but he gradually relaxed and gave her a friendly smile.

None of them cared to play cards or gamble, so they sat on benches in the great hall while a music band assembled and tuned their instruments. From six until eight o'clock the program called for courtly minuets – the women in silk hoop skirts, hair piled high and powdered; the men in colourful, embroidered silk suits and powdered wigs.

Promptly at six, the dance began. To Anne's eye, accustomed to an aristocratic French standard, many of the dancers appeared slightly rustic, lacking the personal grace that the dance required. Their awkward posturing tempted Anne to smile as she exchanged glances with Peter. But Parker and Amelia stood out among the dancers. A powdered wig added to his distinguished appearance. His silver silk suit was embroidered in a luxurious green floral pattern. Amelia wore a light-green silk gown with silver embroidery. She dispensed with the wig and showed off her glossy black hair.

'Who would believe that Parker is in financial distress?' Anne whispered to her cousin.

'The tailor who made that costume,' Peter replied. 'Parker probably owes him thousands of pounds for the clothes in his wardrobe.'

During a long intermission following the minuets, the female dancers changed into less bulky gowns. Everyone else milled about the hall or organized tables for cards and dice. At nine o'clock, the popular, lively country-dances began. Anne threw an inviting glance to her grandfather.

'I'll do a couple of sets,' he agreed, 'then I'll hand you over to your cousin, Peter.' He turned and faced Janice and spoke clearly. 'And when I've rested for a moment, I'll ask this young lady to be my partner.'

André's health was robust for an older man, and the dancing brought colour to his cheeks. After two sets, he signaled his nephew to take over.

Peter proved to be a strong and graceful dancer. His reserve quickly melted away, and his smiles came easily and from the heart. The dance grew livelier with much vigorous skipping and hopping. Anne was nearly breathless when Peter suggested that they had had enough.

Meanwhile, André and Janice danced well together, but they left the floor when she began to tire.

At ten o'clock, they rejoined Anne and Peter and followed the crowd into the Tea Room for refreshments. Anne stole a sideways glance at Janice and was pleased to notice that the young woman had shed the anxiety that seemed to burden her.

A few moments later, Anne recognized Dick Burton, a retired investigator from the Bow Street magistrate's office in London. He was sitting alone at a table, a glass of punch before him. Anne had met him in Bath two years ago in the course of a criminal investigation. Despite certain differences of opinion, they had come to respect each other. Now they made eye contact, and he smiled and beckoned her to join him.

As she greeted him, she recognized the thin scar from ear to mouth on his left cheek, a trophy from his years as a British soldier. The look in his eyes was different. There was loss and sadness, she thought. Had his wife died? They were close.

Anne introduced Janice, her grandfather, and her cousin. They learned that Burton was staying at the York Hotel. From his painful movements – and the cane at his side – Anne could see that he was still crippled by arthritis.

'What brings you to Bath?' André asked.

'The hot baths give relief to my aching joints,' he replied.

'And I meet people of interest to my study of human nature.'

André and Peter excused themselves and went with Janice to the buffet for food and drink. For a few minutes Burton spoke about new acquaintances. Then he paused to sip his punch. That offered Anne an opportunity to ask, 'Now tell me, why are you *really* here?'

Burton smiled. 'I do believe you'd make an excellent Bow Street officer. I can share this much with you. I've been asked to investigate the extent of smuggling in Bath and Bristol. My attention has lately focused on Mr Thomas Parker. I've learned that you know him and his family, so you might help me answer a few questions.'

Anne glanced at the others returning from the buffet.

Burton nodded. 'Tell me when and where we could have a private conversation. The mayor has lent me a small office at the Guildhall.'

'Tomorrow morning after our visit to the Pump Room – say, at ten o'clock.'

'Agreed.'

AN ADULTEROUS WIFE

Bath, Tuesday, 3 November

After a light breakfast, Anne and Janice walked through the city to the Pump Room. Anne cast random, anxious glances over her shoulder. No one appeared to be following them, or perhaps Parker's spies had improved upon their skills. Anne was convinced that he would want to know where Janice was. She meant a great deal to him as a potential financial asset.

The Pump Room was nearly full of patrons. In the background the orchestra was playing a sentimental ballad. Anne and Janice bought the customary glasses of water, then looked around for someone they might know.

Thomas Parker and Amelia had not yet arrived. But Anne recognized Jacob Woodhouse, the young man who had saved

Janice's life three weeks ago in London. He was with his parents, an expression of patient resignation on his face. They were signing to each other.

Anne nudged Janice and discreetly pointed to Jacob, then signed, 'Wouldn't you like to meet the young man who saw the stone fall from the scaffold in London and pushed you out of the way? He can sign, you know.'

Janice stared at Jacob, and her cheeks flushed a soft pink. She bit for a moment on her lower lip. 'Yes,' she signed. 'I'd like to show my gratitude.' She started towards the Woodhouse family, Anne a step behind.

At virtually the same moment, Jacob caught sight of Janice. His eyes instantly brightened, his lips parted as if expecting a kiss. 'Master Woodhouse,' she began in a carefully controlled voice, 'I've so much wanted to thank you for saving me.' Her enunciation was nearly perfect. She and Anne had practiced it in the apartment. She also signed her sentiment to Mrs Woodhouse in case she hadn't read her lips.

'It was nothing,' Jacob replied. His parents gazed at the two young people with incomprehension. Apparently their son had not told them about the incident – he must have only recently arrived in Bath from London. Now he signed to them, 'This is Miss Janice Parker and her friend Madame Cartier.' He explained briefly what had happened. So, Anne thought, he had gone to the trouble to learn Janice's name. He had probably noticed her in the alley on previous occasions.

His explanation seemed to further confuse his parents. 'It appears to me that *someone* cast that stone, but why?' asked David Woodhouse, directing his question to the two young people.

'You both could have been killed,' added Mrs Woodhouse, visibly shaken.

Anne had remained outside the group. Now she moved forward and signed, 'The constable was informed, but since no one was seriously hurt and no assailant had been identified, he's calling the incident an accident.'

Anne surveyed the crowd. Heads were turning. Persons nearby were gawking at this silent, animated conversation. She signed, 'We should continue our discussion in a less public place.'

Woodhouse Senior agreed with a nod. 'I have a key to the Quaker Meeting House. It's only a short walk from here. We wouldn't be disturbed.'

A few minutes later, they gathered on benches in a simple room. Janice and Jacob stole glances at each other and exchanged smiles. Meanwhile Anne described how she was trying to look after Janice, who was still in danger. 'It's too soon to mention his name, but a possible suspect in the attempt on Janice's life is here in Bath.'

'Please keep me informed,' asked Woodhouse, glancing sideways at his son, who was clearly affected by Janice's beauty. 'My son has become involved in Miss Parker's fate.'

Anne gazed at the young couple, then nodded to the anxious father. 'I may need to call upon you for help.'

Anne left Janice with the Woodhouse family and hurried to the Guildhall to meet Dick Burton. The door to his office was ajar. When she knocked, he called out to her to come in.

'Excuse a crippled old man, Madame Cartier, if I remain seated rather than rise like a gentleman to greet you. The arthritis is particularly painful this morning.' She noticed the cane hanging on the arm of his chair. He motioned for her to sit facing him at the table.

They began with an exchange of news since their last meeting in Bath two years ago during his investigation of violent deaths at Combe Park, a manor house on a hill above the city. Anne stayed there while she tutored young deaf Charlie Rogers. At times, her duty to shield the boy from emotional distress conflicted with the Bow Street officer's dogged pursuit of evidence compromising to the boy's mother, Lady Margaret. Nonetheless, Burton gained respect for Anne, and vice versa. Their present meeting began cordially.

Anne understood that the Bow Street officer had come to Bath for police work as well as for relief from his arthritis. And somehow she could be useful to him. So she came directly to the point. 'What are you attempting to do here in Bath, Mr Burton?'

His eyes briefly registered a hint of surprise. But he quickly replied, 'His Majesty's chief minister has asked me to play a modest role in the government's campaign against smuggling, the cause of a significant loss of revenue.'

'I'm aware of the problem,' Anne said, recalling her recent contact with the London milliner's trade in contraband silk.

'Smuggling is a big, complicated enterprise. What part of it are you dealing with?'

'Money,' Burton replied. 'Smugglers need money to build and outfit their boats, to buy products in France – lace, silk, and brandy, for example – to bring into this country, to bribe excise officers and local authorities to look the other way. They also must buy horses and carts, canal boats, and other means of transportation to haul their goods to market. Above all, they need the resources of experienced men of affairs, willing to take great risks for the sake of large profits, tax-free.'

'Can such men of affairs be found in Bath?'

'Their domicile is usually London, but they may come here for the season and meet their associates.'

'And do some of their business here as well?'

'That's true. I hope to uncover them. But I'm in no condition to do it alone – years ago, perhaps, but no longer.' He lifted his cane to illustrate the point.

'Then how can I help you?'

He carefully replaced the cane and asked, 'What can you tell me about Mr Thomas Parker?'

'Where do you want me to begin?'

'I know that he often travels throughout France – you and your husband spent a vacation with him in his villa near Nice two years ago. He finances shipping ventures to our West Indian islands. He lives in grand style, probably beyond his means, as we've seen tonight. Finally, he's estranged from his wife and maintains an expensive mistress. Am I correct so far?'

Anne nodded. 'I have also wondered where his money came from. I've assumed that he has borrowed heavily or was using up a large inheritance, if not from his father, then from a distant relative.'

Burton shook his head. 'I've looked into both possibilities. He *is* heavily in debt, but he can borrow no more. His credit worthiness has declined to zero. He has received nothing from relatives, distant or near. As you know, his father left an enormous fortune to his eldest son, Oliver, and only a modest allowance to Thomas.'

Anne added, 'At Oliver's death, the fortune passed in trust to his daughter, Janice.'

'True,' Burton said. 'Thomas Parker's access to those funds is
strictly limited and cannot lift him out of his desperate financial
situation.' Burton paused, gazed at Anne. 'I suspect that for years
he has supplemented his legal income with money from
smuggling. Unfortunately for him, that resource has diminished
during the past three years due to our free-trade agreement with
France. Lace, silk, brandy, and other popular French products
now enter Britain legally below the smugglers' prices. Furthermore, our excise men have recently become more effective against
smugglers and their associates. If Parker was depending on income
from smuggling, where can he now turn?'

'He would search for a way to get into Janice's trust fund,'
Anne suggested. 'Are you aware that someone has recently
attempted to kill her?'

Burton's eyes widened with surprise. 'I hadn't heard. Parker
wouldn't dare. He would instantly become the chief suspect.
The magistrates would seal the trust fund, at least until he
was exonerated. And that could take a long time.' He paused
for emphasis. 'Unless, of course, her death could appear to
be truly an accident or due to natural causes.'

'That may be true,' Anne granted. She went on to describe
the London incident in detail. 'I haven't discovered any
evidence that would convict him of attempted murder. The
local constable has said it was an accident. I still suspect that
Parker was somehow involved. You might investigate his
connection to Seth Judd, his half-brother, a sea captain, with
a room in London at the scene of the crime.'

'Hmm, I should add him to my list of persons of interest.
Must I go back to London to find him?'

'No, he's lodging in your hotel, the York. On Saturday
evening, Parker paid him a visit. My grandfather observed
them at a coffee-house. Parker looked displeased with Judd
and worried, probably about the London incident.'

'I thank you, Madame Cartier. You've widened the
perspective of my investigation into Thomas Parker's
affairs. He may be more desperate than I had thought. His
dealings with Captain Judd might include murder as well
as smuggling.'

Late in the afternoon after tea, Anne and Janice returned to
their apartment to find Beverly Parker's maid waiting at the

door with a message. Beverly had arrived in Bath, together with the maid and a male servant. She was renting an apartment above a pastry shop on Milsom Street. Could she and Anne meet soon?

Anne replied by the maid with an invitation to supper that evening. Beverly came promptly and alone, looking drawn and tired from a two-day coach ride from London.

Janice served soup, bread, cheese and wine, barely nodding to Beverly, and then withdrew to her own room – as she said – to write letters.

Beverly gazed coolly, and without comment, at the young woman. When she left, Beverly remarked, 'In the year since I last saw her, Janice has grown from a girl into a young lady, but she still lacks good manners.'

Anne acknowledged the remark with guarded displeasure. In Nice, Beverly had nagged the young woman to conform to a prim standard of behaviour. Janice rebelled.

Anne quickly moved past the sensitive issue and asked, 'What have you done since we parted in London?'

Beverly explained that she had spent the past several days with Solicitor Barnstaple, figuring out the lines of a friendly settlement with her estranged husband.

'Frankly, my expectations are low. Barnstaple pointed out that the law gives the husband every advantage in domestic disputes. He could force me to pay dearly for my freedom.' She spoke in a desperate tone of voice.

'Don't give up,' Anne counseled. 'He may yet come to a sense of fairness, or at least desire a quick resolution of this dispute and be willing to compromise.'

Beverly shrugged away these unlikely solutions. There was a moment of silence while she nibbled distractedly on a piece of bread. She lifted up a tablespoonful of soup, gazed at it, and asked, 'Is Janice Parker living here with you?'

'Yes, for her own sake.' Anne described the attempt to murder Janice. 'I'm trying to find out who would want to kill her. The reason may lie somewhere in the past. Can you tell me anything about her family that might shed light on this mystery?'

'As you will recall from our early visits to the Parker estate near Bristol, I knew the family well,' said Beverly.

'Yes,' Anne said. 'Janice's parents were Oliver and Martha

Parker and Janice was their only child. She was ten when they died at sea. Tell me more.'

Beverly nodded. 'Oliver and Martha were in his sloop returning to Bristol from Waterford in Ireland, where he had large holdings of land and other properties. At night, several miles off the southwest coast of Wales, the ship struck a reef and sank. The Parkers and most of the crew were drowned.'

'Who lived to tell the tale?'

'The ship's captain and a seaman are believed to be the only survivors. None of the bodies were ever recovered.'

'That's a strange story.'

'Indeed! An Admiralty Court determined that the first mate was probably at fault. The reef is charted, if not well known. The night was dark. The first mate was at the helm. He was said to drink. The surviving seaman claimed that the mate's speech was slurred and he was unsteady on his feet. He might have been drunk that night. Since he was lost in the wreck, he couldn't testify in his own defence. It's hard to imagine that he would deliberately sink the ship.'

'What was the captain's name?'

'Seth Judd.'

'Judd?' Anne's curiosity was whetted. 'Years ago you warned me about him. Sir Abraham Parker's eldest but illegitimate son and a lecherous bully. I had to draw him off a maid once, made him look foolish. I doubt that he has forgotten. He later went to sea.'

'Yes. When the American War broke out, Oliver Parker outfitted a privateer and put Seth in command. He's apparently an excellent seaman and a ruthless pirate.'

Anne registered surprise at the accusation of piracy.

Beverly smiled wryly. 'The only difference between piracy and privateering, my dear, is that the government sanctions the latter and claims some of the profit. At heart, Seth is a pirate. He has no regard for human life. It's said that he ordered wounded captives thrown overboard. Oliver never complained. Their partnership was a profitable venture, though mostly for Oliver, who received the lion's share of the booty. Seth took great risks, captured many prizes, and became a popular hero. The populace still calls him the Sea Fox.'

'You seem to have kept better track of him than I.'

'He has come to our house in London. and told us about his life at sea. I've also heard stories about him.'

'Did the legitimate Parker brothers, Oliver and Thomas, ever accept Judd as their brother?'

'No, they called him their poor cousin to his face and shared very little of their wealth with him. He needed their financial support for his privateering, so I never heard him complain. But I'm sure there was little love lost between the brothers.'

'Have you heard anything about him lately?'

'Since that incident off the Welsh coast, his reputation is compromised in certain business circles. Investors won't give him command of a ship. But the common people still adore him. He doesn't seem to lack money. I've heard that he owns a few sloops and engages in coastal shipping.'

Anne thought for a moment while sipping the last drops of her wine. It seemed likely that Seth Judd was involved in the smuggling that the Bow Street officer had spoken about. 'It might surprise you to learn, Beverly, that Judd's my chief suspect in the attempted murder of Janice Parker. I don't know his motive, unless he's somehow allied with your husband. Thomas would benefit greatly by her death.'

Beverly gasped. 'I'm more frightened than surprised. Seth is a man without a conscience. I fear him. And if he conspires with Thomas against Janice, he might strike at me. It would be convenient for Thomas to have me out of his way so that he could marry Amelia.'

'Then take care,' said Anne. 'He's here in Bath and has a room at the York Hotel.'

OUTBURST IN THE ASSEMBLY ROOMS

Bath, Thursday, 5 November

For most of the next day, Bath's frenetic social life dulled Anne's sense of imminent danger. The threatening image of Captain Judd, pirate, Sea Fox, receded in her mind.

She had to groom herself and Janice for the Cotillion Ball in the Assembly Rooms. They both looked forward to the evening's good-natured energy and informality, especially the country dancing.

Tonight, André and his nephew, Peter, were to escort Anne, Harriet, Janice, and Beverly. They all met at Harriet's apartment. Prior to leaving for the ball, the women gathered in her parlour to examine each other's costumes. Following a recent trend in fashion towards simplicity, as well as the rustic nature of the dances, the women wore comfortable pastel muslin gowns with matching ribbons. Their hair was left natural and unpowdered. In the same spirit, the Master of Ceremonies had forbidden the wearing of hats and outlandish constructions of hair.

As the party left Queen Square in a coach, everyone seemed to be in high spirits except Beverly. She was unusually quiet for such an occasion. Her jaw was rigid; her lips were pressed tightly together. Anne noticed the woman's distress and leaned towards her. 'What's the matter, Beverly?' she asked softly.

'My husband, Thomas Parker.' Her voice was a hoarse whisper. 'Solicitor Barnstaple has written to him and proposed the terms of a fair-minded separation. I would put up a quarter of my separate property as security for his debts. In return I should have a legal separation from bed and board. Parker replied that he could agree to a separation only if I signed over to him all property held in trust for me. That would put him on the same footing as most other husbands towards their wives.'

'That's not fair,' Anne exclaimed. 'Your father never intended Parker to have the money in that trust. As for bed and board, Parker has given that away to Amelia.'

Beverly sighed, 'I've written to him and asked for a meeting to discuss our differences. He refused to reply. Today, I went to his door in the Circus. I knew he was home but was told he wasn't in. So this evening I'm going to confront him, come what may.'

'Is that wise, Beverly? Visitors come to the Assembly Rooms for entertainment. If your private dispute with Parker were to disturb their pleasure or offend their sense of propriety, they might be annoyed.'

'What else can I do, Anne? I'm at my wits' end. I want to be free of him. It's intolerable to have to beg for his signature in order to spend my own money. He uses that power to humiliate me and to force me to give him my property. That's extortion. I'll never agree to it.' Her voice fell to a barely audible hiss. 'I wish the devil were dead.'

Anne was sorely tempted to second that sentiment, but choked it back lest it fuel her cousin's anger.

In the great hall of the Assembly Rooms, spectators lined its walls; the dancers formed groups of four couples each. With their customary boldness, Parker and Amelia entered a group of distinguished visitors. Beverly disappeared from the hall, apparently unwilling to share it with her husband.

Anne and her grandfather joined Peter Cartier and Harriet Ware, Janice and Jacob Woodhouse, and a young couple, known to Jacob. From the unaffected kindness that they showed to Janice, Anne surmised that Jacob had selected them carefully and had coached them how to communicate with a deaf person.

That afternoon, Anne had learned the evening's program and, once again, had invited Jacob to her apartment to practice the dances with Janice. He treated her like a princess. Her frequent frown vanished. Her face glowed with pleasure. When he left, she signed, 'I'm ready.'

At six o'clock promptly the band struck up the first tune and the dancers went into their figures. After an hour, André yielded Anne to Peter, while Harriet excused herself in order to prepare to sing during the intermission. Other dancers also changed partners. But Jacob always managed to stay with Janice or close to her. She seemed confident, enjoying the music in her head and in her feet.

André retreated to the side, not because he was tired but because he noticed Thomas Parker and his mistress leaving the dance floor. Parker had a scowl on his face and was muttering to her. She tried to calm him. André followed them to chairs alongside the dance floor and sat close behind them. The source of the man's discontent soon became apparent: his eyes were riveted on Janice and Jacob.

Finally, Parker could no longer contain himself. He raised his voice for all nearby to hear. 'That ignorant printer's son is showing too much interest in my ward, Janice. I'll not allow it.'

For another half-hour he continued to fret. Then an acquaintance approached him with a pamphlet and said, 'You ought to read this. Your name is mentioned.'

He scanned the pamphlet with mounting distress. Midway through it he suddenly turned livid. He looked up from the page and glared at Jacob who was dancing right in front of him, his arm around Janice's waist. Parker's hands clenched, he began to rise. André feared that he would bound out on to the dance floor and assault Jacob. Amelia gripped Parker's arm, whispered loudly in his ear, 'Not now, not here.'

André slipped away, found the man who was circulating the pamphlet, and secured a copy. In passionate language it urged Parliament to abolish the slave trade, that 'nefarious commerce in human beings'. It identified Thomas Parker as one of its most greedy, reprehensible defenders and 'an agent of the devil'.

The author of the pamphlet gave his name: Jacob Woodhouse. André sucked in a breath. Anne would now face serious trouble: her Janice appeared enamoured of young Woodhouse and he of her. Parker might take drastic steps. At the least, he would chastise Anne for allowing that romance to bud.

The band came to a conclusion. The Master of Ceremonies announced the intermission, and the dancers cleared the floor for a concert. André searched for Anne. He had to warn her of Parker's mounting anger.

Anne met her grandfather as she left the dance floor. From the anxious expression on his face, she realized that he had serious matters to discuss. With a gracious bow she took leave of Peter, her partner, and followed André into a quiet corner.

'We face a crisis,' he said in hushed tones, and related what he had overheard. 'We must avoid Parker for as long as we can and allow him time to come to his senses. He may choose to avoid making a complete fool of himself.'

She agreed. 'We should listen to Harriet sing. Parker isn't likely to disrupt her in the midst of a public performance.'

Anne sought out Janice and Jacob, warned them of Parker's anger, and urged them to keep out of his sight. 'Your pamphlet, Jacob, has created a stir. Be cautious this evening, if only for Janice's sake.'

The young man listened soberly until she finished, then nodded. 'I'll take back nothing that I've written, but I'll follow your advice and avoid Parker.'

Anne and André found seats in the middle of the audience where Parker wouldn't confront them.

Harriet was in excellent voice, sweet and pure. Her selection of traditional ballads and airs charmed everyone. She closed with a heartfelt rendition of an Irish air, 'The Young Man's Dream', that she learned from a harpist while visiting County Derry. At the end, the touching melody had many in the audience dabbing kerchiefs at their eyes. Anne and André were also close to tears.

The audience rose from their seats and moved like a tidal wave towards the adjacent buffet. 'Look,' said André, 'Parker has placed himself and his mistress at a table that we must pass. Brace yourself.'

Anne hastily screwed up her courage and thought of ways to evade his anger.

But before she could be tested, a commotion erupted a few paces ahead. Someone was shouting. People nearby fell silent to listen. Anne recognized Beverly's voice, uncharacteristically loud and shrill, demanding that Parker treat her fairly and agree to a just settlement of their differences. At the conclusion of her tirade, nearly gasping for breath, she croaked, 'If you continue to deny me justice, you will pay dearly.'

Leaving that threat hanging in the air, she disappeared into the crowd. Parker hadn't an opportunity to rebut her charges. He just sat there motionless, his mouth agape. But a few seconds after Beverly left, he seemed to collect his wits. An ugly, hateful expression momentarily came over his face. He didn't notice Anne and André as they hurried by.

Dick Burton signaled them as they entered the tea room. He was seated alone drinking a glass of punch. 'What was the commotion about?' he asked.

Anne responded with a description of Beverly's confrontation with Parker. 'I fear that she may have compromised her cause, which was weak to begin with. The onlookers probably sympathized with her husband.'

Burton drew the anti-slavery pamphlet from his pocket.

'Parker seems to be receiving an uncommon amount of attention this evening.'

'I, too, have a copy,' said André, 'and have read the reference to Parker. He already resented the printer Woodhouse's attacks on the slave trade. The son's pamphlet raised Parker's temper to the boiling point.'

Anne said, 'I expect to hear from Parker. Given his hostile attitude towards Woodhouse, father and son, Parker will order me to prevent his ward, Janice, from becoming friendly with Jacob.'

'What will you do?' asked André.

'Counsel Janice to be prudent and avoid needlessly provoking Parker. Otherwise he'll ship her back to London under guard or place her here in Bath in close confinement. I doubt that she'll take my advice.'

A waiter approached the table and addressed Anne. 'Madame, I've been asked to deliver this message. I'm supposed to wait for your reply.' He handed the message to her. Burton and André leaned forward, concerned.

She read it and told them, 'Parker wants to see me alone in one of the Assembly's private rooms. Immediately.'

The messenger led Anne to the door. With a sideways glance she saw that André had followed and would be nearby in case she were to call for help. But Anne was confident that she would be safe. Parker was likely to be angry but not violent. She was less sure that she could prevail on him to do the right thing for Janice.

When she entered, he rose and bowed stiffly. His face was set in a frigid frown. He motioned her to a chair facing his.

'Madame Cartier, the behaviour of my ward, Janice, this evening was extremely rude. She chose to dance with the young man who has publicly insulted me.' He tapped on the pamphlet lying on an adjacent side table.

'She didn't know of the pamphlet until after the dancing, nor did I,' said Anne. 'Had I realized the strength of your feeling, I would have counselled that she dance with my cousin, Peter Cartier, instead of with Woodhouse.'

'You are being disingenuous, Madame. This afternoon, you invited young Woodhouse to your apartment, apparently playing the matchmaker. Since you are familiar with Bath,

you must have known that Woodhouse Senior is a rabid abolitionist and my sworn enemy. His son could not conceivably
be a suitable partner for my ward and niece, Janice. I'm deeply
disappointed in your judgement, Madame. I'll not allow her
to meet him again.'

Anne ignored his criticism. 'Sir, she's seventeen and headstrong. Will you shackle her?' Anne added under her breath,
like a black slave. 'Perhaps you don't know that Jacob
Woodhouse is the young man who saved Janice three weeks
ago in an alley off Old Bond Street. He risked his own life
to push her out of the way of a large falling stone. Janice
rightly feels immensely grateful to him. She didn't intend to
spite you.'

Confusion clouded Parker's eyes. He appeared about to
speak but thought better of it. He had heard of the incident
but perhaps not of Jacob's role.

'Furthermore,' Anne continued, 'Janice appreciates that he
knows the language of the deaf and can communicate with
her. I've urged both of them to be prudent during this season
in Bath and to refrain from provocations that could jeopardize
their relationship. If the young man takes my word to heart,
he might be less injurious in what he writes.'

'That's not enough,' sputtered Parker, nursing his wounded
pride. 'You must tell him to make a public apology for his
slurs against me. Until then, I'll not allow him to meet Janice.'
Parker glared at Anne. 'Madame, will you pledge to follow
my instructions in this matter?'

Anne thought hard. If she defied him, he could take Janice
back to his house in the Circus and virtually imprison her.
The consequences could be dire, if difficult to foresee. She
might rebel or even become violent. On the other hand, Anne
couldn't realistically hope to control the two young people if
they fell in love. But the problem might solve itself. They
hardly knew each other and with time might drift apart.

'Sir, I'll speak to Woodhouse Senior. He might be willing
to dissuade his son from personally injurious remarks about
you. I frankly doubt that anyone can persuade him to apologize but if I believe it's feasible, I'll try.' She thought Jacob
might do it to avoid losing Janice. That depended on the depth
of his affection for her, or the lack of it.

Anne had evaded the pledge that Parker demanded of her,

but he seemed slightly mollified and didn't insist. No doubt
he really didn't want to deal directly with Janice's sour moods
and emotional eruptions. They distracted him from the task
of making his mark in society. So, for the time being, Anne
could continue to shelter this troubled young woman.

As they rose to leave, Parker cocked his head in an ironic
gesture. 'I suppose you've heard of your cousin, Beverly's,
outburst. You might warn her. If she tries again to annoy
Amelia or me in the Assembly Rooms, I'll speak to the Master
of Ceremonies and have her banished. She's made her bed,
let her lie in it.'

As Anne left the room, she met her grandfather and described
her meeting with Parker. 'I think I've saved Janice for now.
What do you have to report?'

'I've noticed that my nephew, Peter, and Miss Harriet Ware
appear to enjoy each other's company. They're sitting together
in the Tea Room, drinking punch.'

'And Beverly?'

'I paid a waiter to look after her. She left the Assembly
Rooms in tears, hopefully to return to her apartment.'

'And the young couple, Janice and Jacob?'

'I paid another waiter to watch them. They slipped out the
side door during Harriet's concert, arm in arm.'

'My God!' Anne exclaimed, struggling with a wave of exasperation. 'I hope Thomas Parker doesn't hear of this. He would
assume the worst. I must trust that the young man has escorted
Janice safely back to my apartment on Queen Square. How
shall I save this headstrong young lady from herself?'

André shrugged, then muttered, 'Young people!' He pointed
Anne towards the Tea Room. 'Burton is waiting there. He has
something to tell us about Mr Seth Judd.'

Burton had placed himself at a quiet table where they could
carry on a private conversation. 'Judd was gone for a few days
but has returned to Bath and the York Hotel. I saw him here
tonight for a short while in conversation with Thomas Parker.
I also noticed him speaking confidentially with one of the
waiters, the ruddy-faced one over there. Take a good look at
him.'

Anne drew the opera glass from her bag and discreetly

studied the man on the far side of the room. He was muscular, wore a wig, and was about forty years old. Otherwise, his appearance was unremarkable.

'Why should I pay attention to him?' she asked.

'So that you can better protect Janice Parker from harm. That man is somehow different from the other waiters. He plays his role well enough. He has waited on tables before. I was told that he worked last year at a spa in Bristol. But to my eye he's not genuine. He lacks the deference, the polite congeniality of a typical waiter in the Assembly Rooms. And he has a shifty expression, a sly manner that I've found among men and women on the other side of the law. If I were the Master of Ceremonies, I'd count the silverware. You had better keep Miss Parker out of his reach.'

Anne took another look at the man, watched him move from table to table, and compared him with other waiters. She passed the glass to her grandfather. They agreed that Burton was right on the mark.

'What's his name?' André asked. 'I may learn more about him.'

'Nate Taylor,' Burton replied. 'Tell me what you find. I'll be pursuing Seth Judd and Thomas Parker for a while.'

At eleven o'clock the crowd at the Assembly Rooms had settled down to playing cards, drinking punch and wine, and exchanging gossip. Anne signaled her grandfather that she wished to leave. He had begun to yawn, so he readily agreed. Peter and Harriet left with them in a hired coach. Beverly could not be found.

At Queen Square the women descended and the men followed them to the door and bade them goodnight. Anne's anxiety for Janice mounted as she turned the key in her lock. Was the young woman still out in the city? She might be with Jacob in Crescent Fields, her favourite retreat, enjoying a night-time view over the city, or lying in a meadow counting the stars. At least with him she had protection. He was a brave, stout fellow.

Inside the apartment Anne lighted a candle and surveyed the room. Janice's bonnet and cape hung on a hook. Anne felt relieved; the young woman was home safe. A sound came from her room. Janice appeared at her door in a nightdress, wide awake, a mixture of apprehension and joy on her face.

Anne's feeling of relief quickly changed to irritation. The young woman was remarkably inconsiderate. She shouldn't have left the Assembly Rooms without telling her or André. And it was rash to leave with a young man whom she scarcely knew.

But Anne bit back her urge to scold, signed a greeting, and hung up her bonnet and cape next to the young woman's.

'Please make us a pot of herbal tea,' she signed to Janice. 'I'll change into my nightdress.' She wanted time to prepare for a possible confrontation with the young woman.

While undressing, Anne glanced at a mirror and noticed a cross expression on her face. That won't do, she thought. She forced herself to reflect that Janice had suffered great losses and had had little happiness thus far in her brief life. This evening was a rare, pleasant, and satisfying experience for her. Be gentle, Anne told herself. With luck, no serious harm was done.

Anne drew a dressing gown over her nightdress and joined Janice at the table. The young woman could barely sign coherently, so eager was she to share her good fortune. 'Jacob is a wonderful young man, so light and graceful on his feet, so witty. He's kind . . . and he likes me.'

'I'm happy for you, Janice, that Jacob has come into your life. He seems suited to be your friend. But be patient. It takes a while to get to know a person's true character – whether he's honest and trustworthy, whether he truly has your best interests at heart, whether his affection for you, and yours for him, is genuine and lasting. Let's hope that he *is* what he seems. We all need good friends. I'm blessed with my Paul.'

Janice nodded to Anne's signs, but her mind was elsewhere. Eyes glistening, lips parted, she slowly, quietly, sipped her tea.

Anne then put on a sterner mien. 'Why did you leave the Assembly Rooms without telling me? I haven't bound you with rules, or ordered you to do this or that. But be prudent. Someone has tried to kill you. Until we find the culprit, you are still in danger. I'm trying to help you. So you must keep me informed.'

Janice looked slightly penitent. 'Neither Jacob nor I cared to gamble or play cards or get dizzy on punch. The Assembly Rooms had become hot and crowded. When the dancing ended, we thought only of going outside and enjoying the cool autumn air in Crescent Fields. The sky was clear, the moon bright. We studied the stars in their constellations.' She paused, met Anne's critical eye with a gentle gaze. 'I'm sorry that I was thoughtless.'

Anne mustered a forgiving smile and then signed, 'Jacob's pamphlet has much provoked your uncle. Until the young man apologizes, you may not meet him again – so said Parker. I tried but failed to persuade him to change his mind. Tomorrow, I'll ask Jacob's father what might be done. I fear I can't offer you much hope. But, for the time being, you must obey your uncle and be patient.'

Janice reacted with mounting disappointment and displeasure. 'Jacob showed me the pamphlet. It's true what he writes about my uncle. But, I suppose I have no choice.'

The young woman's signing lacked conviction. Defiance flashed in her eyes. Anne resolved to keep a close watch on her – within reason.

As they finished their tea, Anne signed, 'It's late. But I have a question about your late parents' household. I'm wondering if the threat to your life might come from someone in your family's past. When they died, you were still too young to know much about the world around you. Do you remember the name of a trusted servant, who would know the family's secrets and perhaps your parents' enemies, if they had any?'

Janice thought for a moment. 'My favourite servant was my nanny, Mildred Fox. She lives in Bristol. She was with the family for many years and raised my mother. We exchange messages occasionally.'

'I'd like us to visit her late tomorrow afternoon, if possible.'

Janice brightened. 'I'll write her and ask if she'll see us. She should be at home. She's elderly and seldom travels.'

'Still, we owe her the courtesy of letting her know that we're coming. A courier can take the message at dawn and return before noon.'

Janice went to her room and returned a minute later with the message.

Anne scanned and sealed it. 'And now it's time for bed. Tomorrow will be a strenuous day.'

INTO A MURKY PAST

Bath and Bristol, Friday, 6 November

At breakfast, André and Peter joined Anne and Janice to plan for the day. A courier had left with Janice's message to Miss Fox in Bristol. The two men would go to the Assembly Rooms and learn what they could about Nate Taylor. As they were about to leave, Peter remarked, 'If Beverly doesn't apologize to the MC for her outburst last night, she'll be ostracized. In that case she might as well take the next coach back to London.'

'I agree,' Anne said. 'I'll speak to her this morning.'

In vain Anne searched for Beverly at the Pump Room. But at midmorning she found her at home in her apartment on Milsom Street.

'I'm afraid to show my face in public,' she muttered as they sat in her parlour. 'I lost my temper and my self-respect last night. If I were to go to the Assembly Rooms tonight, the MC would turn me away at the door.'

'He probably would,' Anne remarked distractedly. A sensitive question was nagging her mind but she hesitated to ask it. Finally, she said, 'A mutual acquaintance at the Pump Room this morning told me that she saw you late last night, alone, furiously pacing back and forth along the quay on the Avon River. May I ask what you were doing?'

Beverly flinched and didn't reply. She walked to the window overlooking Milsom Street and stood, shoulders hunched, her back to Anne. Soon sobs racked her body. Anne rose to comfort her and offered a handkerchief.

Between sobs, Beverly explained that, after leaving the Assembly Rooms, she walked south on Horse Street to the river. 'I had just made a fool of myself and intended to throw myself in. But I couldn't muster the courage. I walked back and forth on the quay arguing with myself, cursing my fate. Finally it dawned on me that killing myself was exactly what Thomas would want me to do. He would inherit my property and be free to marry that whore Amelia – without it costing him a farthing. What an idiot I was. I should throw Thomas in the river, not myself.'

She turned and faced Anne, wiped tears from her eyes, and composed herself. In a low, even voice she said, 'I truly hate that man.' Then she added, 'That's a futile sentiment, isn't it. I've come no closer to gaining my freedom.'

'You shouldn't give up,' Anne counseled, grasping at straws, unnerved by her cousin's uncharacteristic vehemence. 'Parker's financial position is so precarious that he might eventually accept a settlement you could afford.'

Beverly shrugged, unpersuaded.

Anne persisted. 'You should re-establish yourself in society and win support for your cause. First, you must apologize to Mr Tyson, the Master of Ceremonies, this morning. Peter, André, and I will be with you and vouch for your sincerity and good character.'

Beverly grimaced as if she had smelled something foul. Finally, she sighed. 'You win. What have I to lose? My pride is gone. I can't sink any lower.'

The two women found André and Peter at a table in the Tea Room. They greeted Beverly cordially, obviously pleased that she would try to make amends. In her dignified contrition she was quite attractive, an advantage in dealing with the Master of Ceremonies.

Peter remarked, 'We've seen Tyson running about. By now, he may have settled down in his office.'

As they entered, he looked up from his writing table. A frown crossed his face when he recognized Beverly. He let the visitors remain standing. 'Your behaviour last night, Mrs Parker, disrupted the good order that our guests expect in these rooms. If they were sufficiently irritated, they might turn elsewhere for their pleasures. Admission to these rooms requires civil deportment, as well as appropriate dress.'

André gave the MC a deferential bow, then spoke on Beverly's behalf. 'Madame Parker is always appropriately dressed and usually civil. Last night, unfortunately, she was taken by surprise and extraordinarily provoked. We, her friends, assure you that it won't happen again.'

Beverly took a half-step forward, bowed slightly to the MC, then acknowledged, 'Last night I acted contrary to my own

best standard of behaviour. I'm sorry for upsetting fellow
guests, and for tainting the good reputation of the Assembly
Rooms. If allowed to return, I'll control my feelings in the
future.'

Her speech was so heartfelt that the MC was visibly affected.
He rose and took her by the hand. 'I'll personally welcome
you in our foyer the next time you come to the Rooms. Will
you attend Thursday's Cotillion Ball?'

Beverly assured him that she would and thanked him for
his generous spirit.

Outside the office the friends breathed a collective sigh of
relief and walked Beverly back to her apartment. At her door
she embraced them. 'I'm so grateful for your support. Now
I feel much better,' she said, and sent them off.

Anne invited André and Peter to her apartment to report on
what they had learned about the waiter, Nate Taylor.

'He lives in a room above a tavern called The Little Drummer
on Avon Street,' Peter began. 'He doesn't associate with other
waiters or workers from the Assembly Rooms, but is usually
seen with sailors and other low-life characters in the neigh-
bourhood. His female companion apparently works at the tavern.'

'I'm familiar with The Little Drummer. Taylor's probably
involved with a nest of smugglers,' Anne remarked.

'Should we talk to his neighbours, and to the barman at the
tavern?'

Anne shook her head. 'Not yet. They would be too frightened to cooperate with you. We'll wait for a better opportunity.'

Late in the morning Anne visited Woodhouse Senior at his
print shop on St James Parade. The print room was crowded
with machinery. Fortunately, it was still. Woodhouse stood
next to a press, reading a proof page and instructing his apprentice. His son was not in sight. Woodhouse saw Anne enter,
smiled, and excused himself for a moment while he finished
with the apprentice.

Woodhouse turned to Anne. 'The press will soon become
quite noisy. We can speak more comfortably in my office.'

She followed him to a small, poorly furnished room in the
rear of the building, more like an animal's den than a business office. He cleared papers from chairs for her and for
himself.

He looked at her with a mixture of apprehension and good humour. 'I understand that Jacob's pamphlet has upset Mr Parker. Has that caused you much trouble?'

'Yes, indeed!' Anne replied. 'He threatens to force Janice to return to his house in the Circus unless your son apologizes publicly. To calm him, I promised to speak to you.' She urged Woodhouse to consider Janice's situation. To be confined to Parker's house would cause her much suffering, especially since the young woman had begun to think that he might be behind the attempt to kill her.

Anne paused, studied Woodhouse's unsmiling countenance. He knew what she was driving at and was sceptical. But she proceeded undeterred. 'Until the investigation is complete and Janice is safe, it would be best if she and Jacob weren't seen together in public.' Anne hesitated but asked, 'Could Jacob be persuaded to apologize to Parker for the pamphlet?'

Woodhouse shook his head. 'I'll try to reason with my son to be more prudent. But I can't promise that he would comply with your requests. I've raised Jacob to pursue truth and justice. His pamphlet cannot be faulted on either count. When you strip away Parker's charm and handsome appearance, what's left is a greedy slave trader. Jacob shouldn't be asked to apologize for stating the truth.'

At noon Anne and Janice set out for the nanny's home in Bristol twelve miles away. She expected them in the afternoon between three and four, the courier had reported. About three o'clock their coach stopped before a weathered brick building in the heart of the city. A cabinetmaker in his shop on the street level confirmed that Miss Mildred Fox lived on the floor above him. 'A determined old lady,' he called her with a hint of disapproval in his voice. 'She has a mind of her own.'

The stairs to the first floor were dark, narrow, and steep, prompting Janice to sign to Anne, 'This is no place for an elderly woman like Mildred. She could break her neck.'

'True,' Anne agreed. 'The Parkers may not have paid her well. She could be poor and this is the best that she can afford.'

They reached the first-floor landing safely and knocked. Janice seemed to grow more expectant by the second.

A grey-haired woman in a simple black gown opened the door,

smiled warmly at the sight of Janice, studied Anne with a sharp eye, and welcomed them. She moved briskly, like a person who paid little attention to the infirmities of old age. Her apartment consisted of one small room, clean but sparsely furnished.

A table was prepared. She poured hot water into a teapot and invited her guests to sit down. As she passed a plate of sweet biscuits, Anne noticed that arthritis had crippled the woman's hands. She knew suffering.

She faced Janice and spoke distinctly being considerate of a deaf girl's needs. 'What have you been up to since we last wrote?'

The young woman recounted the high points of her recent weeks, omitting the attempt on her life. When she reached Bath, she focused on moving from Parker's house into Anne's apartment. 'I'm free to dance and meet kind, friendly people. It's like being released from prison. I'm so happy.'

'That's wonderful,' Mildred said with feeling, then turned to Anne and asked abruptly, 'Why have you come with Janice? Has Parker hired you to be her companion?'

Janice hastened to take the question. 'Madame Cartier is my friend and protects me, in spite of Parker.'

Mildred's brow creased with confusion.

Anne explained. 'Our Janice has become the target of an unknown killer. We don't know why he has attacked her. We wonder if he or she may come from Janice's past, or her family's. You might shed light on details that our investigation has thus far overlooked.' She handed Miss Fox a document with the Bath mayor's seal, testifying to Anne's good character and to her role in the investigation of the threat to Janice.

As Miss Fox read, she frowned with concern. When she finished, she returned the letter and asked, 'What would you like to know? I'll help as much as I can.'

Anne thanked her and asked, 'How did the brothers, Oliver and Thomas, and their half-brother Seth get along?'

'Even while their parents lived,' she replied, 'the boys acted like rivals. From an early age, Thomas, the youngest, resented the greater privileges and parental affection that his older brother, Oliver, enjoyed. Seth, in fact the oldest but illegitimate, was never legally recognized as a son but was commonly regarded as one. He lived with his mother in the servants' quarters. But the three boys played together and the same tutor educated them.'

'How did Seth react to his situation?' Anne asked.

'He never confided in me, nor in anyone else, except his mother, a proud, bitter woman, who strongly influenced him. She still lives in retirement on the Parker estate and Seth visits her. He always deferred to his brothers and outwardly accepted his inferior status in the family. Still, I sensed that he was full of resentment, but kept it locked up.

'When old Mr Parker died, he left all his vast property to the first born *legal* son, Oliver, as the law required. But he had asked Oliver to settle a generous income on Thomas and give a smaller amount of money to Seth. Thomas received less than he expected and complained bitterly to Oliver. Seth appeared to accept his lot.'

Anne said, 'I've heard that Oliver and Seth actually co-operated in maritime commerce and privateering, Oliver advancing the necessary money, Seth commanding the ships.'

'A profitable partnership,' added Mildred, 'though much more to Oliver's advantage than to Seth's.'

'What did Oliver's wife think of her brothers-in-law?'

'She urged her husband not to trust them, especially Seth.'

Anne's face must have looked doubtful, for Mildred added, 'Seth once told a maid that Oliver's inheritance would have been his, the oldest son, had his father done the honourable thing and legally acknowledged his paternity. Seth claimed that he intended to have it all, one way or another. The maid told Mrs Parker who told her husband. Oliver shrugged it off. "Seth sometimes drinks too much ale." But the maid said that Seth was perfectly sober.'

Anne wondered how to interpret Seth's claim. Was it an eruption of deep-rooted frustration or an unguarded moment of candour?

Before Anne could express her quandary, Janice broke in and changed the subject. 'Tell me what you think of Beverly.'

Mildred looked as if she'd rather not answer that question. But Janice fixed her with a penetrating, insistent stare. Finally she replied. 'Beverly married Thomas Parker eighteen years ago, on the assumption that he was rich and socially prominent, as well as charming and handsome. Affection and love weren't part of the contract.'

'How did she feel about me?'

Mildred appeared to be increasingly uncomfortable with

the young woman's line of questions, but she seemed compelled to tell the truth. 'When your parents died, she tried to dissuade Parker from taking responsibility for you. The burden would fall on her. But he confided that he was nearly bankrupt and would end in a debtor's prison unless he became your guardian. For then he would receive a monthly payment from your trust funds and, more important, he would have the likely prospect of soon inheriting your fortune. You were a weak, sickly child. The doctors told Beverly that you wouldn't live more than a few years. In any case, being your guardian and heir would much improve his credit.

'Therefore, Beverly agreed with Parker. She was persuaded that the inconvenience would be brief, the burden light. Afterwards, she seemed indifferent, even negligent towards you, wouldn't let me call the doctor when your condition worsened. It was as if she felt it was fruitless to try to save you, and preferable for you to die quickly rather than to linger.'

Janice turned pale and looked stunned, as if struck by a hammer.

Mildred went on relentlessly. 'I became so angry and upset that I scolded Beverly. She didn't like me anyway and accused me of pampering you. So this was her opportunity to "retire" me with a pitiful pension. She then hired another woman to nurse you.

'When you caught the fever that took away your hearing, that careless and incompetent woman neglected to cleanse your ears regularly. So you lost your hearing, but you recovered your health and confounded both Thomas and Beverly. He had to find money elsewhere, and she had at least to pretend to raise you as her own child.'

Mildred's tone had turned bitter, and her comments dwelled on the darkest side of Beverly's character. Anne's mind baulked at such a thoroughly negative portrait of her cousin. Nonetheless, Anne admitted to herself that Beverly's attitude towards Janice had once included a measure of greed. Now, since her virtual separation from Thomas Parker and his new will in favour of Amelia, Beverly could no longer hope to draw any benefit from Janice's death. She might rather hope for Thomas Parker's speedy death.

A ZEALOUS PARTNER

Bath, Saturday, 7 November

C ould the Parker brothers' quarrel over their father's property have turned poisonous and led one of them to attack Janice? That question had troubled Anne on the ride back to Bath last night. It was still on her mind as she lay in bed this morning. The answer eluded her. The disgruntled nanny's testimony wasn't enough.

Anne rose from the bed and went about her morning toilette. While dressing for the day, she wondered what to do with Janice. The young woman needed something to cheer her up and get her to thinking positively. During the ride home from Bristol last night her expression was grim. Eyes narrowed, she appeared to brood on horrid events in the distant as well as recent past. The visit with her nanny must have reminded her of the many convincing reasons why she so bitterly disliked Thomas and Beverly Parker.

At breakfast Anne proposed to Janice an evening at the equestrian show in Franklin and Ryles's Amphitheatre on Monmouth Street. André, Peter, Harriet, and Beverly would join them. For a few days, a famous London company – including acrobats, strongmen, female slack rope dancers as well as horses and their riders – was performing in Bath.

Janice seemed pleased with the suggestion. She would enjoy the show and her companions, Beverly excepted. The young woman especially liked Harriet, a kindly, sympathetic acquaintance. Janice could also readily understand the singer's natural gestures, distinct articulation, and facial expressions. For Anne the evening would be like reliving a performance at Sadler's Wells, but with horses. Memories of strutting on the high wire to the music of Rule Britannia came back to her. It was exhilarating just to think about it.

Then it occurred to Anne that the performance at the amphitheatre would end late at night. The streets of Bath were mostly well lighted, but there were dark alleys and entryways.

She didn't feel personally in danger but was concerned for Janice. Better to be prepared. She would immediately check her pistol, practice with her rapier, and bring them along this evening. André should bring his weapons as well.

After breakfast Anne and Janice, together with André, Peter, and Harriet, visited the Pump Room, that customary ritual among visitors, and exchanged conventional remarks with Thomas Parker and Amelia. Jacob Woodhouse was there with a few male friends, but they kept a safe distance from Parker.

When Parker and his mistress left, Jacob discreetly greeted Janice. Anne went to the counter for a glass of water to allow them some privacy. But she kept them in view with her pocket mirror. Unfortunately, she couldn't read their lips or figure out the meaning of the sideways glances that they threw towards her. And this air of conspiracy worried her.

Then she noticed the young Oxford scholar, Parker's spy, on the other side of the room. A young woman hurried up to him, spoke earnestly, and rushed off after Jacob, who had rejoined his friends. So, she was the scholar's sister and also a spy – she had hovered by Janice and Jacob while they 'conspired'. For the most part, they had used sign language. Could the spy have understood them? Or, would she overhear Jacob speaking with his friends about his plans?

Anne was about to leave the Pump Room when Dick Burton hobbled in on his cane and caught her eye. Blocked by a line of wheelchairs across his path, he mouthed, 'I want to speak to you.' She left Janice with Peter and Harriet for a few hours of shopping on Milsom Street and met Burton in a relatively quiet corner.

'I believe that Sir William Williams, the retired Welsh judge, is on his way to the Pump Room. We should arrange for a conversation about the attempt on Janice's life and its possible connection to the violent deaths of her father and mother at sea seven years ago.'

Burton had earlier told Anne that Williams, who usually spent the season in Bath, was familiar with the tragic death of the Parkers. Because their ship wrecked off Pembroke on the southwest coast of Wales, the court of inquiry was held in Swansea, the closest major port, and Judge Williams heard the case, the last before he retired. He and Burton had casually discussed it in Bath last season. A few days ago, Burton had recognized the judge's name in the *Bath Chronicle* among distinguished new arrivals in the city.

He and Anne moved to a place opposite the entrance where they could observe the newcomers. Burton gave Anne the judge's description – a short, stout man with a florid complexion and lively gestures. He would wear a full, old-fashioned wig and a long, black coat.

Soon the judge entered the room alone. Anne and Burton waited until he made his way through the crowd to the water counter. When he had nearly finished his glass, they approached him with due respect. Burton introduced Anne as the wife of a French colonel in the Royal Highway Patrol.

Judge Williams' face lighted up. He was clearly pleased to meet Burton in the company of an attractive woman. For a few minutes they exchanged views on the weather, the visitors to the spa, and the prospect for good music and theatre this season.

Burton brought the conversation around to Anne's concern about the recent suspicious accident involving Janice Parker in London. 'When Madame Cartier described the incident to me, I recalled your continuing interest in the Parkers' shipwreck off Pembroke in '82. You might be intrigued by a remarkable coincidence.' He lowered his voice to a whisper. 'Captain Seth Judd was involved in both episodes of violence touching the Parker family.'

The judge pursed his lips, his eyes widened. 'Oh, indeed,' he murmured. 'I would dearly like to hear more.'

He glanced about the crowded room. The band struck up a loud gig. The crowd's chatter rose to a deafening roar. Williams frowned. 'The Pump Room is too noisy and busy for any reasonable conversation.'

Burton nodded. 'What we have to say is also more safely discussed in private. I propose that we move to my office at the Guildhall.' As he took a step, he winced with pain. 'I'll call a chairman to take me there. I've been standing too long. My arthritis is acting up.'

Ten minutes later, Anne and Burton were sitting in his office when the judge entered. He seemed surprised that Anne was there. That reaction prompted Burton to remark, 'We need Madame Cartier with us. She knows the language of the deaf and can speak for Janice Parker. She's also familiar with the rest of the Parker family. I trust her implicitly.'

Williams cast an uncertain glance at Anne and gave her a thin smile. 'Mr Burton has given you a strong recommendation, Madame. I hope that you can help us.'

He settled into his chair. 'I'll begin with the shipwreck. The *Mercury* was a small, fast sloop belonging to Mr Oliver Parker and built to his specifications. It had a tiny cabin for the Parkers and another for the ship's officers. The sails were manned by a pair of seamen who slept in a shelter on the deck. As the ship headed into the Bristol Channel, it had a strong southwesterly wind in its sails and was moving at full speed.

'The sky was dark and overcast, visibility poor. Still, Captain Judd was experienced and had set a safe course south of Pembroke. But during the night the mate was at the helm and allowed the wind to carry the ship off course towards the shore. To this day, the reason for his action remains unclear to me. At the Court of Inquiry the surviving seaman told us that the mate was drunk.'

Anne raised a hand. 'If he were known to drink to excess, why had the captain hired him or entrusted him with the helm alone at night?'

'At the inquiry, and subsequently, Madame, I wondered about the captain's behaviour on this point – as on a number of others. But the inquiry was all about ascertainable facts rather than speculation.' The judge's tone had become a bit testy. Anne resolved to keep her curiosity mostly to herself.

'Near Pembroke,' the judge continued, 'the ship hit a rocky ridge beneath the surface and began to break apart. The great force of the wind carried the wreck over the rocks and into deep water, where it quickly sank. Only Captain Judd and one seaman survived. I really don't know why the others perished.'

The judge leaned back in his chair and gazed at Anne. 'There you have the story in a nutshell, Madame. Now tell me what happened to Miss Janice Parker and what Seth Judd had to do with it.'

Anne replied, 'On the thirteenth of October in an alley off Old Bond Street someone attempted to kill her.' She went on to describe the incident. 'There was no obvious suspect. Her uncle, Thomas Parker, the person with most to gain from her death, was elsewhere. Mr Seth Judd, who rented a room in the building, could have committed the crime, but had no apparent motive. He wasn't actually seen at the site and has an alibi. Later I learned that he had been the captain of the ship that carried Oliver Parker and his wife to their deaths seven years ago. Janice Parker is their daughter and heir to their fortune. Is that not an intriguing coincidence?'

'It is indeed,' remarked the judge, now fully alert. 'Due to lack of evidence,' the judge went on, 'the Admiralty ruled only that the wreck was caused by the mate's error at the helm.'

'Besides Captain Seth Judd,' Burton pointed out, 'you said there was one other survivor. Could you tell us who he was?'

'A young seaman, Nate Taylor. He accused the mate of being drunk at the time. That's as much as I know about him.'

'Then,' said Burton, 'I'll share what I've learned. Taylor came from an innkeeper's family and worked several years as a waiter. Grew bored. Went to sea in 1778 on Judd's priva-teer for the money. After surviving the wreck in 1782, he continued to work in Judd's enterprises.'

'Smuggling perhaps?' asked the judge.

Burton nodded. 'In 1786 he went back to the waiter's profes-sion, first in Bristol, then in Bath. He was a waiter at Thursday's Cotillion.' Burton paused, then added, 'But I've heard that he continues to assist Judd and spies on the excise officers and the military guarding the coast.'

Judge Williams remarked, 'At the time, I had no idea that the captain and seaman Taylor were so close. They may have conspired to deceive me.' The judge appeared chastened.

'We need to look more closely at that wreck off the Welsh coast,' Burton remarked. 'Could you help us gain access to the Admiralty's report?'

Williams nodded. 'A copy of the report should be among my files. I'll send my servant to fetch them. He should be back in a few days. This looks like an opportune moment to revisit that case, especially since the two survivors also seem involved in the present threat to the young lady's life.'

After Anne left Burton's office, Judge Williams asked him for a few minutes of his time. Burton agreed willingly. The judge fussed with a button and seemed ill at ease. He had something on his mind. To encourage his companion, Burton opened a cabinet, took out a bottle of port and two small glasses and poured. They saluted each other.

The judge sipped his port, mellowed slightly, and began, 'I appreciate your high regard for Madame Cartier, and I can understand bringing her here to discuss specific issues that she's familiar with. But is she going to be included in all our conversations as if she were a partner in this investigation? What can she contribute?'

Burton replied with a non-committal shrug. Williams' remarks didn't surprise him. An older man, the judge held stubbornly to traditional ways in his dress and manners.

'Furthermore,' the judge continued, 'Madame Cartier's fascination with crime is unhealthy. It would taint or debase the character of any well-bred woman. In truth, I find women in general to be weak and scatterbrained. Even the best of them are childlike, unfit for men's work.'

Burton caustically reflected that the judge's indictment might be valid for the women in his own life. By contrast, Burton recalled fondly his recently deceased wife: an independent and resourceful woman, clever and wise as well. He felt a pang of loss. They had often discussed his cases. Her advice was always useful.

He took a long sip of his port, then spoke as gently as he could. 'I'll not argue the merits of women in general, sir. But over the years that I've been a Bow Street officer I've found certain women to be remarkably perceptive of human character, good and bad. Madame Cartier has that quality. In addition, she's strong and fearless and can ride and shoot. Her husband and his adjutant have trained her in techniques of interrogation. She understands what's going on and takes good notes. She can even pick locks. A useful skill. Years ago, I was quite clever at it myself. Today, my arthritic fingers can barely turn the key to my own door.'

'Really!' exclaimed the judge. 'I might expect to find that skill in a Bow Street officer, but not in a respectable woman. How *unusual*.' He emptied his glass and smacked his lips.

Burton took the hint and poured more port. 'It's true, sir, that Madame Cartier is not typical in many respects, but neither is she unnatural. Even while investigating crime, she's still a sensitive, caring woman, and attractive as well. I doubt that crime unduly fascinates her. Rather she's passionate in the pursuit of justice, especially for deaf children like Janice Parker, who are so vulnerable. In this case I consider her my partner, and I want her to be well informed so that she can be useful.'

Judge Williams didn't make any further comments, but he left the office looking unhappy.

Late in the morning Anne and Janice picked up mail and returned to their Queen Square apartment to read it. Janice had a letter from Charlie Rogers at Braidwood's institute, reporting on the good times he and other friends of Janice were having, even though they missed her.

Anne sat at her writing table and read a letter from Paul, dated the thirty-first of October, just ten days after she and Beverly left Paris. He reported that the city remained excited, its moods unpredictable. But its administration under Mayor Bailly continued to improve. The Marquis de Lafayette and his National Guard effectively policed the city. Banditry decreased in the countryside around Paris.

But a new crisis loomed. The government would soon seize the property of the Church and sell it to pay off the state's debts and balance its budget. This was a hastily conceived, desperate measure. Paul was sceptical of its success. The sale of so many buildings and so much land over a short period would yield far less than the government anticipated and chiefly benefit wealthy speculators. The state would have to take on the expense of the social services that the church used to provide. In closing he wrote, 'Your husband and your friends miss you already. Fondly, Paul.'

Anne reached for her pen, dipped it in ink, and began a letter to him. She summed up the complicated crisis in the Parker family.

I fear that Beverly has made matters worse for herself. As an adulterous wife, her position vis-à-vis Thomas Parker is hopeless. If she is to be legally separated from him, she must give him all her previously protected property and become a pauper. The law would still bar her from marrying again. Since she's unfit to earn her own living, she would have to return to Italy and be utterly dependent on her lover, Jack Grimshaw. In a few words, her situation is desperate.

Anne laid down her pen, tried to think of something encouraging or uplifting to write. Nothing came to mind. The future for Janice and Beverly seemed bleak. She sighed. Perhaps this evening's entertainment would give her reasons to smile.

MAYHEM IN CRESCENT FIELDS

Bath, Saturday, 7 November

As Anne reached the doors at the Amphitheatre, her skin tingled with excitement. She and her party – Janice, Peter and Harriet, André and Beverly – were among the first to enter, promptly at six p.m. They each paid one shilling and sixpence – a reasonable price – and sat in the first gallery. It offered an unobstructed view of the arena.

The equestrian show was to start at six forty-five p.m. While they waited, Janice eagerly watched the audience drift in, searching apparently for Jacob Woodhouse. Anne lent her the opera glass from her bag.

Suddenly, Janice handed the glass back to Anne and pointed to a man entering the opposite gallery. 'Look, there's Parker's spy, the young scholar from Oxford.'

The spy was talking to a rough-looking man in a sailor's dress. He had a cropped ear and a menacing expression on his face. The spy raised a glass to his eye and aimed it at Anne and Janice. When he saw them looking at him, he lowered it hastily.

'I wonder what that's all about?' asked Anne.

Janice shrugged. 'Parker will never leave me alone.'

Meanwhile, Anne also overheard her cousin, Peter, query Harriet about her summer's entertaining at Sadler's Wells, the music hall a few miles north of London.

Their conversation raised Anne's concern. Peter seemed anxious about Harriet's past. Anne wondered if he might share his parents' low regard for female entertainers, as if the theatre's environment might taint their character.

Anne joined the conversation. 'We loved our work and our companions. For the most part, the audience treated us well.

But sometimes a few men – rogues really – annoyed us or tried to force themselves upon us.'

Peter's brow furrowed. Harriet lowered her gaze.

'On one occasion,' Anne went on, 'they invaded the women's dressing room and harassed Harriet. I had to chase them out with a chamber pot.'

Peter reacted with exasperated fury. 'If they were in my jurisdiction, I would have them whipped and put in the stocks.' He gave Harriet a sympathetic glance. She smiled her appreciation – and relief.

At that moment, the Master of Ceremonies appeared and welcomed the audience. With grandiloquent gestures, he announced 'three stupendous displays of equestrian art'. He signalled and stepped back. Loud trumpet flourishes pierced the air. Signora Rosetta rode into the arena on a great black stallion. Then, balancing on its back, she circled the arena and blew kisses to the audience. The trumpets blasted again and, riding astride, Miss Simonet jumped her white mare through a ring of fire. Finally, the trumpets introduced a six-year-old boy on a pony. He led a troop of six men on Arabians in a series of complicated maneuvers.

The MC returned to announce in deep, suspenseful tones the high wire act. A slender young woman in a shiny silver costume skipped into the arena. A hush came over the crowd. For a moment, Anne was back at Sadler's Wells performing on the high wire in a similar costume. Her heart began to pound, anticipating the thrill and the danger.

The young woman climbed up a ladder to a small platform just below the ceiling. A thin, almost invisible wire stretched across the room's upper, dimly lighted spaces. For a moment she stood poised as if in a trance. The crowd held its breath. Anne tensed; Janice gripped her arm. With a pole for balance, the young woman stepped out on to the wire. A shimmering spectre, she slowly glided in mid-air across the room and stepped onto a distant platform. The crowd breathed out a loud sigh of relief. She bowed to them and received a tumultuous applause.

After the high wire act, Anne followed Janice's gaze and noticed Jacob Woodhouse across the arena in the opposite gallery. Two rows behind him was Parker's spy. Jacob appeared to be alone. Anne doubted that he was there by happy coincidence.

During the following acts featuring the strongman and the acrobats, Janice seemed to lose interest in the performance and looked preoccupied. Then, at the intermission, she excused herself and hurried off to a water closet.

Anne was suspicious but couldn't protest. However, she kept a sharp eye on Jacob who had stood up to stretch and remained near his seat. Then suddenly he was gone, almost certainly to a prearranged rendezvous with Janice.

It was now about eight o'clock and would be dark outside. Anne tapped her grandfather on the shoulder. 'Janice and Jacob have disappeared. We must find them.'

'Do you have your pistol and your sword cane?' he asked. Anne nodded.

'Good. I have mine. Do you have any idea where they might go?'

'My best guess is Crescent Fields, her favourite place.'

At the exit, Parker's spy and his sister stood idle. Anne accosted them. 'Why aren't you following Janice?'

They glanced at each other with alarm. 'A man came from Mr Parker and told us that three sturdy sailors from Bristol would do duty tonight. Bandits were infesting this area. They might attempt to kidnap her.'

Anne was furious, but managed to ask in a level voice, 'Where were the young people going?'

'Into Crescent Fields,' the scholar-spy replied.

Anne and André hurried off in that direction. In the day it was a popular site for walking. At night in cool, early November, it was deserted.

The sky above Bath was cloudless. The moon, a few days past full, shed an eerie blue light over the meadow. Anne saw the young couple about a hundred paces ahead on Gravel Walk about halfway through Crescent Fields. They were walking slowly, arm in arm, on an open stretch of the path.

As they entered a shadowed area, three figures leaped out of a clump of tall bushes and began assaulting them with clubs and knives.

Anne and André dashed towards the fray, drawing their pistols and rapiers and shouting for help. But no one else was in sight. Two of the rogues dropped Jacob to the ground and advanced towards his rescuers. A black mask concealed the lower half of one man's face. The other man grinned malevolently.

Moonlight glinted from their steel blades. A few paces off to one side, the third rogue held a limp Janice on one arm, her head hanging back. With the other arm he raised a long knife and aimed at her exposed throat.

André fired from close range, striking the rogue in the temple. He released Janice and fell to the ground. His two partners halted at the sight of Anne's pistol and rapier. Realizing that the public had been alarmed, they turned and fled. Still, Anne noticed that the grinning rogue had a cropped ear and wore a sailor's garb.

Jacob lay on the path, stabbed and beaten while defending Janice. She was bruised, her gown torn open at the neck. Anne sheathed her rapier and pocketed the pistol. Their shouts and André's shot finally drew men to the scene, including a watchman. They bound Jacob's wounds and hurried the two young people and the mortally wounded rogue to the city's hospital.

At about ten o'clock, messages went out to Parker and to Woodhouse Senior. The latter was at home and came immediately to the hospital, greatly distressed. Parker was attending a private party at the home of an acquaintance and came an hour later. The doctor had sedated Jacob and Janice. So Anne had to tell Woodhouse and Parker what had happened, while André reported to the night constable who had also been summoned.

Woodhouse apologized to Anne for his son's misbehaviour and thanked her for saving him at great risk to herself. He was grief-stricken. His son had suffered knife wounds to his arms and face and had lost much blood. Fortunately, his thick cape had deflected what could have been a fatal blow to his heart.

Parker hardly glanced at Janice resting on a bed, shocked, gasping for air, barely conscious. Anne sat next to her, stroked her brow, and spoke softly to calm her.

'You've not been vigilant enough,' barked Parker at Anne. 'That girl shouldn't have been out there in the dark with that abolitionist.'

Anne stood up to him. 'Your spies were supposed to be vigilant. They told me that you authorized three seamen from Bristol to take over their duty tonight. Is that true?'

'Of course not!' he exclaimed. 'And you shouldn't have allowed

Janice to sneak away in the first place. You knew she's a headstrong, cunning girl. Your responsibility for her is herewith terminated. When she's fit to leave the hospital, I'll take her back to the house in the Circus and put a more trustworthy person in charge of her. My servants will pick up her things at your apartment. As of now, I forbid you to have any further contact with her. And I'll proceed legally against you, if necessary.' He turned on his heels and walked away without allowing Anne to reply.

André put a hand on Anne's shoulder. 'That was unfair. We saved the young woman's life after she put herself and her friend in danger.'

'Parker will confine her like a prisoner.' Anne shook her head. 'This will end badly.'

Near midnight, the constable led Anne and André to the Guildhall. He had already alerted the other constable and the watchmen to search for the two assailants who had fled. The wounded rogue died during the night without regaining consciousness. Because of the brazen nature of the assault and its extraordinary violence, Mr Leonard Coward, the mayor and chief magistrate of the city, had hastened to his office. Anne and André related what they knew.

The mayor turned to the constable. 'What can you add?'

'I've identified the rogue who was shot, Barney Jones, a Bristol seaman and smuggler. Since smuggling has recently become less profitable, he and his two companions, possibly also from Bristol, may have turned to other kinds of crime. We suspect them of several robberies on the Bristol – Bath highway.'

The mayor reflected. 'But it's odd that they would change their habit and come into the city and single out these two young people instead of a prosperous banker and his bejeweled wife. What did they hope to gain?'

Anne raised her hand. 'Janice Parker is a very rich young lady. Her uncle and guardian, Mr Thomas Parker, is a prominent London merchant in Bath for the season.'

'Perhaps the rogues intended to kill her escort, kidnap her, and hold her for ransom,' offered the constable.

'But Jones appeared intent on killing her rather than carrying her away,' countered the mayor.

'That's true,' said Anne. 'This is the second attempt on

Miss Parker's life and may be related to the first.' Anne described briefly the incident outside the milliner's shop in London. 'Someone wants her dead. We're not sure who or why. If you capture the two rogues who escaped, find out who hired them.'

'And their accomplices,' added André. 'Someone must have told the villains when and where to find the young couple.'

Anne thought of the spies hired by Parker. She had noticed them in the morning at the Pump Room, while the young couple was making plans for the evening. Did the spies report that information to Parker and did he instruct them to pass it on to the assassins?

HARSH CONFINEMENT

Bath, Sunday, 8 November – Wednesday, 11 November

Sunday morning, Anne found Dick Burton in the Pump Room. He beckoned her to a quiet corner, eager to hear about last night's attack on Janice and Jacob in Crescent Fields. Rumours abounded in the crowd. Most visitors agreed that it was a failed robbery. That it was so violent and took place within the city aroused great anxiety.

Anne briefly described the incident and concluded, 'Thomas Parker has taken Janice, his niece, to his house in the Circus and placed her in strict confinement. I'm desperate to learn of her condition.' She paused, studying his expression. 'May I ask an unusual favour?'

He nodded with an indulgent smile.

'If you have a spy in Parker's household to report on smuggling, could he or she also report on Janice for me?'

'I must compliment you, Madame Cartier. As you rightly suspect, I've recently engaged one of Parker's maids, Gracie White, to help me. She's a trustworthy, local woman. How effective, I cannot say. Thus far she hasn't uncovered Parker's secrets, but I'll gladly add your concern to her responsibility.'

'Janice has mentioned her. Where may we meet?'

'She usually worships in the Abbey Church on Sunday

morning. In the afternoon she has tea with Madame Gagnon on Milsom Street.' He raised a warning hand. 'I know you will be cautious. It could be dangerous to expose her.'

Early in the afternoon, Anne found Miss White in Madame Gagnon's shop. It was closed for business, but the two women were visiting over a pot of tea and a basket of brioches. Anne was invited to join them. She learned that Amelia Swan had often sent the maid to the shop to pick up a ribbon or place a simple order. Madame Gagnon took a liking to the maid and invited her to stop and chat on Sunday when the shop was closed and Madame was free. Miss White might find employment there at the end of the season, when Mr Parker moved back to London.

Gracie White was a thin, plain-looking young woman, well mannered and intelligent. She spoke the King's English with hardly the hint of a country accent. Those were uncommon qualities in a simple domestic maid.

Anne was intrigued and asked her, 'We've nearly finished tea. Could you and I have a conversation in the back room?'

'I don't know,' the maid replied, confusion and fear in her eyes.

'You can trust Madame Cartier,' said the milliner Gagnon with an encouraging smile. 'I'll leave in a few minutes to run an errand.'

The maid still hesitated and her hands shook, nearly spilling her tea. But finally, she acquiesced and followed Anne into the back room.

'I realize that you rightly fear your master and mistress,' said Anne, as she and the maid sat down at a small table. 'I'll be very careful.' Anne handed her a sealed message from Dick Burton.

She broke the seal and read intently, murmuring the words. From time to time, she glanced up at Anne. Finally, she returned the message and said, 'Mr Burton speaks well of you and writes that I should help you look after Janice. I'll do so gladly, but I must be very cautious, lest I be found one day floating in the River Avon.'

'Really?' Anne tilted her head, pretending to be surprised at the threat of violent death.

'Oh yes, Madame,' the maid replied. 'I fear Captain Judd.

He's king of the smugglers in the West Country and is known
to be merciless when crossed. He often comes to the house
and appears to do business there. He would be very angry to
discover me spying, as would Thomas Parker and Amelia
Swan.'

Anne reassured Gracie, then probed into her background.
She was the only daughter of the recently deceased vicar of
a country church. He gave her a good education but left her
penniless. Soon after she arrived in Bath looking for work,
Amelia hired her. She quickly grew to dislike the former courtesan but tried to appear loyal and obliging. When Burton
offered her a small sum to spy on the Parker household, Gracie
was ready to accept.

'I pity Miss Janice who must live in that pit of vipers. I'll
do whatever I can for her.'

Anne thanked the maid and rose to leave. 'By the way,
Miss White, I couldn't find you at the Abbey Church this
morning. I was told that you worshipped there.'

'I had no choice. Mr Parker ordered me to go with him to
the hospital to fetch Janice.'

'So soon after the assault? She hardly had time to recover
from the shock.'

Gracie nodded. 'She was still weak and under the influence of a sedative, in no condition to protest her uncle's action.
He took her back to his house in the Circus and strictly ordered
us servants to prevent her from leaving – by force if necessary. We should also speak to no one about her, but I'll keep
you informed as best I can.'

Later on Sunday afternoon, Gracie White and several of
Parker's servants arrived at Anne's door to carry away Janice's
things. Anne inquired about Janice, but they shook their heads
and refused to reply. Nonetheless, she showed them to the
young woman's room, opened an armoire and several cabinet
drawers, and observed while they carefully packed clothes,
shoes, and other personal items into a chest. The variety, beauty,
and expense of her gowns surprised Anne. Indifferent to
fashion, the young woman rarely wore them. Without a doubt
Amelia had chosen them – and probably purchased them with
Janice's funds.

Gracie slipped away from the others for a moment. Anne

followed her, and they met in Anne's dressing room. The maid spoke in a frightened whisper. 'Miss Parker is beginning to come out of the sedation and wants to walk in the garden. Mr Parker demands that she remain in her room and he says he'll hire a guard to keep her there. He has ordered me to bring her food.'

'Encourage her if you can,' said Anne. 'Now you had better go.'

As the maid left, she said, 'I think it's wrong to treat her like a criminal, but most of us are afraid of Mr Parker and will do as he says. Don't let anyone know that I've spoken to you. He'd punish me.'

Anne promised.

For the next three days, Janice remained strictly confined to the house and isolated in her room from all visitors. Anne could only imagine the young woman's state of mind. Bruised and shocked by the assault, she must be tortured by regret for the folly of her actions and for the grave injury that they had caused Jacob. Unfortunately, she had no wise, kindly person to whom she could unburden herself. She was locked into an uncaring, suspicious, and hostile environment.

But Anne was sure that the young woman's grief and self-pity would be followed by anger. Janice was far too headstrong to submit to Parker's tyranny for very long. She would soon look for ways to elude him and his jailers and to escape from his chains. And if that were impossible, what then? Anne shuddered. Would the young woman's frail health be under-mined beyond repair? She might give up on life.

Meanwhile the search continued for the two missing rogues who had attacked Janice and Jacob. But any hope of finding them was dwindling. They had probably shipped out of Bristol within hours of their failed assault. The police lacked their names or a good description but were confident that they were sailors or smugglers.

Anne and André visited Jacob Woodhouse daily in the hospital. He was a weak, crestfallen young man, blaming himself for Janice's misfortune. But his strength was slowly returning. He would go home in a few days, and then he would ponder Parker's harsh treatment of Janice. His anger would grow along with his desire to exact retribution. Could his father restrain him from violence? Anne was not certain.

*   *   *

Wednesday morning at the Pump Room, Anne, André, and
Beverly were drinking the water, listening to the musicians,
and chatting with acquaintances. Beverly's mood was
subdued, her smile forced. Anne tried unsuccessfully to
cheer her up. The conflict with her estranged husband
obsessed her.

Dick Burton shuffled into the room on his cane, drew close
to Anne, and whispered, 'Judge Williams just told me that he
has received his file on Oliver Parker's shipwreck. He also
wants to hear from you about the assault on Janice Parker.
Come to my office at ten and join us.' Anne agreed and Burton
moved on to the water counter.

She then gave a brief explanation to her grandfather who
gallantly offered to escort Beverly to the morning prayer
service at the Abbey Church, another social ritual of the season.
Afterwards they would treat themselves to hot chocolate and
brioches at Sally Lunn's tea room.

At ten Anne entered Burton's office. The two men were
waiting for her with concern plainly etched on their faces.
Judge Williams asked, 'What happened on Saturday night in
Crescent Fields? Rumors abound. For the most part, the public
thinks it was a failed robbery. But the police aren't saying
anything.'

'They're searching for the assailants,' Anne replied guardedly.

'And for the person who hired them,' added Burton under
his breath.

'Then it wasn't attempted robbery, was it?' asked Williams,
meeting Anne's eye.

'No,' she replied. 'This was the second attempt to kill Janice
Parker.' She cautioned the two men to be discreet and went
on to describe the attack. 'Since one assailant is dead and the
other two have escaped, we don't know yet who they are or
who hired them.'

'But we can fairly guess,' Burton added. 'A trio of smugglers engaged by Seth Judd.'

Judge Williams nodded. 'And how are their victims doing?'

'Young Woodhouse is improving and will go home in a
few days to convalesce. Janice has recovered physically but
I'm concerned for her mental state. Her uncle has harshly
confined her to the house in the Circus.'

For a moment the two men stared silently at Anne. Finally,

Williams said, 'Our investigation is more urgent than ever. The late Oliver Parker and his daughter may have in common a persistent and ruthless enemy.'

'True,' said Anne, 'and we must find him soon. His third attempt might succeed.'

The judge opened his file on Burton's writing table. He also circulated notes he had taken during the inquiry and a copy of the Admiralty's report that attributed the wreck to the mate's error.

With a nod to Anne, Williams continued. 'Let's turn again to the death of Oliver Parker. At the time, I was unhappy with our conclusion. So a few months after the inquiry, I sailed to Waterford and engaged at my own expense a trustworthy solicitor to investigate Oliver Parker's businesses, properties, and other dealings in the southeastern Irish counties. Over the next few years the solicitor gathered new evidence that altered my view of the case. His main discovery was that Oliver Parker had secretly carried with him on the sloop a large cache of gold coins from his joint privateering ventures with Judd.'

'How could the solicitor find out?' Anne asked. 'Did he contact someone who actually saw Parker put the gold in a chest and carry it on board?'

'Not exactly, Madame. He spoke to Parker's banker who knew that Parker kept gold coins in a strongbox in the bank. With imprudent pride he had once shown the banker his horde of Spanish gold escudos. Shortly before sailing, Parker came to the bank and emptied his strongbox into a chest and carried it away. A guard on the quay recalled Parker carrying a small but heavy chest with unusual care into the sloop.'

Burton asked, 'Were the ship's crew, or at least its captain, Seth Judd, unaware of a treasure on board?'

'A good question,' replied the judge. 'Greed can be a powerful motive for mischief. At the official inquiry I asked the captain and the seaman if the sloop were carrying anything of great value. They said no. So our court went on deliberating in utter ignorance of Parker's secret. Had we known, we would have questioned the two survivors much more closely and searched for signs of sudden extravagant spending and for other evidence of new, stolen wealth.'

Anne asked, 'Why was Parker so secretive? Did he have any reasons other than the safety of his treasure?'

'Yes, my Irish solicitor thinks Parker was concealing evidence of serious fraud. A few months earlier, Captain Judd had captured a Spanish treasure ship. It was badly damaged in the battle and later sank. The manifest of its cargo was burned; its captain and other ship's officers were killed. But through a local agent in Cartagena, the ship's port of departure, the solicitor received a copy of its manifest. He found a discrepancy between the gold listed in the ship's manifest and the amount of gold that Parker and Judd declared to the Admiralty. They must have hidden part of the trove in order to cheat the Crown, the crew, and minor investors of their full share in the prize. The rogues must have then divided the hidden gold between themselves, with Oliver most likely taking the lion's share.'

'So,' Anne continued tentatively, careful not to irritate the judge. '*If* Captain Judd were to find out Parker's secret, he might have plotted to steal the gold and wreck the ship in order to conceal his crime.'

Burton seemed doubtful. 'But did he also *have* to murder Oliver and his wife?'

'No,' said Anne. 'Judd could have found another way to steal the gold. Murder wasn't necessary and would add greatly to the risk. Oliver couldn't take Judd to court to recover the stolen property. He would have incriminated himself.'

Williams sighed. 'Even with the solicitor's report, there's much about the case that's murky. We, the members of the Court of Inquiry, were uneasy with Captain Judd's version of the wreck. It simply seemed odd that an experienced captain would place an incompetent mate with a weakness for drink at the helm of the ship during the most dangerous part of the voyage. How was it that the captain and one seaman could escape and the others could not? Had he wrecked his own ship? We couldn't figure out why he would do that at the risk of his own life and his reputation.'

Anne suggested, 'Perhaps he had other, darker reasons, besides stealing the hidden treasure aboard his ship. Family resentments, perhaps.'

When Anne returned to her apartment at noon, she found a note under her door. Its message was cryptic: ribbons at three o'clock. That was a simple code between Anne and Gracie, the friendly maid in the Parker household. They had earlier agreed to meet secretly when the maid had news and could safely leave the house.

At the appointed hour, disguised as a domestic servant in a simple grey woolen gown and plain white cotton bonnet, Anne entered Madame Gagnon's shop on Milsom Street. Gagnon was serving an elderly lady, but she recognized Anne and nodded towards the back room.

Gracie was already there, nervously pacing the floor. She stammered, 'Miss Parker will attend the Cotillion Ball tomorrow night, the first time outside her room in days.'

'How is her health?' Anne felt helpless.

'She's over the initial shock, but her asthma is getting worse. She's restless and angry.' The maid hesitated to say more.

Anne urged her on. 'Why angry?'

'Mr Parker has hired a woman to "look after Janice", as he says. Janice hates her. She was a warden for female inmates at one of the prisons in Bristol. Watches me closely when I bring meals into the room and prevents me from conversing with Janice. On Monday at supper she insulted the woman – called her a stupid cow. The woman said nothing. But as soon as I left the room and shut the door, she slapped Janice. Hard. I could hear it out in the hall. So could Mr Parker. He was walking by and opened the door. I could see Janice rubbing her face. It was red on one side. But she wasn't crying. Parker warned her that he wouldn't tolerate impertinence, then he instructed the woman to be firm but not to leave marks.'

'Do you think that the woman abused Janice again?'

'I don't know. She doesn't trust me any more and won't let me into the room. When I bring food, I must leave it with her.'

Anne left this meeting with pity for the young girl's plight. But at least in the short run Parker felt constrained to present Janice to the public in outwardly decent condition. Still, how long will her frail health endure the stress?

A POISONED PUNCH

Bath, Thursday, 12 November

Anne spent the next day busy preparing for the weekly Cotillion Ball, troubled by lingering fears that Janice might not attend after all. So she was relieved when Parker and Amelia Swan entered the Assembly Rooms with the young woman in train. To outward appearances she had apparently recovered physically from Saturday night's ordeal. Her breathing, however, was laboured. A slender woman, she had lost weight and appeared frail. Any facial bruises were skillfully concealed by cosmetics. In a pink muslin gown and a string of pearls around her neck, she was quite attractive.

Anne had arranged to go with her grandfather, Peter, and Harriet. At the last minute Beverly joined them. Though she had apologized to the Master of Ceremonies for her bad behaviour the week before and promised to avoid any more of the same, she was still anxious as she walked through the foyer. Anne held her under the arm and whispered encouragement. Then Beverly saw him approach and her arm tensed. She almost stumbled. But he smiled, bowed nicely, and greeted her loudly enough for everyone in the room to hear. She breathed a soft sigh of relief and relaxed.

While Anne's companions made up a set for the country-dances, Anne sat among the spectators along the sidewall and scanned the hall with her opera glass. Parker and Amelia Swan joined a set but Janice remained seated with her guard, like a condemned felon awaiting execution. Her face – pale and drawn – lacked any joy. She ignored the dancers and stared over their heads at an invisible spot on the opposite wall. Her guard, a large, hard-faced woman, was dressed in an expensive black silk gown and adorned with paste diamonds. But neither the costume nor Amelia's skilful application of cosmetics could conceal the woman's base origins, unfeeling spirit, and vulgar tastes. She made no attempt to break into

the young woman's silence but gazed at the festive scene
before her with a careless, indifferent expression.

When the dancing ended, the crowd rushed to the Tea
Room's buffet of ham and turkey, bread, cheese and fruit, and
great bowls of punch, sweet green tea laced with rum or
brandy. Anne and her companions waited a few minutes for
the rush to subside. As they entered the room, they passed Mr
Burton alone at his usual table, with a glass of punch before
him, his cane at his side. He gave Anne a warning glance.
She lingered. He silently mouthed, 'Seth Judd is here tonight,'
then directed her gaze to a tall, broad-shouldered man a few
steps ahead of her. She mouthed back, 'Thank you.'

The captain seemed at ease in the company, nodding to
acquaintances and greeting friends with a broad, confident
smile. He walked with a seaman's gait to the buffet. The waiter,
Nate Taylor, handed him a glass of punch, and they exchanged
a few words. As Judd turned around, he gazed at Anne with
a look of instant recognition. Had he recalled her from years
ago at the Parker estate, or had he spied on her recently? Either
alternative was unnerving.

For a long moment they assessed each other. His eyes were
pale blue, full of intelligence but cold and hostile. Sun and
wind had weathered his strong, broad face to the colour
and texture of brown leather. He took a sip of the punch, gave
her just the hint of an ironic smile, then turned and walked
away. She knew with a sudden frisson of fear that this man
was her lethal enemy.

Anne and André chose a small table with the best possible
view of Parker's group, partially obscured by the crowd's
frequent milling about. While André went to the buffet for
food and drink, Anne adjusted the swivel lens of her opera
glass ninety degrees so that she would not appear to be looking
at Parker's table.

Amelia sat on Parker's right side, Janice on his left. To her
left was her guard. Two young, wealthy, carefree couples
completed the table of eight. In an expansive mood, Parker
had engaged Nate Taylor to bring food and drink from the
buffet.

Neither Parker nor anyone else at the table paid attention
to Janice, who sat quietly picking at her plate of ham, bread,
and cheese and ignoring her glass of punch. Her ill-mannered

guard attacked the food as if she hadn't eaten in days and drank punch like water. Soon, her eyes were half closed and her head was lolling on her shoulders.

Anne occasionally scanned the crowd. At a table for two Peter and Harriet were chatting like best friends. Beverly had wandered away from them and stood against a wall near the buffet casting furtive glances at Parker's table. Her expression was inscrutable.

Burton was still sitting by himself, gazing over the rim of his glass of punch. His attention appeared to be devoted to Seth Judd, who sauntered through the crowd like a successful man of affairs among his clients. Some of them, Anne had learned, were excise officers.

André returned with food and punch. But Anne had become too engrossed to eat or drink. Instead she trained her spyglass on Parker himself. With each glass of punch he grew giddier, regaling the table with anecdotes, caressing Amelia, teasing the female acquaintances across the table, joking with their male companions.

Amelia grimaced at her lover's behaviour, apparently embarrassed. After several minutes, she began to cast anxious glances at Janice. Finally, Amelia got up from the table, whispered into Parker's ear – which he appeared to ignore – and left in the direction of the water closet.

Parker signaled Taylor for more drinks. He served everyone at the table except Janice, who pointed to her glass that was still full. At that moment, Amelia returned and appeared to scold Janice. Parker turned to Amelia, and they spoke earnestly to each other. Anne tried to read their lips but failed. Others at the table were engaged in general hilarity. Janice still kept to her withdrawn, unsmiling posture. Parker rose to propose a toast. He raised his glass. 'To beautiful Amelia,' he nearly shouted, and emptied his glass in one long gulp. He sat down, exchanged a few words with Amelia, and beckoned the waiter for more punch.

Several minutes passed, Parker waxing loud and witless. Then a strange expression of unease or fear came over his face. He began to pant. Suddenly, he clutched his throat and gasped, tried to suck in air, seemed to choke. His arms started to flail about wildly, nearly striking Amelia, who reared back in horror. Janice leaped from her chair, her eyes wide with fright. Her drunken guard woke up startled and fell backwards with a loud crash. The others at the table sat spellbound.

Parker slid out of his chair to the floor and lay there, twisting and jerking for a few minutes, while a waiter rushed up and loosened the stricken man's shirt at the neck so that he might breathe.

Alerted by the commotion, André turned to Anne. 'What's happened?'

She replied softly, 'This may have been an accident or someone may have just killed Thomas Parker. We must try to find out.'

They joined the circle of the curious who had quickly gathered around the prostrate man. When the Master of Ceremonies arrived, together with a medical doctor from the crowd, Parker lay still, his eyes open, staring, but sightless.

Mr Tyson and a couple of waiters tried to push people back. 'Clear the room,' he shouted. 'The Tea Room is now closed.' He turned to the members of Parker's table. 'You must stay here until the constable arrives.' They sat down, benumbed by shock. Amelia had thrown herself on to her dead lover. Nate Taylor and Seth Judd appeared, pried her loose, and sat her down. She seemed barely conscious. The two men propped up Janice's drunken guard in a chair. Janice stood apart from the group, dazed, wheezing, shaking.

Anne wrapped Janice in her arms, comforted her for a few moments, and then lowered her into a chair, Anne on one side, André on the other.

Dick Burton shuffled up to Mr Tyson. 'May I be of assistance, sir?' Meanwhile, the waiters and other servants steered the agitated crowd out of the room, and shut the doors.

'By all means, Mr Burton.' The Master of Ceremonies knew him to be a retired police investigator and apparently assumed that he had a special mission in Bath. 'I've sent for the constable. What else should I do?'

'Don't disturb the body. Parker may have been poisoned, but a medical examiner must determine the precise cause of death. Bring pen and paper. The constable will need to take statements from all these witnesses.'

Burton approached Anne and said in a low voice, 'We need to talk.' They moved to a small table off to one side. 'We were both observing Parker's table – you with that swivel-lens opera glass. One of my informants watched you. Can you tell me who poisoned Parker?'

Anne was surprised that Burton so quickly decided that Parker's death was murder. 'I didn't see anyone put poison in his glass. But how could I know? His drink was punch and it looked like everyone else's. Of course it could have been tampered with before the glass reached his table. I can't say for sure. My view was sometimes obstructed by people passing between my table and Parker's.' She paused and asked, 'Are you certain that it was murder?'

'Had this happened to his niece, I might have said that it was an asthmatic attack. But Parker was a healthy man with no history of breathing problems.' Burton met Anne's eye and asked carefully, 'Could you see your cousin, Beverly Parker?'

For a moment Anne was tempted to invent an alibi for Beverly; she was obviously a strong suspect. Her quarrel with Thomas Parker was notorious. But Anne quickly gave up the idea. Burton was far too perceptive and would detect – and resent – any attempt to deceive him. Anne wanted to keep his trust, so she said, 'Before the incident, I saw her standing alone near the buffet table watching Amelia Swan and Thomas Parker. Then I lost sight of her.'

Burton said, 'I'll refrain from judging her. The death of Thomas Parker and the attempts on his niece may be linked in a wider scheme. Someone other than Beverly may have designed a plot to wipe out the Parker family. After all, Oliver Parker and his wife died under suspicious circumstances. I'll need to question Amelia Swan and Seth Judd.'

'Sir,' Anne remarked, 'you've made me more concerned than ever for Janice's safety. With her life still in danger, she shouldn't return to the house in the Circus into the clutches of Amelia and that dreadful guard. Couldn't we persuade Mayor Coward to temporarily let her live with me again?'

'The mayor will be here shortly. We'll speak to him. I'm sure he'll agree to your proposal at least for tonight.' He hesitated, then gazed at Anne with an ambiguous expression. 'You must realize that Miss Parker is also a potential suspect. Her unhappiness with Parker is well known. She could have carried that poison to the Tea Room on her person and secretly dropped it into Parker's glass of punch without you noticing. That has to be among the possibilities that a magistrate would consider.'

Anne protested. 'That magistrate should be informed that Janice did not have access to poison during the past several days. She was unconscious in the hospital. Then Parker strictly confined her and hired a guard to watch her. Parker has spied on her ever since she arrived in Bath.'

Burton conceded, 'We may also discover that she hasn't purchased poison from any of the chemists in Bath. However, the poison is probably a massive dose of tincture of laudanum, a drug that is common in households. She could have slipped out of her room this morning while her guard was drunk or sleeping and found the poison.'

Anne shook her head. She was about to challenge him again. He seemed to have slipped back into the role of a Bow Street officer, single-mindedly pursuing a culprit, oblivious to the injury he might cause to a frail bystander like Janice. But now he waved his hands. 'Enough speculation on that point.'

'Will you conduct the investigation?' Anne asked.

'Bath has no experienced investigator. Complicated, serious crime is rare here. I assume the mayor will ask me to investigate this one, especially since I've showed him my commission from the government to investigate Parker's role in West Country smuggling. I want to begin immediately. Bring Miss Parker to my office tomorrow morning and help me get her story.'

His brusque tone annoyed Anne, so she challenged him. 'Because of the horror that she has undergone, her mental state is sure to be fragile. If you have any concern for her welfare, as well as for the truth, may I suggest that you visit her in my apartment?'

Burton blinked as if offended. With a hint of irritation in his eyes, he gazed at Anne for a long moment. 'I hadn't intended to browbeat her into confessing to a crime that she hadn't committed. But your suggestion has merit. Shall we say tomorrow at ten in the morning in your apartment?'

'Yes,' Anne replied, then conceded, 'We must discover the true killer, if we are to clear Janice – as well as Beverly – of suspicion.'

'And that won't be easy,' added Burton.

Almost an hour passed before the mayor and the night constable arrived. After conferring with Burton and the Master of Ceremonies, they took statements from the people at Parker's table, then from Nate Taylor who had served it, and finally from Mr Tyson himself. Meanwhile several watchmen urged patrons to leave the building or at least tried to keep the curious at bay.

Anne and André remained at Janice's side. Her asthma impeded her breathing. When asked to give a statement, she couldn't speak, so she signed and Anne translated for her. Janice's statement revealed little. She seemed lost in a trance. At Anne's request, Burton persuaded the mayor to authorize her and André to temporarily care for Janice until a court could decide what should be done with her.

When they were finally allowed to leave the Tea Room, they met Peter, Harriet, and Beverly waiting in the foyer. Suddenly, Amelia appeared, a wild expression on her face. She charged towards Beverly, shaking her fists and screaming, 'Assassin, assassin, you killed my Tom.'

Beverly shrank back while Peter stepped between the women and seized Amelia by the arms. She tried to kick him but became entangled in her skirt and started to fall. Seth Judd moved swiftly and caught her.

'Come with me, dear,' he said. 'I'll take you home.'

Beverly had turned deathly pale and was breathing with difficulty. Peter and André carried her to a waiting coach and set off for her apartment. Anne and Harriet put Janice in another coach and rode towards Queen Square. Janice began to revive. Anne asked, 'What did Parker say to you, while you were sitting next to him at the table?'

'He and Amelia insisted that I should drink my punch. It was rude of me not to, since they had paid for it and given it to me. I didn't want to drink the punch. I've never liked it. I also resented that they were badgering me. For the past few days, my uncle had been very mean. Last night, I demanded to be set free. He said I was an ungrateful, disobedient bitch. I talked back, called him a brutal bully. He went into a rage and ordered that dreadful woman – my guard – to whip me, "But do it lightly so it wouldn't show", he said. Nonetheless, my back is still sore.

'Tonight I knew that he couldn't behave like that in the Tea Room, so I defied him and refused to drink. In the back of my mind was also the idea that the drink might be poisoned.

Ever since he locked me up, I've had that fear. When the maid brought my food, I had her taste it first.'

She paused and switched to signing. 'In case you are wondering . . .' She looked Anne straight in the eye. 'I didn't kill Parker but I'm glad he's dead.' She lapsed into a profound silence and stared at the floor of the coach.

Anne and Harriet exchanged worried glances. Finally, Harriet shrugged, and then mouthed, 'Later.'

After seeing Janice to bed, Anne stood outside the door for a moment pondering the young woman's ambiguous reaction to Parker's death. She concluded that there were dark areas of Janice's mind that needed to be explored.

Anne went downstairs to Harriet's apartment. She had changed into her nightdress and had put on a robe. The fire was low and the room cold. The two women pulled chairs close to the hearth's dying heat.

'What do you make of it all?' asked Anne.

Harriet replied with another question. 'Why would anyone kill Parker in the most public place in Bath? There were perhaps five hundred people in that tea room.'

'Is it really such a strange idea?' Anne asked. 'The room was crowded – men and women milling about, distracted, chattering with each other, tipsy from strong punch. It wouldn't be too difficult to administer a poison unobserved.'

Harriet nodded. 'Thanks to Amelia's outburst, the public's suspicion has fallen on Beverly. But there must be other suspects.'

'Very likely,' Anne agreed. 'Thomas Parker was much involved in legally dubious business affairs. To credit Dick Burton, Parker also engaged in smuggling. He could have made many enemies whom we wouldn't know.'

'True,' Harriet added. 'One or more of them could have been in the Tea Room tonight.'

Anne bade her friend goodnight and started for the door. 'And we shouldn't overlook Amelia and Judd. They may have motives still hidden from us.'

SUSPECTS

Bath, Friday, 13 November

Early the next morning, Anne checked on Janice. The young woman woke up tired but relieved that she was free from Parker's prison and safe for now. She would rest at home with Harriet and Peter to look after her until Burton arrived at ten. A city watchman would stand guard outside the building.

Anne and André set out to visit Beverly, who was also resting in her maid's care. On the way, André described what happened when he and Peter brought her home. 'She was in a state of nervous exhaustion. Peter found a tincture of laudanum that she had been taking recently and gave her a dose. Her maid helped her to bed.'

'Even before Amelia accused Beverly last night, you must have realized that Beverly would be suspected,' Anne said.

'Of course. His death saved her dowry and freed her to marry Grimshaw, two powerful motives in the eyes of the law. She was also in the Tea Room with us and perhaps had an opportunity to poison his punch.'

'Unfortunately, that's what the public is thinking right now.'

'Yes,' he agreed. 'But the public doesn't know, any more than we do, whether she actually killed him.'

When they reached Beverly's apartment, the maid told them that she was asleep. Anne said that they would come back later. As they were about to leave, Anne thought that the maid looked upset. She asked, 'What's the matter, dear?'

She hesitated to reply and appeared embarrassed. 'Mr Burton came here early this morning with two constables. They looked so serious. They found Mrs Parker's laudanum and asked if any was missing. I said I didn't know.' She paused anxiously. 'Is she suspected of killing her husband?'

'It's probably too early to say,' Anne replied. 'I'm sure Mr Burton has to investigate several people in addition to

Mrs Parker.' To herself Anne admitted that Beverly must be high on Burton's list.

Anne and André walked the short distance to Parker's house in the Circus. The maid, Gracie White, showed them into the front parlour. Anne told her, 'We've come to arrange for Janice's things to be taken back to Queen Square.'

'I'll see to it,' said the maid. 'No one else seems to be in charge here.'

'Is Miss Swan at home?' Anne asked out of courtesy. At the death of Parker, the position of his mistress became problematic. Anne had heard that Parker's recent will made Amelia heir to his property, a doubtful blessing since it was heavily encumbered with debt. Anne didn't know what else, if anything, he might have given her. Could she maintain the rented house in the Circus, or the much more expensive one leased on Berkeley Square in London? Would the law allow Beverly to contest the will? She was legally still the dead man's wife. At the very least, she could put the inheritance in legal limbo and deny Amelia any benefit of it.

'She's in mourning and told us that she wouldn't see anyone.' The maid hesitated. 'But she's had to see Mr Burton, who was here at the crack of dawn with a pair of constables. Over her objections, they searched the house from top to bottom. She was most distressed.'

'What were they looking for?' Anne asked.

'They wouldn't say.'

Laudanum, Anne assumed, but Burton must also have used this opportunity to search for evidence of Parker's connections to smugglers. She closed the parlour door and asked in a low voice, 'Did Mr Seth Judd visit Miss Swan last night?'

The maid hesitated, appearing to assess this question in the light of her changed circumstances. With the death of Parker, his household would most likely disperse, each one looking for other employment. Anne had learned from Janice that the servants did not like Amelia, felt no loyalty to her, and expected little consideration from her.

'Yes,' she replied cautiously. 'He left at dawn with several boxes, just minutes before Mr Burton arrived.'

Anne turned to André. 'Judd must have spent the night searching through Parker's papers for anything that could incriminate him, especially all references to their partnership in smuggling.'

'Yes,' André agreed. 'Burton surely was disappointed. And there's nothing more for us to do here. We should return to Queen Square. You and Janice are to meet Burton at ten.'

As they left the parlour, Anne asked Gracie, 'Does anyone in this house use laudanum?'

'Yes, Madame. Mr Burton also asked me that question. I told him where to look in Miss Swan's room. He found a bottle of highly concentrated laudanum there. There was a similar supply in Parker's room. He took it in diluted doses to calm his nerves and to sleep better.'

'Was it possible for Janice Parker to steal some of that laudanum?'

'No, she couldn't leave her room. It was too closely guarded. The guard actually searched me for contraband, weapons, and the like when I brought the meals.'

For the moment, Anne felt immensely relieved.

Burton was already at the entrance to the house on Queen Square. He had come by sedan chair and had struggled to the door on his cane. He looked weary.

Anne greeted him. 'My friend Harriet has lent us the use of her ground-floor parlour so you won't have to climb up the stairs to my place.'

'Her kindness is much appreciated, Madame.' He followed her into the parlour. Janice was seated, calmly waiting. She rose to greet him with a bow. Burton accepted an offer of tea. She left the room to fetch it.

Burton leaned his cane against his chair and sighed. 'It's been a long morning.'

Anne smiled sympathetically. 'We heard that you visited Parker's house in the Circus.'

'In vain, I regret to say. Since Parker died suddenly, unexpectedly, he must have left behind some evidence of his smuggling. But there was nothing of interest in the house. I did find a large supply of common tincture of laudanum in Parker's room and another in Madame Swan's. In fact, I believe she was under the influence, nearly out of her mind.'

'How unfortunate for you, sir. Just a few minutes ago, your spy, Gracie White, told me that Seth Judd spent the night in the house and left with several boxes shortly before you arrived.'

'So that's why I found nothing. Why didn't she tell me?' He seemed irritated. 'Don't I pay her enough?'

Anne came to Gracie's defence. 'Judd probably had threatened the servants just before you arrived. They were still frightened to death, including Gracie.'

At that moment, Janice came with the tea, poured, and sat down – hands folded, eyes lowered. She had closed a door or two in her mind.

Burton began gently. 'I realize you've had a trying time here in Bath, Miss Parker. Last night's tragedy must have been especially upsetting. I hope you're feeling better.'

Anne signed his remark to Janice, who replied with a grateful smile. A frail young woman with a resilient spirit, she seemed rested and, on the surface, not much the worse from her ordeal. Some anxiety hovered in her eyes, however.

'I have to ask a few questions about last night.' He paused as if giving her an opportunity to protest. She nodded for him to continue.

'You told Madame Cartier that you hated Thomas Parker because he had mistreated you. Is that correct?'

'Yes, to put it mildly.'

'That hatred could have moved you to take laudanum from the house in the Circus to the Tea Room. Since you sat next to Parker, you could have put it into his punch. Is that correct?'

'No, it isn't. I'm sure that you didn't find the laudanum in *my* room. I was imprisoned and didn't have access to the rest of the house.'

Burton stroked his chin and gazed at Janice. 'I concede, young lady, that we found the laudanum in Miss Swan's room and in Parker's. Nearly everyone in Bath has a supply, or so it seems. I'll not speculate now on how you might have obtained it.' He turned to Anne who had been translating Janice's signing. 'I think that will do for now, Madame.'

Anne offered a question. 'Janice, who brought you the glass of punch?'

Janice read Anne's lips. 'The waiter who usually served our table and served Thomas Parker.'

Anne and Burton exchanged glances. 'Nate Taylor,' they said together.

Burton rose, took leave of Janice. Anne saw him to the door and asked, 'Have you asked your spy, Gracie White, about Janice?'

He nodded. 'She denied supplying Janice with laudanum. Anyway, she wouldn't have dared. It was too risky. The guard watched her like a hawk.'

'So, where does Janice stand in your investigation thus far?'

'I start from the fact that Janice hated the victim and sat next to him. If I were to discover that she could have obtained the poison, I would be obliged to regard her as my chief suspect.'

His words were discouraging but not surprising to Anne. 'Could you pursue Nate Taylor, since he brought the poisoned drink to the table?'

Burton replied, 'I haven't thoroughly investigated him yet. He lives on Avon Street. I don't have trustworthy informants there. It's truly a den of thieves, whores, and smugglers. They can smell police, such as me, a mile away.'

'Perhaps I can help you,' Anne offered. 'I've made a few friends there.' Burton appeared to raise an eyebrow, but Anne continued. 'You might remember the seamstress, Sarah Smith, and her friend, Lord Jeff, Harry Rogers' black slave. Two years ago, the printer David Woodhouse took up Jeff's cause and won his freedom. They remain in contact.'

'I recall the incident. Yes, pay Miss Smith and her friend a visit. They might know Taylor.'

Sarah Smith's seamstress shop was closed when Anne arrived early in the afternoon. A sign indicated she'd be back in an hour. Anne had dressed as a poor male domestic servant in a worn, plain grey suit. Her face was darkened with powder, her hair concealed by a cheap wig. Rather than wait on the street, she entered the tavern next door, The Little Drummer, hoping that someone else might also know Taylor. She thought it likely that he would be familiar to a certain class of women.

The Little Drummer hadn't changed in two years. Anne sat at a small table in the large wood-paneled public room. The ceiling was low, the interior dim. Thin rays of light struggled in from the street through small, high windows. The wooden furniture was battered but decent.

The clientele was sparse at this hour and mostly male – artisans from nearby shops, servants, a few of the cleaner and better-dressed sort of day labourers. A few sat alone, most were chatting and playing cards. They scarcely gave Anne a passing glance. At a table near the stairway to the upper floors sat an attractive young woman playing solitaire, a bored expression on her face. Probably one of the Nymphs of Avon Street, she appeared to be waiting for a customer. Anne took notice of the young woman's low-cut red silk gown. Its material was of exceptionally high quality and expertly sewn. How was that possible?

A waitress approached Anne. 'What will you have?'

'An ale,' Anne replied, pitching her voice low to suit her disguise, then asked casually, 'Has Sarah Smith been here this afternoon?'

'Stepped in for a few minutes,' the waitress replied. 'Said she was going to the hospital to visit young Mr Woodhouse who was attacked Saturday night in Crescent Fields. His father, the printer, told her that his son was doing poorly today. Had a bad night.'

Anne was concerned. She hadn't seen the young man since yesterday morning. If he had taken a turn for the worse, could he cope with a visit from Janice? Had he heard the news of Parker's death?

While Anne was mulling over these questions, Sarah Smith walked in. The waitress addressed her, 'There's a gentleman asking for you.' She pointed to Anne.

Sarah approached Anne tentatively, her brow furrowed with confusion. But when she was a few feet away, her eyes began to brighten. Anne raised a finger to her lips. Sarah smiled and sat down. 'Don't worry. Your disguise is good. I'm the only one who could recognize you. Because of your kindness to Jeffery and me, I'll always remember you.'

Anne ordered ale for Sarah. While waiting, they caught up on the news of the past two years. 'Jeffery still works as a footman at the York. They treat him with respect, feed and clothe him, but don't pay him much. Still, we are content: my mother and I do well enough in the shop.'

Anne pointed to the Nymph in the red silk dress. 'Is that your work?'

'The dress?' she asked, a teasing smile on her lips. 'Yes, I finished it for her a few days ago. The silk is of the highest quality. Fanny has a steady man with money and is my best customer. He supplied me with the silk cloth a few weeks ago. I've been working on the gown ever since; he'll pay me this afternoon.'

Anne's curiosity was aroused. 'Tell me about him.'

'He's a waiter at the Assembly Rooms, lives in a top-floor apartment of this building. He seems clever but erratic: sometimes charming, sometimes rude. On the street he's feared because he's reputed to have close ties to smugglers.'

'Could that explain how he got the fine silk cloth?' Anne asked.

'I don't know,' Sarah replied. 'I've learned not to ask questions about the business done on this street. The waiter is notorious. If anyone crosses him, he threatens to have his friends break their heads.' Sarah leaned forward and whispered, 'Lately, he has begun to talk as if he were rich, or expecting to be. That's odd, because most smugglers complain that their business has recently slumped.'

'Is he called Nate Taylor?'

'Why, yes. Do you know him?'

'Slightly. I recognize him. He's connected somehow to Captain Seth Judd.'

'I've heard the name Judd but can't match it with a face.'

Anne described him in detail. 'We think he might be behind the attempts to kill Miss Janice Parker.'

Sarah's eyes widened. 'I heard that her uncle, Mr Thomas Parker, was poisoned in the Tea Room last night. How ghastly!'

Anne nodded. 'Nate Taylor served Parker's table. Seth Judd was in the room.'

Sarah's mood turned sombre. 'In my business on Avon Street I'm obliged to deal with dubious characters. These two men seem much more threatening than most.' She paused. 'But I must go. I'm expecting Taylor any minute now at the shop.'

Just as she was rising from the table, Taylor walked in the door with Seth Judd. Fanny hailed them and they walked directly up to her. She showed off her gown, her eyes bright with delight. Taylor smiled politely. Words were exchanged. Voices were raised. Fanny's face turned red with anger. 'You can't cheat her,' she shouted. 'That's not fair!' She nodded her head towards Sarah. The men had not noticed her. She had stopped halfway across the room, Anne a step behind her.

Taylor glared at Sarah with a mixture of embarrassment

and contempt. 'I'm not paying any more for Fanny's gown. I've spent enough on the cloth. You'll have to get the rest of your money from her.'

'But we have a contract,' Sarah insisted. 'Have you no honour? I'll bring my complaint to a magistrate.'

'There's nothing on paper.' Taylor's face twisted into a cruel grin. 'Black lady, it'd be your word against mine. Guess whose would prevail. If you persist, you might anger my friends on the street. There's no telling the damage they could cause to your shop.'

Seth Judd had stepped back and stood near the stairway, observing the quarrel, a wry smile on his lips. Now he called out to Taylor. 'Nate, leave her be. Come, we have business to discuss.' The two men ascended the stairs.

The public room had become a theatre. For a few brief minutes the patrons had suspended their card playing and conversation and had stared at the conflict. Now they went back to their pleasures, ordered more drinks.

Sarah introduced Anne to Fanny as Mr Cartier, keeping up her disguise. They sat at Fanny's table. Sarah looked pale, dispirited. 'This isn't the first time that I've been cheated. I'd better not tell Jeffery. He'd become angry and might knock Taylor's head off.'

Fanny whimpered, 'I'll try to pay you something. But I think Taylor's going to leave me. I won't earn much any more.'

Sarah shrugged. But her lips began to quiver.

Anne remarked, 'I got the impression that Seth Judd and Nate Taylor had something important to talk about. I wish I were a fly on that wall.'

'You're right,' said Fanny, drying tears from her eyes. 'Mr Judd seldom comes here, and then only on business.'

'Do you think we could search Taylor's room? We might find evidence to support Sarah's claim against him for the gown. And there could be things of interest to you, Fanny.'

Sarah and Fanny seemed intrigued but doubtful. 'How shall we get in?' asked Fanny.

'Leave that to me.' Anne put an extra dash of male authority into her voice.

Before long, the two men came down the stairs, Seth Judd with a bundle under his arm. They walked out into the street,

ignoring Anne and the other two women as they passed.
When the entrance door closed behind them, Fanny said,
'Nate is going to his job in the Assembly Rooms – he'll be
there until eleven o'clock. This is a good time to search his
rooms.'

Hoping for this opportunity, Anne had brought along the
tools for unlocking a door. When the barman was busy elsewhere, the three women stole up the stairs. Fanny led the way
to Taylor's door and Anne set to work. 'It's a simple lock,'
she told the others. 'It should open quickly.'

Taylor's principal room was spotless and in good order,
reflecting a passion for detail. The plank floor was polished,
boots lined up neatly by the door. His writing table was free
of clutter, paper stacked in well-organized piles. Writing materials were clean and near at hand. Against a wall stood a large,
open armoire, where his clothes hung neatly on racks. Two
pistols lay on the mantel; a pair of cutlasses hung on a wall.

Anne warned her companions to return everything to its original position. Taylor must not find out that his room had been
searched. While the others attacked the writing table, Anne
searched for hiding places: loose floorboards or windowsills,
false walls and hidden cabinets, faux books. He would most
likely be keeping records or a diary of his activities.

She found his financial register in a secret drawer of the
writing table. He had entered the full sum that he had promised to pay Sarah Smith for Fanny's gown. He added that he
intended to give her only the silk cloth. She couldn't force
him to pay for her work. Anne showed the entry to Sarah.
She clapped her hands, smiling with relief. 'This is the proof
I'll need to force him to pay me.'

'But you must wait until we are ready to arrest him,' Anne
cautioned. 'Right now we need to gather evidence of his many
other crimes.'

Even skimming through the register Anne could see that it
recorded Taylor's significant part in the West Country smuggling's system of distribution. Seth Judd's name was missing,
but he was probably there under a pseudonym. Burton would
be pleased with this discovery.

'Oh, no,' cried Fanny. 'He's found another girl.' She handed
Anne copies of a recent exchange between Taylor and a prosperous lace merchant in the smuggling trade. According to

Taylor, the man's daughter was common looking but docile and rich. 'At least,' wrote Taylor, 'she's not a whore that I have to share with every man on Avon Street.'

'Don't weep for him, Fanny,' Anne counseled. 'He's not worth your tears. He's bound to come to a bad end.'

Anne's search for a diary or for any reference to Janice Parker was thus far in vain. It wasn't to be found in any of the usual hiding places. She glanced upward. The low ceiling was wood rather than plaster. If a man stood on a chair, he could easily remove a loose board. She found the diary directly above the writing table.

Her hands trembled as she began to browse. The first entries were in 1784 – after the shipwreck, unfortunately. And it was written mostly in code. Burton could find an expert to read it. Anne returned the diary to its hiding place.

She walked to the window and reflected. She had found no mention of Seth Judd or Thomas Parker or Janice, nor any correspondence between Taylor and Judd. It's likely, Anne thought, that Judd had just removed any papers that might incriminate him in Parker's death or the attacks on Janice.

The sky outside was growing dark, time to leave before a rougher crowd of sailors and prostitutes took over the building. The women had been in the room for an hour and had also explored Taylor's other, small room with a sleeping alcove. He stored contraband there: fine French wines, silk, and lace.

Sarah asked, 'Shall we take some of these papers and books with us?'

Anne shook her head. 'No, we're here illegally. I'll describe to the mayor and Mr Burton what we've found. They'll come themselves or send someone with a search warrant. In the meantime, don't tell *anyone* what we've done. Taylor must not find out or he'll remove the most damning material.'

They left the room as they had found it and hurried down the stairs. Fanny returned to her table, Sarah to her shop. Anne walked north on Avon Street, hoping desperately that her two companions could keep the secret.

A HARD BARGAIN

Bath, Friday, 13 November

Back in her apartment, Anne studied her disguise in a mirror and decided to keep it on. She could foresee being involved in the effort to seize Taylor's papers. She alone knew their location and the safest way to reach them. She could also act quickly, and speed was imperative.

But she would need a trustworthy male companion, someone who could credibly carry a search warrant. The local constables wouldn't do. They were typically slow, stolid, unimaginative men, and some of them took bribes from the smugglers.

Her cousin, Peter Cartier, was certainly incorruptible. Swift, brave, and strong, he was also resourceful, though Anne hadn't known him long enough to be aware of his limitations. As a Justice of the Peace, he would be familiar with legal searches.

Anne knocked on Harriet's door. Her friend opened. For an instant she frowned, confusion in her eyes.

'Is Peter here?' Anne asked, teasing in her male voice.

Harriet brightened and replied with a mischievous smile, 'Who may I ask is calling for him?'

'A cousin in need of help.'

'Then you may speak for yourself.' She led Anne into the parlour where Peter was seated, having just finished drinking tea with Janice. A chess game was laid out on the table between them. They looked up with surprise at the shabbily dressed stranger. As she drew close, they recognized her and broke out in laughter. Janice rose to clear the table, yielding her place to Anne. Harriet sat next to Peter.

Anne removed her wig. 'I'm in disguise, Peter, because I've just come from Nate Taylor's rooms on Avon Street. I've found his personal papers related to smuggling and, I'm sure, to other crimes. Mr Burton will be ecstatic. This evidence should go a long way towards putting Captain Judd in prison and out of Janice's life. My search was illegal, so I left the room as I found it. I must quickly go back there with a warrant and retrieve the papers. Otherwise Taylor will soon become suspicious and remove them. I need a companion I can trust.'

She caught Harriet's eye and pleaded, 'Would you mind if I borrowed Peter this evening? I'm very sorry to have to ask.' She also signed the message to Janice who had just returned to the room.

'Yes, of course you may,' Harriet replied, 'though Janice and I shall miss him.' She cast a fleeting glance at the chess set that was to provide the evening's entertainment. Janice frowned.

Anne felt a stab of regret but she pressed on. 'Peter, would you go with me?'

Peter leaned back in his chair, momentarily at a loss for words. 'Anne, I'm amazed. You've taken on an extraordinary task. I'd be happy to help you finish it.' He hesitated. 'How will you get the search warrant?'

'I trust that Dick Burton will get it for us. We'll find him at the York Hotel.'

'And how shall I be able to help you? Look at me.' He pointed to the silver floral embroidery on his elegant buff silk suit. 'Even if I were to dress in my simplest rags, I could hardly be of use to you anywhere on Avon Street among its thieves and smugglers. I'd stand out like a sore thumb.' He studied Anne. 'How have you managed to transform yourself into a bankrupt solicitor's clerk?'

She put on her wig. 'I've watched such men, then acted rather like them in small comic roles on the London stage. But for tonight's work, you won't need special training, only a suit like mine. Come with me to Madame Gagnon's shop. She'll fit you out.'

It was early in the evening when Anne and Peter reached the York Hotel. She was still in her disguise. His costume was similar to hers: the dull, grey woolen suit and ill-fitting old wig of a lowly domestic servant. She had quickly explained to him what she had found in Taylor's rooms above The Little Drummer and the need for haste. Burton ought to know about the hidden evidence of smuggling as soon as possible. She sensed that Fanny would want revenge on Taylor and be too excited to keep the search a secret for very long. Anne had a plan to retrieve the papers that very evening.

Anne found Burton in the hotel's dining room at supper

with a man whose back was towards her. The two men sat facing each other in earnest conversation. She hesitated to interrupt. Still, she felt that she must. As she approached the table, Burton glanced at her, puzzled, then irritated. Only when she was a few paces away, did he finally recognize her. She beckoned Peter to join them.

Burton and his companion had almost finished the meal, and their brandy glasses were nearly empty. Burton turned to his companion. 'Mayor Coward, may I present Madame Cartier and her cousin, Peter Cartier, a London Justice of the Peace – both of them well disguised, if I may say so. They have been assisting me in the investigation of the Oliver Parker shipwreck as well as the recent attempts on the life of Janice Parker. I think they may have news for us.'

Anne bowed to him. 'Thank you, sir, for the compliment. We've hastened here with a report because you may wish to act on it immediately. This afternoon, I discovered strong evidence of smuggling and possibly other crimes in the rooms of Nate Taylor. If you wish to seize it, you should do so before eleven o'clock when Taylor will leave his work at the Assembly Rooms. If he learns that he's been searched, as is likely, he'll remove or destroy the evidence. Seth Judd has already taken away valuable papers this afternoon.'

Burton quickly scanned the room. It was almost empty, and no one was within hearing distance. 'Sit down both of you. Tell us more, Madame.'

Anne described the register that recorded in detail the distribution of smuggled goods throughout the West Country. 'I also discovered Taylor's diary for the past five years. Most of it is written in code, but you could find an expert to read it. You might learn more about the attempts on Janice Parker's life. There's also a cache of contraband in one of his rooms.'

When Anne finished, Burton saluted her. 'Madame Cartier, you've given us an excellent opportunity. I'd like to seize that evidence with as little commotion as possible. We can't employ uniformed officers or we'd have a riot. Furthermore, I hope to use the evidence to force Taylor to incriminate Seth Judd, the chief target of my investigation.'

'Sir, I know a way to remove the evidence without a fuss. Peter and I can enter The Little Drummer by the rear stairway. I'll open Taylor's door and seize the register and the diary.

Peter will simply verify the contraband and we'll be out of the building in five minutes. If you wish, the excise men can pick up the contraband later.'

Burton and the mayor glanced at each other, astonished. Burton asked, 'Would you lead the search, Madame?'

Anne glanced at the cane hanging on the arm of his chair. 'Sir, I'd gladly yield the honour to you, but I suspect that you wouldn't want to climb up the steep stairs to the top floor.'

Burton smiled. 'You've read my mind, Madame.'

She turned to the mayor. 'Do you approve, sir?'

'I'll follow Mr Burton's advice.'

'It's the best plan that I can think of, sir.'

'Then I'll deputize cousin Peter Cartier as an extra constable and give him a search warrant.'

Anne paused as a thought came to her. 'To be safe, Mr Burton should tell the Master of Ceremonies at the Assembly Rooms that a young lady named Fanny, a Nymph of Avon Street in a red silk dress, may attempt to accost one of his waiters, Nate Taylor, this evening. She must not speak to him. The MC should send her away.'

The mayor nodded and turned to Burton. 'We'll go to my office in the Guildhall. It's on the way to Avon Street. I'll write out the warrant and affix my seal.'

At nine o'clock, armed with the mayor's warrant, Peter and Anne stole through a dark passage to the back door of The Little Drummer. They had left Burton at a safe distance back in his office. Off to one side of the tavern's door was a bin of stinking trash. Broken glass and other debris littered the ground. The door was locked but not barred. Anne breathed a sigh of relief. 'I can open the lock but not the bar. They'll bar the door later when the tavern closes. We'll be long gone by then.'

She took up her tools, recalled the instruction Georges Charpentier had given her, and set to work. Peter remarked, 'A useful skill for an investigator. I should take lessons.'

Anne merely nodded. She focused intently on her task. And within a minute, she succeeded. 'It's open,' she whispered.

Anne and Peter raced up the stairs in the dark, Peter carrying a shuttered lamp. At each landing they heard shouts, voices, drunken cries. The brothel on the floors above the tavern was doing a lively business. On the top floor, they caught their breath. Anne unlocked the door and they stepped inside. After she relocked the door, Peter unshuttered the lamp as little as possible. Anne retrieved the register and the diary, while Peter studied the contraband. He had just completed an inventory when Anne heard steps and voices outside on the landing.

'Quick. Shutter the lamp and jump into the armoire,' Anne whispered.

They slipped behind Taylor's rack of clothes, just as a key turned the lock and the door opened. Someone walked in. Anne peered through the clothes. Seth Judd was carrying a lighted candle. Amelia Swan followed him.

'What exactly are we looking for?' she asked.

'A register of Nate's transactions with smugglers and West Country businesses. He gave me a register this afternoon, but many entries appear false. I think he's trying to cheat me out of my share. He probably keeps an accurate register hidden somewhere.'

Anne's heart skipped a beat. Judd might search the armoire. Would he show respect for Peter's search warrant?

'Try the writing table,' suggested Amelia. 'That's where he'd keep it.'

'I see a hidden drawer,' said Judd. 'It's locked. I'll force it open.' There was a loud smashing blow, then the sound of splintering wood. 'Nothing here,' he said, anger creeping into his voice.

'Let's go.' Amelia sounded impatient. 'This is a waste of time. Make him tell you where it is.'

'I'll confront him in the morning before I leave for Bristol. Shall we go back to your house?'

'I'd rather go to The Saracen's Head for supper.'

'You're supposed to be in mourning. Remember?' He smiled and drew her into his arms.

She kissed him passionately. 'Right, we'll go to my place.'

The door closed and was locked. The footsteps on the stairs faded away.

As Anne and Peter left the armoire, Anne asked, 'What was that all about?'

Peter replied, 'From his perch down in hell, Thomas Parker has just learned there's no honour among thieves.'

*   *   *

Back in Burton's office, Anne and Peter took turns reporting on what they had observed. Be brief, Burton had cautioned. They must catch Nate Taylor as he finished work at the Assembly Rooms.

'Of the two financial registers that Taylor was keeping, we apparently have the honest one. He's taking a great risk trying to cheat Seth Judd,' said Anne.

'I'll remember that when I question him,' Burton remarked. 'It's a good lever for prying the truth out of him.'

'Do you suppose Thomas Parker knew that Captain Judd and Miss Swan were intimate?' Peter asked.

'Just imagine,' Anne added, 'if he discovered her infidelity three or four days ago and said that he would strip her from his will. How would she have reacted?'

Burton replied, 'She might have poisoned him before he could change his will. During this morning's search of the house, we found it properly signed and sealed.' He glanced at a clock on the wall. 'The Assembly Rooms will soon close. Let's listen to what Mr Taylor has to say.'

They reached the Assembly Rooms twenty minutes before closing, and joined André and Harriet at a table in the Tea Room. The crowd was still lively and loud, boisterous at times. In the next-door gaming room gamblers of both sexes crowded around the tables, playing faro, though it was illegal, and casting dice.

An hour earlier Harriet had sung a program of ballads and airs, and was now resting with a cup of warm herbal tea. Throughout the evening, André had kept a sharp eye on Nate Taylor. 'He seemed preoccupied this evening, bumped into people, nearly dropped his tray.'

'I'm not surprised. He has much to be worried about,' Burton remarked. 'I'll speak to the MC about interrogating him.'

A few minutes past eleven, as the last stragglers were cajoled out of the building, the MC approached Burton and said to follow him. André would escort Harriet to her apartment on Queen Square. It was late and she was tired.

To Anne, still in disguise, Burton said, 'I'd like you to sit to one side. Take notes, observe Taylor.' To Peter he said, 'I'll lead the interrogation, but ask any question that occurs to you.'

He gazed at them with anticipation. 'I think Taylor is our key to resolving several crimes: the death of Thomas Parker, the attempts on Janice Parker's life, the shipwreck of Oliver Parker in 1782, and large-scale smuggling in the West Country. They are all somehow connected to Seth Judd – the Sea Fox.'

The MC arranged a small storeroom near the kitchen for the interrogation and supplied Anne with pen and paper. As he left, he said, 'I'll be back in a minute with Taylor.'

The waiter entered the room hesitantly, his eyes clouded with confusion and anxiety. Recognizing Burton, he stammered, 'I told you before. I've done nothing wrong, just ordered the drinks from the barman and delivered them to the table. I'd no idea there was poison in one of them.'

Burton said nothing, gestured Taylor to a seat at a table, and sat opposite him. Peter sat next to Burton. They were silent, unsmiling for a few moments, staring at Taylor. His discomfort increased. He clenched his hands in his lap.

'So why am I here?' he finally complained.

Burton nodded to Peter, who reached into a portfolio, pulled out Taylor's financial register, and opened it on the table. 'Do you recognize this?'

Taylor glanced at a page, gasped, and turned pale. 'How'd you find it?'

Burton tapped it solemnly, ignoring the question. 'It convicts you of five years of distributing smuggled goods worth thousands of pounds.' He paused for a moment, glaring at the waiter. 'That's a hanging offence. But if you have a kind magistrate, he might send you for life to our new penal colony in New South Wales.'

'Or,' Peter added, 'we might arrange for Seth Judd to see this register and compare it with the false one you gave him this afternoon. He already suspects that you've cheated him and intends to confront you tomorrow morning. Can you imagine his anger?'

Taylor had begun to perspire. The knuckles on his clenched hand had turned white. 'What do you want?' he croaked.

'The truth,' Burton replied softly, measuring the words. 'If you cooperate with us, we'll protect you from Captain Judd and persuade the magistrate to reduce your punishment. If you try to deceive us, you will most likely hang.'

Taylor took a deep breath, leaned back, and tried to gather courage. His mind appeared to struggle with the threats he had heard and was desperately calculating his options.

Burton nodded to Peter again, who drew the diary out of the portfolio and laid it on the table. Burton showed it to Taylor. 'It's in code, mostly, but rather simple to read, like many amateur codes I've read for the Bow Street magistrate. I've seen enough to realize that you've kept a detailed record of your correspondence with Seth Judd and his associates, as well as daily notes of your own affairs. So we should be able to catch you, if you lie to us.'

Taylor's shoulders slumped in a sign of surrender. 'What can I tell you?'

'Seth Judd doesn't appear in the financial register. How is he involved?'

'He's there under the code name Cain. He gives me money to buy goods from the smugglers. Then I sell the goods to merchants at double or triple the cost. The captain receives forty per cent of the profit. I'm entitled to ten per cent.'

'And what was Mr Thomas Parker's role?'

'He gathered money from rich investors and sent it to Captain Judd for the purchase of goods, ships, weapons, and other equipment – and bribes to excise men, royal officers, watchmen and the like. In return, he received fifty per cent of the profit to be shared with the investors. That's generally how the system works.' He hesitated.

'Anything else?' Burton tilted his head in a skeptical gesture.

'I believe that the captain also has a smaller, personal business outside the system, using his own cutters and resources to smuggle high-quality silk and tobacco for sale to prominent rich customers. I've no record of it. Someone else must keep those accounts.'

'Is Parker in your register?'

'Yes, he's Abel, to Judd's Cain. The captain chose the names. They seem to fit.' A nervous smile flickered on Taylor's lips. 'They were brothers, you know.'

'Indeed, that brings me to the next question. Who killed Thomas Parker? Was it Seth Judd?'

Taylor studied the ceiling, chewed on his lower lip. 'I served everyone at that table, including Thomas Parker. But I didn't put poison in his glass, and I don't know who did. My tray is numbered like the chairs at the table. When I fill or refill a person's glass, I put it on his or her number. Anyone could figure out those numbers and poison a certain person's glass. Mrs Parker – Beverly – was near the counter where I placed my tray. While I was talking to the barman, or otherwise distracted for a few minutes, she could easily have put poison in her husband's glass. The counter was crowded and busy.'

Anne pondered Taylor's explanation. It sounded reasonable up to a point. Without hesitation he had assumed that Beverly was the chief suspect. It hadn't occurred to him to mention others who had the same opportunity as she.

'Was Seth Judd ever at the counter?' Burton asked.

Taylor took a moment to think. 'Yes, when Miss Swan and Thomas Parker were arranging with me to serve their table, the captain joined us.'

'What does "arranging" your service entail?'

'The eight people at the table wanted different drinks: white wine, red wine, punch with spirits, punch without spirits. Miss Swan and Thomas Parker told me each person's preference. They made the same arrangement for the food. That made serving much easier and quicker for me, since I didn't have to run back and forth through an impatient, hungry, and thirsty mob.'

Anne raised her hand. Burton nodded for her to go ahead, and he drew back to observe. 'So,' Anne began, 'Seth Judd, Amelia Swan, and Thomas Parker had the same opportunity as Beverly Parker to put poison in one of the drinks.'

Taylor shrugged. 'That's true, I suppose. But I can't imagine why Mr Parker would want to poison his own drink. I don't know why Miss Swan or Captain Judd would want to kill him.'

'Tell us the kind of drink you served each person at that table.'

He thought for a moment and replied, 'I served punch with spirits to Amelia Swan, Thomas Parker, Janice Parker, and her companion. To the other persons at the table I served one white wine, one red wine, and two punch without spirits.'

'To the naked eye, then, there were six identical punch glasses on your tray, distinguished only by the numbers that they stood on. Couldn't someone accidentally exchange the one with poison with a harmless one?'

'Yes, that could happen while the tray was on the counter and I didn't have my eyes on it.'

Burton stood up and addressed Taylor. 'That's enough for tonight.' He turned to Peter. 'As deputy constable, would you please take Mr Taylor to the city prison on Grove Street. The MC has called for the night constable who will assist you. A constable will pick up Mr Taylor in the morning at about ten and take him to my office in the Guildhall. Judge Williams will join us there for more questions.'

'Why won't you let me return to my apartment?' asked Taylor peevishly.

'I fear that Seth Judd might have discovered your betrayal and be unable to contain his anger. You wouldn't live through the night. The prison isn't comfortable, but you will at least be safe.'

As Anne was about to leave the storeroom, she remarked to Burton, 'Taylor admitted that the poisoned glass could have been intended for someone other than Thomas Parker but was accidentally – or deliberately – switched.'

'Yes,' Burton replied. 'The intended victim could have been Janice. We know of two previous attempts on her life and in both of them Seth Judd was involved in the background. This could have been his third attempt. But by mistake the poisoned glass was accidentally served to Thomas Parker.'

Anne continued with her theory. 'Imagine that Miss Swan, and perhaps Captain Judd, studied Taylor's tray. They weren't looking for Parker's spot at all. They determined which glass was destined for Janice and poured in the poison.' She paused. 'Come to think of it, Parker was positioned to do the same thing.'

Burton pursued Anne's idea. 'Someone else may have noticed them, perhaps Beverly, who then moved the poisoned glass to Thomas Parker's number on the tray.'

'I'd rather think that the switch of the drinks was accidental,' Anne countered, wishing to exonerate her cousin in this speculation.

Burton smiled sardonically. 'Thomas Parker may have unwittingly poisoned himself.'

Anne wondered aloud, 'Janice is asthmatic and occasionally has severe attacks. I've seen her fall to the ground struggling to breathe. Her symptoms resembled Thomas Parker's tonight. Could the poisoner have wanted to mask her murder as an asthmatic attack?'

'Yes, it's possible,' Burton replied with an involuntary yawn. 'Sorry, Madame. It's late. I'll add your suggestion to the others. One of them may eventually explain this murder.'

RECOLLECTIONS OF A LETHAL SHIPWRECK

Bath, Saturday, 14 November

Anne smelled the morning coffee while she was still half-asleep. A few minutes later, Janice knocked, and entered the room with a breakfast tray. She set it on a table by the window. There was a chill in the room, so she stirred up a fire in the hearth. Anne pulled on a robe and joined her at the table.

Janice poured the coffee. 'You came home late last night. I let you sleep and made the breakfast.'

'Thank you, Janice, that was kind of you.' The young woman's thoughtful gesture was touching.

After serving the bread, Janice asked, 'May I ask what happened?'

'We discovered strong evidence of Seth Judd's smuggling and found a witness to testify against him. Unfortunately, he is still free. You have to fear another attempt on your life. Be careful.'

'Why don't you just put him in jail? Then I'd be safe and you wouldn't have to worry.'

'Yes, it's frustrating to watch him swagger through the Assembly Rooms, free as a bird. Unfortunately, Judd is clever and has powerful friends. No court would dare to put him on trial at this point. We must produce still more evidence of his crimes and at least one more witness.'

'Why would he want to kill me? I've never understood.'

Anne sighed. 'His motives have also seemed unclear to me.

I used to think that he wanted you dead so that your wealth could go to his partner in smuggling, your heir, Thomas Parker. With Parker's death, that wealth could still go to Amelia, Parker's heir and Judd's lover.'

'But Beverly is Parker's wife. Couldn't she challenge the new will?'

'True, she could and probably will do so. Seth must realize that.'

A wry look came over Janice's face. 'If Beverly were convicted and hanged for her husband's murder, there would be no one to challenge his will.'

'That's plausible,' Anne conceded. 'But let's return to our most pressing problem: Seth Judd still threatens your life. On the bright side, we're making progress towards arresting him.'

When breakfast was finished, Anne asked Janice, 'How are you feeling? You've had a dreadful ordeal.' Anne thought of the years of loveless neglect that the young woman suffered under Parker. Then recently she had to endure several days of abusive imprisonment at his hands, and finally the shock of his murder.

Janice slowly cleared the table. 'I feel relieved that Parker is dead, almost giddy. It's as if a heavy stone has been lifted from my spirit. But I'm also uneasy about the future. What's to become of me?'

'In four years you will come of age and can begin to manage your own affairs. In the meantime, however, law and custom decree that you must have adult supervision. A court will soon decide who shall be responsible for your welfare.'

'That's what I'm afraid of. Will anyone listen to what I want?'

'If you were poor, you might be left to your own devices. Or, you could be apprenticed to a dressmaker, or become a domestic servant. But you are heir to a large fortune and must be looked after. In particular, should you wish to marry a young man, you would need the consent of a legal guardian.'

'Who would the court pick?'

'A magistrate's first choice would probably be Beverly Parker. For better or for worse, she has had the care of you since the death of your parents. But he might look askance at her estrangement from Parker and her adultery with Grimshaw.'

Janice grimaced at the mention of Beverly. 'We really dislike each other.'

'Then who would *you* prefer?'

'If it were left to me, I'd choose the printer, Mr David Woodhouse.'

'But you've only met him once two weeks ago. You hardly know him.'

'I was with him and his family for several hours that day. His son speaks well of him. Even his enemies among the slave traders respect him.' She met Anne's eye. 'And you admire him too – I can tell. He's generous and kind, and he and the rest of his family can sign. I feel at home with them.'

'A court might find him acceptable if no suitable or willing relatives could be found. Do you know if your father had any cousins or distant relatives?'

'I've never heard of any. I suppose if you searched long enough you'd find one under a rock somewhere. He might be willing to take responsibility for me and hope to skim money from my inheritance.'

Anne inwardly flinched at the young woman's cynical remark, a likely consequence of years of abuse by negligent or covetous adults. 'The mayor has said that I'll be your temporary guardian while we are in Bath. Mr Burton wants you to remain here until your uncle's murder is resolved. Mr Barnstaple, the solicitor who oversees your estate, will continue to send you a monthly allowance. He also looks after my affairs. I'll write to him today and explain your situation. Give him time. He might think of a solution you could live with.'

Janice smiled in agreement, and their conversation moved on to the plan for the day.

As Janice was about to leave with the breakfast tray, she grew pensive. 'I'd like to visit Jacob Woodhouse in the hospital. He's been there a week. Do you think he's well enough to receive visitors?'

'Yes,' Anne replied. 'I'll send a servant to make sure. I'll omit the Pump Room this morning and go with you as a precaution.' Anne didn't mention that she would bring along her pistol and sword cane.

*   *   *

At the hospital an attendant led them into a large, airy room of many cubicles divided by hanging curtains. The attendant pulled aside a curtain to reveal Jacob sitting up in bed prepared to greet his visitors. His face was pale and drawn. The attendant said, 'Mr Woodhouse had received a severe blow to his head, cuts on his arm, and a knife wound to his chest. He's recovering nicely but tires quickly. Don't be long.'

'Good morning, Janice,' Jacob signed with a heartfelt smile. 'I'm so happy that you've come.'

Her lips quivered, her eyes glistened. But she bravely blinked back her tears and signed in return, 'I'm pleased that you're doing better, Jacob. I thank you for saving my life a second time and regret that you were wounded so badly.' She paused and then signed hesitantly, 'You know that my uncle is dead and I'm living with Madame Cartier. If you wish, we could meet again – when you are well, of course.'

He mustered a thin smile. 'I would like that very much, Janice. The very thought should speed my healing.'

The visitors were preparing to leave when it occurred to Anne to ask Janice and Jacob together, 'How did your assailants know where to find you?'

Janice replied, 'Parker's spy, the one you confronted in Queen Square, was at the Pump Room with his female companion that morning. The young woman came close to us when we made our plans to walk to Crescent Fields.'

'I see,' said Anne. 'She could have passed that information to the three villains waiting outside.' She suspected that Seth Judd instructed them to work together with Parker's spies.

Jacob waved feebly as they left. 'Visit my mother. Tell her I'm looking forward to going home.'

At the printing shop the family and its apprentices gathered in a solemn conclave to meet Anne and Janice. They reported on their visit to the hospital and assured them of Jacob's improvement. Relieved, the men went back to work at the presses. Judith Woodhouse took the visitors upstairs to the family's rooms.

'Never mind the mess,' she signed. 'My maid is ill, and I'm busy preparing a room for Jacob. He'll need air and light.'

'Can I help?' Janice asked.

Mrs Woodhouse appeared to appreciate the offer but hesitated to accept it.

Janice insisted, 'I may be rich but I also know how to work.
I would especially enjoy doing something for Jacob.'

Mrs Woodhouse relented with a gentle smile. As Anne left,
she felt relieved that Janice was safely occupied for the day.

While Anne and Janice were visiting Jacob Woodhouse in the
hospital, Peter and Harriet went to the Pump Room. He was
curious how well the 'secret' of Nate Taylor's detention was kept.
As soon as they entered the room, they noticed that the crowd
was even more animated than usual. Word was passing from
one person to the next that Nate Taylor, waiter at the Assembly
Rooms, had been arrested and put in prison. His rooms had
been searched and important documents seized.

'A constable's tongue must have come loose,' Peter observed
grimly.

'Do you think Captain Judd has heard?' Harriet asked.

'Perhaps not,' Peter replied. 'One of Burton's spies told me
that Judd was with Miss Swan all night. I look forward to
seeing how he will react to the news.'

'There he is,' said Harriet. He stood just inside the room,
surveying the crowd in his usual sharp-eyed, self-assured
manner. He strode towards the water counter. An acquaintance hurried up to him and spoke a few words. Judd stopped
in his tracks as if struck. He frowned, gave a tight-lipped reply,
and continued on to the water counter.

'He apparently just learned that Taylor's been arrested,'
Peter whispered to Harriet. 'Burton's investigation into
smuggling now seriously threatens him.'

At the water counter Judd joined friends and acquaintances
and ordered a glass. For a short while the men acted casually, pretending that the news meant nothing to them. One by
one, they drifted away from the counter with their drinks.
Soon, however, they met at a table in a far corner of the room
and began an earnest discussion.

Peter said to Harriet, 'I must find out what Judd plans to do.'
He signalled to a young servant. The boy was hardly more than
twelve years old, but remarkably quick-witted. Peter had
befriended him earlier and used him as a spy. Peter discreetly
pointed to Captain Judd. 'Find out what he's saying to his friends.'

'Yes, sir,' the boy replied. 'I'll collect their empty glasses,
wipe the table, and listen.'

The boy came back a few minutes later. 'The captain says he must leave Bath and return to Morland Court. His friends should finish their business with him as soon as possible. He might soon embark on a journey.'

Peter gave the boy a coin, then turned to Harriet. 'Judd feels the noose tightening around his neck. In the next few days, he'll become desperate and either flee or fight.'

At ten o'clock in the Guildhall, a constable arrived with Nate Taylor, unshackled. Judge Williams and Dick Burton were waiting at the writing table. Taylor stood before them. Anne was off to one side with pen and paper, aware that the judge was casting sideways glances at her. Were they friendly? Perhaps not, to judge from his finger tapping on the table and the downward curve of his lips.

The judge fussed with his wig, then began, 'Tell us, Mr Taylor, what really happened off the south coast of Wales in June 1782. At the inquiry seven years ago you told us that the sloop *Mercury* crashed into the rocks because the first mate at the helm was drunk and steered too close to shore. Is that correct?'

Taylor glanced at Anne, then answered with a weak, 'Yes'. He appeared confused by her discreet, yet mitigating presence in what was otherwise looking like a grim magistrate's inquisition.

The judge went on, 'Let me tell you, Taylor, I have subsequently investigated the mate's background. There's no evidence of him ever being drunk on duty. In Bristol taverns he was known to drink a pint of ale, but no barman could remember him ever drinking to excess.' The judge waved a finger at Taylor. 'You're off to a poor start. Furthermore, you told us that the sloop wasn't carrying anything of value. We have since discovered that a large quantity of gold was on board.'

Burton added, 'I must warn you, Taylor, this investigation will continue beyond today for as long as necessary. We'll be checking the accuracy of everything you tell us against your records and other evidence we've discovered. If you lie to us, we'll show you no mercy.'

For a few moments, Taylor stammered, as if desperately thinking of ways to escape. Beads of perspiration appeared on his ruddy forehead. Finally, he nodded.

'Now that we understand each other,' continued the judge, 'first tell us who really was at the helm that night.'

Taylor averted his eyes, licked his lips. For a moment the room was silent, except for the muffled rumble of traffic out on the street. 'It was all his idea,' he began. 'Captain Judd's. He took me aside shortly after the sloop lost sight of the Irish coast. He said he trusted me – we'd sailed together, risked our lives taking the Spanish ship, yet we received only small portions of the legal prize. He said his brother, Oliver, a greedy man living in a magnificent manor house and dining on delicacies, had secretly taken a chest of gold and had refused to share. That chest had to be in Oliver's cabin, the captain said. He had seen it come aboard. This was a God-given opportunity to take our due.'

Taylor paused. His tone had grown self-righteous. He glanced at the others in the room, inviting their approval, but they gave him no encouragement. The judge waved him on.

'I told the captain that I agreed with him and asked for more details. Then he laid out his plan. During the night, he would surprise Mr Oliver at gunpoint, take most of the gold and leave him with ten per cent. He couldn't complain to the authorities because the gold was contraband. It hadn't been properly declared as a prize of war.'

Burton interrupted. 'This is beginning to sound like a pact between thieves.'

Taylor shrugged. 'The plan was risky and illegal, I admit, and the captain's reference to his gun made me hesitate. But murder wasn't part of the plan. Captain Judd was a brave and daring sort of man, one of the best privateers in the American War. So I trusted him.

'At midnight, the mate was at the helm, and I stood near him. The captain broke into Mr Parker's cabin to demand the gold. A minute later, I heard a shot. The mate told me to see what had happened. I entered the cabin and found Mr Parker lying in a pool of blood. Captain Judd was leaning over Mrs Parker, her throat cut from ear to ear, a bloody knife in his hand. I cried out, "What's gone wrong?"

'Captain Judd replied that he had shot Parker who had pulled a hidden pistol from under the bed. And he had killed his wife when she tried to seize the pistol.'

Taylor paused again, this time nervously, apparently

concerned that these ghastly horrors were reflecting back upon him.

Anne grimaced at the account that she had just written. She could feel little sympathy for Oliver Parker, a fraud who profited from smuggling as well as from trading in slaves. But his wife was an honourable woman who deserved a better fate. She had been a kind and generous mother to Janice.

Taylor pressed on. 'What shall we do now?' I asked. 'The pistol shot will have alarmed the rest of the crew.' The captain ignored me. He wiped the blood from his knife on the bedclothes and seized Parker's pistol.

'On the way out we met the mate. He had handed the helm over to Grimes, the other seaman. He demanded to know what we had done. The captain said it was none of his business. He should return to the helm. The mate darted past us and tried to enter the cabin. The captain shot him in the back and threw him overboard. The seaman at the helm stared at us, frozen with fear. The captain confronted him, the knife at his throat.

' "Either you're with us, Grimes, or you're dead."

' "I'm with you," he said.

' "Then you must have a share." The captain left me holding the knife and went into the cabin. A minute later, he came back with a small pouch. "Ten pieces of gold. It's blood money. If you try to betray us, you'll still hang with us. Sail out on the next ship to Africa, China, or wherever. Open a grog shop. Never let me see you again in Britain."

'We lowered the ship's boat near Pembroke and sent him off. That's the last we saw of him.

'By this time, with no one really minding the helm, we had sailed off course perilously close to the shore. The captain took the helm. I tried to work the sails. But we hit the rocky ridge. The sloop was lightly built and began to break up. The captain seized the chest of gold before we slipped off the rocks and sank. We had lashed broken spars together into a raft. Now we drifted ashore with the incoming tide. No one on shore had noticed us. So, before raising an alarm, we waited for the outgoing tide to carry the sunken ship into deep waters, where the bodies wouldn't be discovered.'

'What happened to the gold?' Williams asked.

'We hid it, went back for it later, and divided it, two-thirds for the captain, one-third for me.'

'Then you agreed on the story that you would tell to the Court of Inquiry.'

He nodded. 'A year later, when the war and privateering ended, smuggling picked up and he asked me to work for him.'

'What did he do with his gold?'

'With some of it he bought two cutters for the smuggling trade. I think he hid the rest.'

'And your portion?'

He hesitated. 'I've saved it to buy a shop and get married. But first I wanted to give up smuggling. However, the captain wouldn't let me. Said I knew too much. If I were to try to leave, he would kill me.'

'You will sign the statement of your testimony that Madame Cartier is preparing. I have no more questions now, perhaps later.' The judge turned to Burton, who shook his head.

As the constable was about to take Taylor back to the prison, Burton stayed him with a gesture and asked Taylor to describe the missing seaman, Grimes.

'I didn't know him well. This was the first time he sailed with us. He said he was twenty, came from Bristol and had relatives there. He was living at the White Gull on the quay when the captain hired him.'

'What did he look like?' asked Anne, interrupting her writing.

Taylor grimaced with the effort to recall. 'He was of average height and slender, had dark hair, sallow complexion.' He paused and smiled. 'Now I remember that he had an odd look – one eye was blue, the other green.'

Burton glanced at Anne and the judge. They both shook their heads, no further questions.

During the next few minutes, Anne finished her summary of the interrogation and handed it to Judge Williams, who scanned it and gave it to Taylor. He signed it and the constable took him away.

The judge turned to his companions. 'At the inquiry in 1782, I wondered if anyone had survived the wreck, besides Judd and Taylor. I knew the seaman's name, Isaac Grimes, and that he came from Bristol. For a few months thereafter my clerk surveyed lists of ships' crews in vain. It was like looking for a needle in a haystack. If Grimes had survived, he might live under an assumed name, or have settled in one of our colonies. With the additional information that Taylor has just given us, I think we should renew the search.'

'As secretly as possible,' Anne added, risking the judge's displeasure. 'Seth Judd and his smugglers mustn't find Grimes first.'

After the interrogation, Anne asked Judge Williams, 'What would happen to Janice's inheritance if she were to die? Would it go to the estate of the late Thomas Parker?'

'That would depend,' the judge replied. 'As Thomas Parker's still legal wife, Beverly Parker could challenge the recent will. The judicial process could take as long as she and Amelia Swan are potential suspects in Parker's murder. His creditors could also lay claim to much of the estate. Only the remainder – perhaps still a considerable amount – might eventually go to Miss Swan.'

'Then Janice is still in danger,' Anne said.

'Yes, unfortunately.' Williams' expression softened. 'The girl's wealth hangs over her like a sword of Damocles.'

SEARCH FOR CLUES

Bath, Saturday, 14 November

Early in the afternoon, Anne and Peter met Burton and a city constable in front of Parker's house in the Circus. Peter reported Judd's Pump Room remarks about finishing business and going on a journey.

Burton received the information with a frown. 'We must move swiftly or Judd will slip out of our hands. I'll alert my spies.'

At Burton's request, Anne had brought along pen, ink, and paper to record the interrogation. In the course of the investigation she had already produced a thick file of testimony. She had asked Burton once, what purpose the file would serve.

He had answered, 'Madame, my memory is not what it used to be. The file is a useful crutch. I'm also looking ahead to the trial of Judd and others at the Admiralty in London. That's months away. Our witnesses might die or simply disappear. At least I shall give the court an accurate paper record of their testimony.'

As they walked up to the entrance, Burton said, 'Miss Swan's grief is mostly feigned. But, I'll offer my condolences anyway. Then, regardless of her tears, I intend to interrogate her – and Judd too. I've learned that Captain Judd is with her "to offer consolation".'

'Why would Miss Swan poison Parker?' Anne asked. 'True, she's his heir. But she would receive nothing from him but debts – unless of course Janice were to die and her fortune would augment his estate.'

'Madame, if I were to hazard a guess, I'd say that Miss Swan is praying earnestly for the young woman's speedy demise. Judd is more pragmatic and not inclined to pray. I imagine him devising another plan to kill Janice.'

Burton knocked. The maid, Gracie White, opened the door, hiding her role as his spy. With the slightest hint of a smile, she announced, 'I've been instructed to say that Madame is in mourning and will not receive visitors this afternoon.' She started to close the door.

Burton stopped the door with his cane and took a step forward. The maid retreated. Burton handed her his Bow Street card and said, 'Take this card to Madame and tell her that we'll expect her in the parlour within ten minutes. Then, if she hasn't come to us, we'll go to her.'

The maid bowed and led them into the parlour. As she passed Anne, she whispered, 'Seth Judd is with her. Do you want him, too?' Anne passed the question to Burton. He told the maid, 'We'll speak with Madame, first, alone, then with Captain Judd.'

When the maid left, Burton told Peter and the constable to search the house from top to bottom. 'Question the servants concerning Parker's state of mind, as well as Janice Parker's confinement.'

Burton turned to Anne. 'Watch for more signs of intimacy between Miss Swan and Seth Judd that could have a bearing upon the death of Parker. He wouldn't be the first victim in a murderous triangle of love betrayed.'

A few seconds short of the deadline, Amelia swept into the

parlour, her full, black silk dressing gown swishing behind
her. In the ten minutes allotted, she had managed to groom
herself tolerably well and to assume a haughty attitude.

Seth Judd entered at her side, his throat tight with indignation. 'Have you no shame!' he sputtered. 'How dare you
intrude into Miss Swan's private grief?' He glared at Burton.
'Do you have a warrant?'

Burton rose painfully on his cane, retrieved the mayor's
warrant from his pocket, and showed it to Judd, then to Amelia.
'Excuse us, Madame, but we must question you concerning
the death of Mr Thomas Parker.' He turned to Judd. 'And you,
sir, must wait outside. We'll speak to you shortly.'

Judd glared at Burton, then at his companions. Finally, he
stalked out. Peter and the constable followed him. Burton
motioned Amelia to a chair facing him. Anne sat with pen
and paper at a small table off to one side.

'Now, Madame,' Burton began, 'tell us when and where
you first met Mr Thomas Parker.'

She fussed with the folds of her gown while she seemed
to consider her response. 'I believe it was in the fall of 1786
at a soirée in London in an elegant house of pleasure in Mayfair.
He was a charming but lonely gentleman, married to an
unfeeling woman. He and I soon became best friends and
lovers. For the past two years we've lived together virtually
as husband and wife. He would have divorced his wife, and
we could have married, but the process is nearly impossible.'

'I understand the difficulty of divorce,' said Burton, then
went on. 'Madame, I've learned that Thomas Parker changed
his will recently in Bath. You became his chief beneficiary.
Was the will ever an issue between you?'

'We discussed it at length, but in a friendly way. Since he
couldn't marry me, I wanted evidence of his often-stated conviction that ours was a lasting relationship, akin to marriage.'

'Were you aware that his financial situation was desperate
and, if he were to die, you might inherit his huge debt?'

'He did not discuss his business affairs with me. But I knew
that financial ventures could be risky. Storms sink ships, or
pirates steal their cargos. Thomas might sometimes lose, but
I had confidence in him: in the end he would win.'

'Did you know that some of his ventures, such as smuggling,
were illegal as well as risky?'

'Thomas a smuggler? Sir! You besmirch a gentleman's honour!' Her lips tightened with indignation.

'Madame, I have the evidence to convict him. I'll also submit it to the tax authorities. They will add their claim upon his inheritance to that of his creditors.'

She became silent and still, her mind busy calculating.

'Did you know, Madame, that one of Parker's chief business associates was Mr Seth Judd?'

'They were acquainted. Judd has been our guest in London as well as in this house. He was one of the many men with whom Thomas did business.'

'Where did he reside in London?'

'Why do you suppose I would know that?'

'He rented a room above the millinery shop you frequented in the alley off Old Bond Street. You must recall the spot. It's where someone dropped a large piece of masonry on Miss Janice Parker.'

'The constable judged that to be an accident.'

'His wasn't the last word on that incident. He was ignorant of many important facts. But we are beginning to stray from the point. Are you aware that Mr Judd is suspected in that attempt to kill Miss Parker?'

She paused, met Burton's eye, and said levelly, 'You give too much weight to a coincidence. I hold Mr Judd in high regard. He has been helpful to me since Thomas' death.'

'In what way, Madame?'

'What can you possibly mean, sir?'

'He has helped you go through Parker's correspondence and other papers. Has he removed any such material from this house?'

She hesitated, appearing to calculate again how much Burton might know and what she could safely reveal. 'We went through the accounts for this house and other expenses of this season in Bath. He took with him bills that should be paid to merchants, here and elsewhere.'

'A caring friend, this Seth Judd. Did Parker ever accuse you two of intimacy?'

'Really, sir, you go too far.'

'Not as far as I might, Madame. Credible witnesses observed you and Mr Judd in an embrace that could enrage even a tolerant man like Thomas Parker. In view of your background as a courtesan, he might reasonably infer that this was not the first and only instance.' Burton paused for a moment, then speculated. 'Perhaps Parker had not yet discovered your infidelity. To prevent him from doing so – and then removing you as his heir – that's in itself a sufficient motive for murder.'

'Mr Burton . . .' She let out a great sigh of exasperation.

'Apart from your motives,' Burton went on, 'you had an opportunity that night in the Tea Room to poison him. You were with Judd and Parker at the bar, ordering drinks for your table and could watch the waiter place the drinks on his tray. You could slip poison into the one that was going to Parker.'

'Others could have done the same.'

'You have accused Beverly Parker. Why?'

'She was also at the bar. It was busy. Many people were trying to order at the same time. In the confusion she could have poisoned Thomas' drink.'

'Did you actually see her do it?'

'No, I didn't. But she must have. She was the person with the strongest motive and had quarreled with him in front of everybody.'

'That will be all for now, Madame,' said Burton abruptly. 'Please tell Captain Judd that we'll speak to him in fifteen minutes.'

Amelia rose hesitantly from her chair, her face a picture of anxiety and confusion. Burton's questions had shaken her and thrown her off-balance.

After Amelia left the room, Burton settled back in his chair, tilted his head to a sceptical angle, and asked, 'Madame Cartier, what do you think of our courtesan's performance?'

Anne broke off writing, laid down her pen, and blotted the page. 'She remains a suspect. Her liaison with Judd could have led to conflict with Parker and she might then have poisoned him. But thus far, Parker hasn't given us any reason to believe that he suspected her infidelity.'

'I agree,' said Burton, almost reluctantly. He appeared to have a visceral dislike for the woman.

'What shall you ask Judd?' asked Anne. 'He's implicated in so many crimes where evidence is lacking or incomplete. His interrogation could be complicated and unproductive.'

'Your concern is well founded,' Burton replied. 'I'll focus

on Thomas Parker's death and return to the other issues later. Please tell him to come in.'

When Anne opened the door and looked out, Seth and Amelia were together in the hall, several paces away, face to face, speaking intensely. They didn't notice her.

She called out, 'Captain Judd.' They both spun around towards her, with startled expressions. For an instant Judd appeared to seethe with anger. His lips parted, his teeth clenched. Then suddenly he seemed calm and collected, like a man who had nothing to hide and no reason to be concerned.

Anne returned to her table. As Judd passed by, he gave her a chilling glance. But he said nothing and settled into the chair facing Burton.

'Mr Judd, we are trying to determine who might have caused the death of Mr Thomas Parker two days ago. You were not at his table, but witnesses have placed you at the bar when the waiter prepared a tray of drinks.'

'I was one of those near enough to have put poison into his glass. But I didn't do it and had no reason to. I counted Parker as a business associate, an acquaintance of long-standing.'

Burton added, 'And a half-brother, as was Oliver Parker.'

'That's correct. They raised money for my voyages.'

'Describe your relationship to Amelia Swan, Parker's mistress.'

Judd's face registered a brief flash of indignation. 'In a word, proper. We've met on social occasions, Parker usually present.'

'When and where did you first meet her?'

'After the American War, about six years ago. I began to visit her house of pleasure when I was in London.'

'Did you introduce Parker to her?'

'Yes. They seemed suited to each other.'

'Were there any hard feelings when she became his mistress?'

'No, I remained on good terms with both of them.'

'That will be all for now, captain.' Burton paused and met Judd's eye. 'I expect you to remain available for more questions.'

As Judd passed by Anne, he said beneath his breath, 'I haven't forgotten.' She instinctively shuddered but didn't mention the threat to Burton.

For a few moments Burton reflected, then asked Anne for her opinion.

'I watched his reactions carefully,' she said. 'He didn't betray any motive for killing Thomas Parker. I'm not surprised. He's a clever man. But, if I may speculate, it's in his interests that both Janice and Parker die, so that his "friend", Miss Swan, could inherit Oliver Parker's fortune. He would then marry her. As her husband, he could persuade or force her to share her wealth, even though it would still be in a trust.'

Burton added, 'Once the captain was Miss Swan's heir, he could have her killed. Then he'd own the entire Parker estate and be lord of the manor. Perhaps that's what he dreams about.'

'He's clever and ruthless enough to realize that dream,' Anne reminded him. 'They call Judd "The Sea Fox" for good reason.'

'Your idea, Madame, is not far-fetched. But it needs the solid footing of evidence.'

Anne agreed. 'My idea rests partly on the captain's very real attempts on Janice's life. Why else would he want to kill her? For that reason I would consider him as a serious suspect in her uncle's murder.'

'As do I,' Burton said. 'But now let's hear what Peter and our constable have found.'

Peter spoke for both of them. The maid, Gracie White, had proved to be the most helpful and perceptive of the servants. She noticed recent signs of mental anxiety and physical decline in Thomas Parker. He cursed and drank more than usual and groomed himself with less care. He snapped at the servants, sometimes at Miss Swan.

Anne remarked, 'We know that he mistreated Janice, even had her whipped when she defied him.'

'A spirited young lady,' Burton remarked.

'And a bit foolish,' Anne added.

'Let's get back to Thomas Parker's odd behaviour,' said Burton. 'What does it mean?'

'Perhaps his financial difficulties had unhinged his mind and were driving him towards suicide.'

'That's plausible, if not convincing. Still it remains as a possible explanation.'

*   *   *

It was midafternoon when Beverly and her maid returned home from a walk. Anne and Burton had waited in the parlour of her apartment. Burton had sent Peter and the constable to see that Nate Taylor was safe and secure in prison. Beverly appeared unpleasantly surprised by the unannounced visit.

'The November wind from the west in Crescent Fields was brisk and biting. I must look like a scarecrow.'

Indeed, her creamy complexion was tinged with pink to the colour of peaches, her dark-brown hair was tossed over her shoulder and hung in lovely waves, and her golden-brown eyes were wide and glistening. The walk had invigorated her and heightened her beauty. Anne said as much when she greeted her.

The compliment soothed her irritated spirit. She invited them to a small table for tea and sweet biscuits. The conversation soon touched on Thomas Parker.

Beverly remarked levelly, 'If you've come to console me on the death of my husband, you'll quickly discover that I feel no grief. To my shame, I never loved him, and shouldn't have married him. Nor did he ever love me – as far as I could tell. It was a marriage of convenience.' She paused for a moment, as if recalling a typical episode of their unhappy common life. 'I'm glad it's over. I wish that it could have ended civilly, without recriminations.' She shook her head, trying to banish an ugly sight. 'I truly regret his ghastly death.'

Burton nodded to Anne. She brought out her ink and paper. Beverly looked askance. 'What kind of visit is this?'

'Business mixed with pleasure.' Burton met her eye. 'The mayor needs to know what happened Thursday night when your husband was poisoned. So he has asked me to question all those who were with Parker or near him. We've just come from speaking with Amelia Swan and Seth Judd. Like them, you were near the drinks counter. Did you notice any suspicious behaviour?'

'I suppose if anyone's behaviour looked suspicious, it was mine. At the least I looked foolish. Why was I near those people whom I detest? In addition, I lacked an escort or companion. Evil demons, or a mixture of fascination and hatred, seemed to disarm my reason and drew me to that counter in a kind of stupor. I feared that Mr Tyson would surely notice and cast me out of the Assembly Rooms.

This afternoon's long walk in the cold has cleared my head and I see all of Thursday's horror in a better light.'

'Tell me about their drinks, especially Parker's.'

'I don't recall – I wasn't paying attention to them. Amelia and the others had noticed me and kept throwing sidelong glances in my direction. I could read my name on their lips. I tried to figure out what they were saying.'

'How did Parker look?'

'He has acted strangely since coming to Bath. He was all joy and gladness to the world outside. But when he thought no one was watching, a desperate, wild look came into his eyes. And that's how he was Thursday night.'

Burton leaned forward. 'What do you mean?'

'I felt that he couldn't continue to carry on like that. He was bound to break.'

'That's probably true, Madame. We're aware that he might have taken his own life. But we have no proof, merely specu-lation. We'll stop now.' Burton turned to Anne. 'Finish writing the deposition and I'll ask Mrs Parker to sign it.' He turned to Beverly and thanked her. 'I may have a few more questions another day.'

To escape the November chill Anne and Burton entered the pastry shop below Beverly's apartment on Milsom Street, sat at a small table in a private corner, and ordered more tea. Anne could see that Burton wanted to talk.

After the tea was served, he said, 'You know Mrs Parker better than anyone, Madame. What do you make of her comments?'

Anne had to carefully consider her reply. 'She didn't poison Parker's drink and doesn't know for certain who did. But she suspects that Parker poisoned himself.'

'Yes, she gave me the same impression. Her suspicion has merit. A coroner's jury might agree that Parker committed suicide, being of unsound mind. But I can't accept that verdict.'

'Why not?' Anne stirred sugar into her tea.

'The question in my mind is why would he do it in the Tea Room? True, his finances were in ruins. He was unable to tap into Janice's fortune, his only recourse. He also might have been involved in the attempts to kill her, but unwillingly or in spite of himself, at great cost to his conscience. This latest conflict with Janice could have tipped the uneasy balance in his mind.' Burton paused for Anne to follow his thought. 'But why would he kill himself so publicly? Why not do it in the privacy of his bedroom?'

'A good question,' Anne agreed. 'Perhaps he wanted his death to look like murder, committed by his beautiful, adulterous wife. If judged guilty, she could draw no advantage from his death and never marry his rival, Grimshaw. Parker would thus have the added satisfaction of believing that she would be hanged in a public spectacle at London's Newgate prison.'

'Madame Cartier, you continue to amaze me. That was a bizarre scenario but plausible. It's quite possible that her open infidelity stung him much more than we realized.'

Anne felt her cheeks flush. 'Mr Burton, I'll take your remark as a compliment.'

He gave her a friendly smile and reached for his cane. 'That's enough for today concerning the death of Thomas Parker. We have examined several suspects, but discovered none that is clearly guilty. I'm intrigued by your idea that Parker's death might fit into Captain Judd's grand design to eliminate the obstacles to his becoming the lord of Morland Court. Come to my office this evening. We'll talk with Judge Williams.'

THE MISSING SEAMAN

Bath, Saturday, 14 November

Early in the evening, Anne met Judge Williams and Burton in his office. Upon seeing Anne, the judge pursed his lips in disapproval – probably unconsciously. Anne gave him a polite smile in return. Having noticed this exchange, Burton winked to Anne, greeted her warmly, and directed her to his right hand at the table. He and Anne summarized the day's interrogations for the judge.

Burton concluded the report with a caution. 'I limited my questions to Seth Judd to his possible role in poisoning Parker.

He's probably not directly involved, at least in this crime. I deliberately refrained from probing into the shipwreck of 1782 and the deaths that occurred there, as well as his role in West Country smuggling. Now we need to discuss how to deal with those issues.'

'The matter is urgent,' Anne added. 'Seth Judd is most likely the devil behind the attempts on Janice Parker's life. Only when he is hanged or securely in prison will she be safe.'

'I agree,' said Williams with a hint of impatience. 'But we don't have sufficient evidence yet to convict him. It won't be easy. His exploits during the American War earned him a hero's reputation among the common sort of men. He's also wealthy and well-connected, and has damaging information that he could use to extort support from prominent persons on his behalf.'

'True,' Burton growled. 'Many of the excise officers are in his pay. If we can trust Nate Taylor's financial records, Captain Judd also supplies half the merchants in this part of the country with smuggled goods.'

'Taylor's testimony is not enough,' Williams continued. 'At a trial, it would come down to his word against Seth's. We need a second, independent witness.'

Burton nodded. 'That would be the missing seaman, Isaac Grimes.'

'Yes, if indeed he reached shore alive,' Williams said. 'Odds are that he's dead. But in case he might have survived, I've placed a spy, a maid, in his circle of family and friends. She has ingratiated herself with his mother. Today she told me about a man vaguely resembling Grimes at the Infirmary in Bristol.'

'Why is the Infirmary significant?' Anne asked.

The judge replied, 'A few weeks ago, Agnes Grimes, the seaman's mother, was taken there, gravely ill. The stranger visits her. But Mrs Grimes won't reveal his name or the nature of his visit. She did mention in passing that he came from Charleston in the United States.'

Burton showed interest. 'Hundreds of men could vaguely resemble Grimes. But the coincidence should be pursued.' Burton turned towards Anne. 'Madame, you have a kindly way with people in distress, and you aren't a police agent. People are more inclined to open up to you. And you've even experienced hospitals, though that was in Paris. Would you care to pay Mrs Grimes a visit?'

'I could be persuaded,' Anne replied, reminded of her search for a missing prostitute in the Salpêtrière, the French city's huge, notorious institution for sick and indigent women. 'Perhaps I could talk to the judge's spy, visit Mrs Grimes, and learn more about this stranger who visits her. If he's our man, I might find a way for us to approach him. Tell me about the Bristol Infirmary and how it operates.'

'As merely a visitor to this area,' Burton admitted, 'I know very little. But consult your friend, Mr David Woodhouse. Quakers are among its chief supporters. He has written about it, extols its merits.'

They rose to leave Burton's office. Anne turned to the judge. 'Would you tell me about your spy? Since she has Agnes Grimes' confidence, she could help me approach her.'

Williams frowned, as if reluctant to share a secret. He hesitated, and then said, 'Her name is Mildred Fox. Several years ago she and Agnes Grimes were servants together in the Parker household.'

'Thank you, sir. You've made my task a little easier. I've met Miss Fox. She was Janice Parker's nanny.'

Late in the evening, Anne was alone in her rooms, writing a letter to Paul in Paris and feeling anxious. The Bristol *Journal* had reported ongoing unrest in Paris. Following the fall of the Bastille in July, a clique of traitors had tried to assassinate him. Now, horrid images from those days surged into her mind: a baker's body hanging from a lamp post, wild-eyed men and women with long bloody knives dragging a headless corpse through a narrow street. Was Paul still in danger, and would he tell her, even if he were?

She shook herself and gazed fondly at his portrait in miniature on the table before her. Her gifted friend, Michou, had painted it, a faithful study of his thoughtful, handsome features. For a long moment she imagined him across from her, smiling, gazing into her eyes. He would listen to her and offer advice. Somehow he helped her to think more clearly.

Then her thoughts began to wander back to the violence she had witnessed. This was unhealthy, she told herself. Return to work. She finished writing the news from Bath, signed and sealed the letter, and kissed it.

She reflected on the progress of the investigation thus far. Tomorrow's short trip to Bristol might produce evidence of Isaac Grimes, the missing seaman and witness to Seth Judd's crimes on the *Mercury* seven years ago.

The door to the house slammed. Steps sounded on the stairs. Janice must be returning from a day with the Woodhouse family. Anne had almost forgotten her. It was late and dark outside, not the best time for her to be moving about the city.

The young woman entered the room, followed by Mr Woodhouse. 'My apprentice and I have brought her home safely,' Woodhouse remarked, looking relieved. 'I engaged a watchman to accompany us. He's waiting outside, alert to any suspicious persons. Sorry to be so late. We celebrated Jacob's return. Time flew. Janice is welcome tomorrow at our place if she wishes to come. She's very bright and eager to help. There are many useful skills she could learn in a busy printing shop, as well as in the house.'

Anne asked if she could offer him and his apprentice a hot drink. It was quite cold outside. He declined politely, thanked her, and left.

Janice took off her cape and her bonnet and shook her hair loose. There was color in her cheeks. She looked happy and very pretty. 'Jacob came home a few hours ago,' she signed rapidly. 'We talked for a little while. He's getting better.'

'What did you learn about the Woodhouse family?'

'They are peaceful and happy, and work well together. They laugh and tease each other. Mr Woodhouse is mostly in the shop with the presses. He also helps his wife gather the news and the announcements for their weekly newspaper. Together they decide the layout for the printing. She also keeps the accounts.'

'I don't really know her. She must be a talented, skilful woman. Do you like her?'

'Very much. She's kind and generous. And it's such a relief to be with an intelligent signing person. She smiles easily and tells amusing stories. We understand each other perfectly. I helped with cleaning and preparing the meals, and joined in the family prayers.'

'Tell me about their prayers.' A few years ago, Anne had lived with a devout Quaker family in their country home near London, hired to tutor their deaf son and daughter. The daily routine included minutes set aside for quiet meditation.

'They are still for a few moments before and after meals. During the day, Mrs Woodhouse takes short pauses, becomes very still, as if asking God for direction, or sharing a problem with Him. I'll go to their Meeting tomorrow.' She paused with a teasing smile. 'It's Sunday, you know.'

'Would you like to have more time with the Woodhouse family?'

'Yes, as long as I can be useful. But I want to live here and receive your guidance.' She paused, gave Anne a generous smile. 'This season in Bath has become for me an opportunity to go from Braidwood's school out into the world. At times, it's frightening and confusing. But I've grown so much already that I hunger for more.'

'I'm happy for you, Janice. Would you mind if I accompanied you tomorrow morning to the Meeting House? Afterwards, I'd like to speak to Mr Woodhouse. He might help me find a certain missing witness to the deaths of your parents.'

Janice's eyes widened with curiosity.

'I'll tell you when I know more. Let's go to bed.'

PURSUIT

Bath and Bristol, Sunday, 15 November

The following morning, Anne and Janice joined the Woodhouse family at the Quakers' service of worship in the plain square room of the Meeting House. About thirty persons had gathered on rows of wooden benches along the walls. A secretary sat with pen and ink and an open book at a table near the door.

The white walls were bare. There were no crosses or other religious symbols, no altar or communion table. Light poured in through high windows of clear glass. Two elderly men in plain black suits and wide-brimmed black hats occupied a raised platform next to the secretary. 'Those are our Elders, wise and prudent men,' David Woodhouse whispered to Anne. 'They give us counsel and advice, help us better understand the movements of the Spirit.'

Anne believed in God. How else could she account for the complex universe that she lived in? A Supreme Intelligence must have created it, then stepped aside to allow it to function according to its natural laws. At least that's what the philosophers of the day asserted. She doubted that anyone really understood how the world worked. That conviction grew stronger, especially as she encountered cruelties such as the slave trade and other absurd human evils. Some people thought that invisible powers – whether the Holy Spirit, or angels, devils, ghosts and the like – played a role in human affairs. But she believed that she alone was responsible for what she did – and so were others.

The atmosphere of the Meeting House set her to thinking about spirits. 'By their fruits ye shall know them,' she recalled from the Bible. Whatever spirit moved David Woodhouse must be good. The Quaker was honest and truthful, and he advocated liberty for black people at a risk to his own life. Anne was inclined to think that goodness was natural to him rather than from an outside force.

Participants in the service took their seats in silence. Anne and Janice sat with David and Judith Woodhouse and the young apprentice. Most of the male participants, including Woodhouse and his apprentice, were dressed in plain black suits and broad-brimmed hats like the elders. Judith Woodhouse and most women wore unadorned black gowns and bonnets. But several men and women, presumably visitors like Anne and Janice, had arrived in more colorful, fashionable dress.

'We call ourselves Friends,' David had told Anne before the service. 'You should feel welcome.' He had explained that there would be several visiting Friends and visitors from other Christian denominations, attracted to Bath by the spa. Friends came from many different walks of life, David had said. The Bath Meeting included a prosperous banker; others were artisans and housewives, grooms and scullery maids.

'Men and women, rich and poor, all are equal in the Society of Friends. We have no pope, or bishops, or paid priests,' he had insisted. 'At our Meetings, we observe a religious silence and wait for God to speak to our hearts and minds. Sometimes a Friend feels called to stand up and share a message with the rest of us. That might happen three or four times in the hour.'

Gradually, as the latecomers settled down and the children were sent out to play, a profound silence came over the Meeting. Finally, an elderly man rose – a nodding acquaintance Anne and Janice met while promenading on Queen Square.

Now he took off his broad-brimmed hat and began to speak out against slave trading. Anne drew closer to Janice and signed the gist of his speech. The evils of that commerce were countless, he said, and he had described them at an earlier Meeting. This time he would dwell on the damage they did to those most directly involved in the trade: wealthy investors, ships' captains and crews, plantation owners in the colonies. Their hearts became hard as rock, their minds blinded, their souls twisted. They shut God out of their lives – however loudly they might pretend otherwise, giving free play to the greed, lust, and other destructive forces of an apostate world.

He spoke slowly and distinctly in solemn, elevated tones. Utter conviction brought youthful colour to his grey, wrinkled face and made his voice strong and vibrant. Janice seemed riveted to his lips and appeared to comprehend every word he said. She probably thought he was describing the degradation of her father, Oliver, and his two brothers, Thomas and Seth. They exemplified the wages of sin. Exposed as criminals, the first two died violently; the third, a murderous monster, was likely to hang.

Anne wondered if the speaker had recognized Janice and had directed his comments to her. Even if they were unintentional, they could serve as a warning. Her tainted family fortune had already inspired two attempts to murder her. What must Janice think of the wealth she had inherited? Thus far in her brief life, the young woman might never have considered that the traffic in slaves had enriched her family and had compromised its honor. Her new association with the Woodhouse family would surely force her to confront the issue. That could help her to grow up and take responsibility for her life, as well as her fortune.

In conversation with the family at the noon meal, Anne learned that the Society of Friends had condemned the slave trade years ago. In 1783 it banned its members from taking part, the first Christian denomination to do so.

She turned to David Woodhouse and asked about the Bristol Infirmary. He had not only written a piece on the Infirmary but had also remained involved in its care of the sick and the infirm. The Infirmary's treasurer, a fellow Quaker, was his friend.

Anne told him, 'I want to question Mrs Agnes Grimes, one of the patients there. Would the staff limit my access to her?'

'No, their rules are reasonable,' he replied. 'They open the Infirmary for visitors between nine and ten in the morning and between three and seven in the afternoon.' He added, 'Of course, as a stranger, you might find both staff and patients reserved or diffident. You need someone to smooth the way for you. I'll recommend you in a message to the matron in charge of the ward.'

Later that afternoon, accompanied by her cousin, Peter, Anne traveled to Bristol. While Peter visited the city's constables and watchmen to prepare for the apprehension of Grimes, should he be found, Anne returned to the room of Mildred Fox. It was shortly before three o'clock. She was preparing to go to the Infirmary with undergarments she had laundered for Mrs Grimes. Anne had brought along sweetmeats, hoping that the patient would be well enough to enjoy them.

Anne showed Miss Fox a message from Judge Williams, ordering her to cooperate with Anne and explaining the need to question Mrs Grimes. Miss Fox became uneasy, stammered that Grimes was too weak to speak and quickly tired. Her mind was often confused.

Anne wondered about Fox's reluctance but concluded that she apparently felt exposed and compromised. Anne reassured her: the judge carefully concealed their connection – he valued her service. However, the case was so important that he had to take certain risks. Anne and Mildred must identify Mrs Grimes' visitor.

'If he's her son,' Anne said, 'we have to learn how to approach him.'

Mildred nodded agreement. 'According to the matron, he goes by the name of Mr Henry Groves. He visits Agnes alone. If I'm there when he comes, she tells me to leave.'

'Have you noticed anything distinctive about his appearance?'

'His suit is plain but cut from fine woolen cloth. He has a

neatly trimmed black beard – and wears a black patch over
one eye.'

'What's the colour of the other one?' The patch was
intriguing.

'It's blue, I believe.'

Anne remarked, 'If this man is Grimes, he has prospered
in America and can afford to keep his mother in a private
room.'

'Oh,' Miss Fox added, 'even before Agnes took sick, she lived
comfortably. She couldn't do that on a pension from the Parkers.'
A hint of bitterness had crept into Mildred's voice. 'For several
years, someone has been helping her. She won't say who.'

At the Infirmary, Anne handed Woodhouse's message to the
matron. She read it, nodded, and showed the two visitors to
Mrs Grimes' room. On the way, the matron commented on
the bearded man who visited Mrs Grimes. His visit was
unusual. A stranger, he took a personal interest in her.

'Had he explained why he came?' Anne asked.

The matron smiled sardonically. 'He told me that he was
a relative and had heard that she was dying. He feared that
she wouldn't receive a Christian burial. The medical doctors
at the Infirmary would take her cadaver and dissect it in their
anatomy lessons.'

Anne was appalled. 'Would the doctors do such a thing
without her expressed approval?'

'Yes, indeed, they need cadavers badly. The supply of
condemned felons is scarce. But Mrs Grimes will be properly
buried. The stranger has seen to it.'

The Grimes room was bare and small but had a window.
Anne noticed that the woman enjoyed more privacy than any
other patient in the building. Most of them lay in a large ward.
Only curtains separated them from one another.

Miss Fox noticed Anne's reaction and whispered, 'I've asked
who is paying for her care, but the matron told me to mind
my own business.'

Agnes Grimes lay still, eyes closed. Beneath the bedclothes,
her body seemed little more than skin and bones. Anne thought
she might have died, until she noticed a slight heaving of her
chest.

'You have visitors, Mrs Grimes,' the matron announced.

The patient's eyes opened, her head turned. The rest of her body didn't move. It was as if only her head was still living.

'Ah, Mildred,' she said in a faint, cracked voice. 'Who is with you?'

'Anne Cartier, teacher of deaf children, friend and tutor of Miss Janice Parker.'

Anne stepped forward. 'I bring her greetings to you. She's indisposed today but she sends along these treats. Hopefully you will soon feel well enough to enjoy them.'

The patient's eyes widened with growing interest. 'Thank Janice for me. I recall her: a lively, bright child.' She glanced at Mildred. 'You looked after her until her terrible sickness.' She shook her head. 'Unlucky child! She lost her parents, then her hearing.'

'And you lost *your* son,' Anne gently added. 'Those were dreadful times. How you must have grieved for Isaac. But it's good that Mr Groves looks after you. I see that he has brought you a yellow rose. What a thoughtful gift in gloomy mid-November.'

Agnes gazed at the flower in a vase at her bedside. 'He brought it this morning – it's from the bouquet that he'll give to his bride tomorrow. I'd love to go to the wedding but lack the strength. The flower is the next best thing.'

'Where's the wedding to take place, Agnes?' asked Miss Fox, slipping into her role as spy.

Mrs Grimes hesitated for a second, eyes half-closed, then said, 'At a church in the city. Don't remember which one.' She seemed compelled to add, 'He's my nephew. Lives in America. You wouldn't know him.'

She appeared to grow tired and closed her eyes again.

Anne signaled Miss Fox. They quietly left.

Anne and Miss Fox walked together to the Infirmary's exit, where they parted. Anne would speak to the matron again. Fox said she would go back to her room and set off in that direction. Anne stepped into a shadowed corner, replaced her white bonnet with a brown headscarf, turned her cape inside out, and smeared grit on her hands and face. This was the best disguise she could adopt on short notice. She hobbled bent and stiff-legged after Fox. She was reassured that many poor old women on the street looked like herself.

From two encounters, Anne had come to distrust Miss Fox. As Anne suspected, she didn't go home but went instead to a seaman's tavern on a narrow side street near the harbour and the White Gull. Anne followed her into a crowded, smoky barroom. Men and women were lined up at the bar buying ale. Anne joined them, while she searched the room for Mildred. Finally she saw her at a table with a seaman, sharing a jug of ale. They were bent towards each other like two thieves in conversation.

Anne pulled the scarf as far over her face as she dared and bought a mug of ale. Then, at the risk of being detected, she sat at the next table with a clear view of Mildred. Fortunately, the woman was nearsighted and preoccupied. Peering over the edge of her mug, Anne could hear a few words and read others from the woman's lips.

'He'll be married tomorrow at a church somewhere in town. The old lady wouldn't tell me which one. I think they'll leave the country soon.'

Anne figured out that Fox's companion would report everything she said to a person they called 'the captain', Seth Judd, no doubt. When she finished, the sailor pushed a coin across the table to her. She stuck it into her pocket and hurried out of the room.

Still in disguise, Anne hastened to the White Gull. Peter was alone at a table. He blinked as she approached, bent and shuffling. Then he recognized her and smiled.

'What have you been up to?'

'I've talked to Mrs Grimes at the Infirmary. I'm convinced that her mysterious visitor is her son in rather thin disguise. I followed Mildred Fox and learned that she has betrayed Grimes to Seth Judd.'

Peter appeared alarmed. 'Is Grimes in immediate danger?'

'I doubt it. Judd doesn't know where Grimes is hiding any more than we do. He doesn't even know which one of a half-dozen churches in Bristol Grimes has chosen for his wedding. In any case, Judd might decide to do nothing, since Grimes will soon be out of the country and no threat to him. Or, since he's aware of our active interest in Grimes, he might assassinate him before we can persuade him to testify.'

'A crisis is upon us,' Peter said. 'While you were at the

Infirmary, I learned that the city's chief constable is aware of our investigation. I sensed that he could be trusted and brought him up to date. I've arranged to meet the mayor this afternoon as soon as you returned from the Infirmary.' Peter studied Anne's disguise with a critical eye. 'Can you come with me?'

'Yes, as soon as I clean the grime off my face. We'll need the mayor's help. Tomorrow we must try to attend Grimes' wedding. Judd's men might be there.'

To Anne's surprise Peter took her to the mayor's home rather than to his office. As they drove through a gate to the entrance, Peter explained that the meeting had been hurriedly called, since the suspect was about to leave the city within a day or two.

'On a Sunday afternoon, public offices should be closed. Judd's spies may be watching the mayor's office for signs of extraordinary activity. So our meeting with the mayor will be disguised as a social visit.'

Anne understood the reasons for caution. The investigation closely touched the Sea Fox – a popular naval hero, as well as a wealthy and powerful member of the community. Even the city's highest officers had to pay careful attention to what they were doing.

A servant led them to the mayor's study, where Mayor James Hill had already seated Bristol's chief constable and an eager young excise officer. Introductions were made. The mayor rang a bell. Servants arrived with port wine and sweet biscuits, poured, and then left the room.

The room's atmosphere turned serious. 'Let me explain,' said the mayor for the benefit of Peter and Anne. 'Our new excise officer, Lieutenant Howe, has recently come to us from the Excise Office in London. The government has put him in charge of anti-smuggling operations in the Bristol area. His predecessor lacked conviction and energy. Smugglers like Captain Judd were free to do as they pleased. Lieutenant Howe will enforce the law without fear or favour.'

Peter then showed his papers to his companions and was acknowledged as the agent of Judge Williams and Dick Burton. They would come later if necessary to further the investigation. Peter described Anne's familiarity with the Parker family and her role in locating the missing seaman, Isaac Grimes.

When the three Bristol men exchanged enigmatic glances, Anne began to feel anxious. They could object that this attempt to confront the alleged Mr Groves was hasty and complicated. They would need more time to plan and to execute their measures. In the meantime, Mr Groves might slip through their fingers and disappear forever.

The mayor addressed Peter in a non-committal tone. 'Judge Williams has informed us that Nate Taylor has accused Seth Judd of the wreck of the *Mercury* seven years ago. Why is this missing seaman so important?'

Peter summarized the case. 'With Grimes we would have the two eyewitnesses we need to prove that Captain Seth Judd is guilty of piracy and murder in the wreck of the sloop *Mercury*.'

'I understand,' the mayor said. 'Crimes on the high seas are often difficult to prosecute, since the witnesses – usually seamen – are easily bribed or intimidated or leave the country. For this case to prevail at the Admiralty, we would have to be severe with our two witnesses. Nate Taylor is already in custody. We would also have to hold Grimes.' He turned to the chief constable. 'How should we go about it?'

The constable reflected. 'If we find him at tomorrow's wedding, I could bring him to your office for a hearing. Then you could hold him in a secure room at the Mint.'

'The Mint?' Peter and Anne asked in unison.

'The Mint is the city's workhouse,' the constable explained. 'It has nothing to do with coinage.'

Anne waved a hand. 'We must take his bride into custody as well. Otherwise, Captain Judd's men will hold her hostage and threaten to harm her if her husband were to testify against Judd.'

'But we can't hold her for long without accusing her of a crime,' the mayor observed, then added, 'Perhaps you, Madame Cartier, could persuade her to retreat to a safe place until the judicial process is over and Seth Judd can no longer threaten anyone.'

'And how long might that be?' Peter asked.

'At the Admiralty in London, this case could take three or four months.'

'That's a challenge,' said Anne, 'but we have no choice.'

'Then this is how we shall proceed,' said the mayor. 'If we

can discover the church, we'll apprehend Grimes after his wedding tomorrow and bring him to my office. Then we'll call Judge Williams and Mr Burton from Bath to take part in a hearing. If Grimes can be persuaded to testify, Seth Judd will be arrested and moved to London for trial.'

Up to this point, Lieutenant Howe had been attentive but silent, still a stranger to the area. Now the mayor gestured towards him and said to the others, 'Previously, we could not trust excise officers to move against Captain Judd.' The mayor asked Howe, 'Can we count on you?'

Howe sat upright and looked the mayor in the eye. 'Absolutely, I'll put a cutter and a dozen armed, honest men at your disposal.'

Anne and Peter exchanged glances. The investigation had just moved a long step forward.

That evening, having returned to Bath, Anne and Peter met Burton and Judge Williams in Burton's office. Peter informed them of the meeting with the mayor. 'Assured of the excise officer's cooperation, the Bristol authorities are preparing to move against Captain Judd.'

'But,' Anne pointed out, 'before seizing him, we must gain the testimony of our second witness Isaac Grimes.' Anne reported on what she had learned at the Infirmary. 'Mr Groves is probably Grimes in disguise and wouldn't want to be brought into our investigation of Judd.'

Peter added, 'It would be too risky. Judd might have him killed. The Bristol authorities think that the two of you should hold a hearing at their mayor's office late tomorrow afternoon. We hope to have Grimes in custody by that time.'

Williams and Burton nodded their approval.

Anne asked Burton. 'Could we offer him a reward?'

'I can arrange something,' Burton replied. 'Would he trust us?'

'We could earn his trust,' Anne replied, 'if we guarantee that he wouldn't be charged with complicity in the Parkers' murder. Furthermore, he and his bride must be protected.'

Burton turned to the judge. 'Could we assure Grimes that he's wanted only as a witness, not as an accomplice in Judd's crimes?'

Williams had thus far added little to the conversation. Now

he stroked his chin for a long moment, then replied, 'Taylor's story of the shipwreck satisfies me that Grimes played no part in the murders and had a knife at his throat when he took the ten pieces of blood money. If he testifies against Judd, he'll receive a reward.'

Anne began to feel encouraged. 'Still, if we leave him exposed to Judd's ruffians, I fear he might disappear again, this time for good.'

'His protection could be difficult,' the judge continued. 'The only safe place that I know of is the city jail. He might not agree to stay there until the danger is past.'

'Besides, we must think of his bride,' Anne said as she rose from the table. 'Now I need some sleep before tomorrow's task.' She turned to Judge Williams, 'Before I go, I must warn you that Mildred Fox is spying for Seth Judd as well as for you.'

Williams' lips parted in disbelief and embarrassment. 'Treacherous woman!' he sputtered and shook his head. He neglected to thank Anne. She wasn't surprised.

Peter and Judge Williams left the office, having agreed to adjourn to the Assembly Tea Room for a game of cards and a bottle of port. Anne lingered. She asked Burton, 'Have you questioned Janice's guard about her access to the poison that killed Thomas Parker?'

Burton evaded Anne's gaze, rubbed the head of his cane. 'Under questioning, the guard insisted that no laudanum could have gotten past her watchful eye.'

'She confirmed Janice's story,' exclaimed Anne.

'I'm not surprised. The guard would want to appear vigilant,' retorted Burton. 'A magistrate might concede that we don't know *how* Janice could get her hands on the poison. Nonetheless, she is still a suspect, though not the strongest one.'

'Who is the strongest?'

'Beverly Parker.'

A STRANGER'S WEDDING

Bristol, Monday, 16 November

The early morning air was damp and cold. Anne wrapped herself in a woolen cape and climbed into her cousin Peter's rented coach. In a thick mist they set out for Bristol, an hour's drive away. They were to search for Isaac Grimes. The mayor of Bath had deputized Peter for this mission. His charge didn't give him any jurisdiction in Bristol, but he could expect support from local authorities, if he were to need it.

Anne and Peter wanted to blend into the city's harbour area, so they disguised themselves in plain, worn clothing from Madame Gagnon's shop on Milsom Street. They would pose as sister and brother, would-be immigrants to America, she a domestic maid, and he a clerk.

Peter seemed anxious. Anne was puzzled why. He was a brave, resourceful fellow. Perhaps he was concerned for her.

'You needn't worry about me, Peter,' she assured him. 'I can take care of myself. Besides, I don't expect to encounter any serious danger today.'

'Frankly, that's not the problem, Anne. I'm still not comfortable being anyone other than myself. Acting like someone else is like trying to make oneself understood in a foreign language. I feel uncomfortable, awkward, and inept. My speech and my manners betray me.'

Anne tried to explain. 'No one can play a role that they don't understand. They may recite the lines and make the gestures, but they won't fool anyone. Great actresses like Sarah Siddons have the rare ability to grasp the inner qualities of the characters they play and then portray them. Her Lady Macbeth is an utterly plausible murderess.'

'You're right, Anne. I've watched Mrs Siddons on the stage. And as a magistrate, I've also encountered murderers who could pretend convincingly that they were honest men. So what shall we do?'

'We'll play ourselves, Peter, speak in our own voices, use

the manners and gestures that we're accustomed to. But let's imagine just for today that fortune has turned against us here in England, and we must seek a better life abroad.'

'Do you have a story for us?'

'Yes, indeed.' She went on to concoct a tale about their father dying bankrupt, leaving them poor, their family reputation tainted, all avenues of improvement closed.

'As a magistrate, Anne, I've observed people in that situation, desperately trying to avoid a debtor's prison. I can put myself in their shoes.' He gazed inquiringly at her. 'And you have acted for a time on the stage. Why did you move to the music hall, and later to the school for the deaf?'

'As an actress, I wanted to be as good as Mrs Siddons. Anything less seemed false, like going through the motions, merely posturing. Besides, actresses are poorly paid. Unless I could act as well as Mrs Siddons, I would starve. I found that my talent lay in singing and dancing – entertaining the audience rather than uplifting them. When I'd had enough of that, I started to teach deaf children, and lately – as you know – I've also learned how to outwit criminals.'

'Tell me about your life in Paris.'

For the rest of the ride she recounted episodes from the last two years of sharing in the work of her husband, Colonel Paul de Saint-Martin, provost of the Royal Highway Patrol. She had described the wave of assassinations that followed the storming of the Bastille, when he raised a hand. 'Later I must hear more. But now we have arrived in Bristol.'

They left the coach and the horses in a stable and walked a short distance to the inn, the White Gull, where Grimes used to live. A large stone building, it overlooked the quay. On the ground floor was a busy tavern.

They sat at a table and surveyed the room. Nearby, a group of men who appeared to be ship's officers and shipping clerks were enjoying foaming tankards of ale and loud conversation. The group soon broke up, leaving one of their number behind to finish his drink.

Peter and Anne approached him with studied deference. Peter inquired about cheap passage to America. 'We've heard,' he said, 'that a ship has recently arrived from Charleston. Would it take on passengers and return to the same port? We would be interested.'

'You're in luck,' the man readily replied. 'I'm the purser on that ship, the *Molly Anne*. We've been in dry dock for a couple of weeks. The ship should be ready in two days to set sail for Charleston with a cargo of fine cloth, household furniture and table service, and other luxury goods for the rich planters. Passengers are welcome.'

'Could you tell us,' Anne asked, 'who would be familiar with conditions there and would have recent news?'

'If you are contemplating a new life in America and want to know the challenges you might face, I can't help you – I wasn't on shore long enough to learn much about the place. But you could speak to one of our passengers, Mr Groves. He lived in South Carolina for several years. But I haven't seen him in two or three days. He seemed friendly with the barmaid and her daughter. You might ask them.'

The purser finished his ale, wished Anne and Peter good luck, and left the tavern. They waited for a few minutes until a barmaid approached their table. A sturdy woman in her mid-forties, her face was etched with lines earned from a harsh life. She examined these strangers with a practised eye and asked in the routine manner of her profession what they wanted to drink.

'Ale,' Peter replied.

When the barmaid was beyond earshot, Anne whispered to Peter, 'Refer to Grimes by his own name. Let's see her reaction.'

When the barmaid returned with the drinks, Peter innocently asked where Mr Grimes could be found and briefly explained their desire for information about Charleston.

Instantly, the woman's eyes narrowed, her lips tightened. Anne could virtually read the suspicions growing in her mind. Two strangers inquiring about Grimes somehow meant trouble, even danger.

'He's not here, haven't seen him in years, and I don't know when he's coming back.'

'Oh!' Anne feigned surprise. 'A few days ago, we met a man on the quay who saw Grimes, said he was here. If you see him, say that we'd like to meet him. We'll come back later.'

The barmaid mumbled, 'As you wish,' and returned to the bar.

Once outside, Anne whispered, 'She'll send someone after him. We'll follow.'

Peter pointed to a large wagon on the quay. 'We can hide behind it and observe the tavern door.'

Anne shook her head. 'The tavern has a back door. I'll watch it. You had better find a constable. We'll meet here in an hour at the latest.'

Anne barely reached the back door in time to see a young boy come out, furtively glance left and right, then dash up narrow, crooked passages towards Corn Street. Anne followed him past the Corn Exchange to the portal of All Saints Church. The boy stopped, looked about, then slipped into the church. Anne waited a minute, then entered as well.

The light was dim. As her eyes slowly adjusted, she saw a small group gathered in a side chapel. An elderly, black-robed minister was raising his arm in a final blessing, and the group began to disperse. It was the conclusion of a private wedding.

The boy had stopped off to one side, impatiently waiting. Now he approached a young man, the bridegroom, to judge from his ill-fitting dress suit, probably rented for the occasion. He had a black beard and a black eyepatch.

From hiding, Anne observed the scene through her opera glass. The boy's message caused the bridegroom to frown and pause for thought. Finally, he patted the boy on the head, bent over and whispered a message into his ear, and sent him off.

The bride and the other members of the group had stood waiting, confusion etched on their faces. The bridegroom waved away the incident and said for all to hear, 'Now let us celebrate at the Rummer.'

The inn was located in the market only a few steps away. Anne followed the group into the inn and watched as they settled around a large table in a secluded corner. A thin screen partially separated them from the rest of the customers.

Anne hastened back to Peter outside the White Gull.

'Our man Groves has just married a local woman named Joan, daughter of the White Gull's barmaid. I hope that Seth Judd doesn't hear of it. If Groves is truly Grimes, he has risked a great deal. How shall we approach him?'

'We'll join the party, Anne. We must at least get close enough to eavesdrop on what they say.'

*   *   *

The bells of All Saints tolled the noon hour as Anne and Peter entered the Rummer. The wedding celebration had begun. Drinks were served and food would soon arrive. Conversation was lively.

Anne and Peter chose a table near the party. Through an opening in the screen Anne could see Groves and his bride at the head of the table, as well as most of the half-dozen guests. Unfortunately, Anne's table was too exposed to public view for her to use her opera glass. Without the glass she read their lips poorly. Still she could also learn something from gestures and facial expressions.

Peter ordered lunch and cider. Gradually, the party heated up and voices grew loud. For the most part the conversation seemed to consist of the conventional banter on such occasions. From a waiter Anne learned that the bride, Joan, was twenty-one years old and a chambermaid at the White Gull. She had a pretty face, a generous smile, and a sturdy body.

As the bride returned from a visit to the water closet, her face flushed from drink, she received congratulations from a woman at the table next to Anne and Peter.

'Are you going to leave Bristol?' the woman asked her.

'Oh yes,' she exclaimed, throwing caution to the wind. 'I'm looking forward to America.'

'And what will you do there?'

'Serve grog in Isaac's tavern.' Unmindful that she had revealed her husband's identity, she blew him a kiss. It seemed to Anne that she must have known him for a number of years. Despite Seth Judd's warning, Groves surely visited Bristol more than once since the shipwreck of '82. Since he had escaped Judge Williams' notice, he had used the assumed name and given it in the public banns of his marriage.

The cider for Anne and Peter arrived with a large platter of broiled fish, potatoes, and green vegetables. Peter poured and they set to eating. Anne quickly lost interest in the food. Her mind was focused on the wedding celebration.

Nothing noteworthy appeared to be happening. The celebration's tone in fact had become rather muted. Groves tried to live up to what was expected of a bridegroom, but his smiles grew thin, his laughter forced. He looked preoccupied and anxious.

Anne lifted her glass of cider as if to drink and surveyed

the room again over the rim. She stopped suddenly at three sailors gathered around a table.

'I know that man with the cropped ear,' she whispered to Peter, pointing discreetly. 'He's one of the three who attacked Janice and Jacob that night in Crescent Fields. I wonder if he'll recognize me.'

The three sailors, too, were closely watching the wedding party. From time to time they leaned forward and exchanged whispers with each other, throwing side glances towards Groves.

'I've posted my constable and a watchman outside the door,' Peter said softly. 'I'll ask the watchman to follow the sailor. At an opportune time and place, the constable will arrest him and arrange to transport him to Bath to face charges.'

At that moment the sailor glanced towards Anne. For an instant they locked eyes. Then he swung around and spoke a few hurried words to his companions. They rose together from the table and strode from the room.

Peter followed them, was gone for a few minutes, and then returned. 'The sailors have disappeared. My constable and the watchman had wandered off into the market and didn't see them leave the inn. The watchman claimed that there are dozens of cropped-eared men in Bristol.'

'Groves is in trouble,' said Anne. 'The sailors might know by now that he's hiding in the city, probably at the White Gull.'

Peter nodded. 'They also know who we are and what we're doing here. We must be careful. Without a doubt they belong to Seth Judd's gang of smugglers.'

'I think we should warn Groves, assure him of our protection, and try to persuade him to tell us his story.'

'How can we approach him in such a public place and in the midst of his wedding celebration? He's drinking heavily and hardly sober enough to understand us. He could become belligerent and cause a commotion.'

'We must talk to the manager. I have a plan.'

As the celebration wound down and guests rose to leave, the manager approached the newly married couple. When they had bid goodbye to their guests, he asked them to come to his office to receive a modest gift.

With the aid of his Bristol constable, Peter had made an arrangement with the manager. In the office Peter and the constable were to confront the couple and warn them that their lives were threatened. They would be taken by closed carriage to the mayor's office in the Council House on Corn Street.

The ruse worked. Groves and his bride went gladly to the manager's office. They weren't disturbed to find others in the room and were pleased to receive a small purse from the manager. Then Peter approached Groves, showed his official papers, and pointed to the mayor of Bristol's seal. 'Mr Isaac Grimes, we want you and your bride to come with us to the Council House. This is for your own protection and for safe keeping. We have observed three sailors spying on your wedding party. They are working for Captain Seth Judd and would do you or your wife harm.'

The man glared at Peter. 'My name is Groves and I can take care of myself and my wife. What kind of trick is this? I've done nothing wrong. You can't arrest me.'

'For a start, you gave a false name to the church for the banns of marriage. Remove the patch over your eye. We'll see who you are.'

'I refuse!' shouted the man. 'How dare you!'

Peter signalled the constable, who took a step forward.

The bride stepped in front of the officer, then turned to her husband, began to weep, and removed his patch. The eye was normal except that its colour was green. The contrast to the blue eye was striking.

'So you are clearly Mr Isaac Grimes after all,' Peter said. 'You will have to appear before an ecclesiastical court for giving a false name in the banns of marriage. More important, the Admiralty in London wants you, Isaac Grimes, as a witness to piracy and murder on the sloop *Mercury* on the twenty-first of June 1782, off the coast of Wales. We'll hold you in custody until you testify at the trial of Seth Judd.'

Joan Grimes took her husband by the hand. 'Come, Isaac, we'll settle this misunderstanding in the mayor's office.'

A RELUCTANT WITNESS

Bristol, Monday, 16 November

At the Council House Anne looked after the newly-wed, Joan Grimes. The surprising turn of events had left her pale and teary-eyed, wavering between grief and anger. Anne ushered her into an anteroom of the mayor's office and ordered herbal tea. The chairs were comfortable; the room was quiet and heated by a glowing fireplace. A maid served the tea. Anne started a calming, reassuring conversation.

'May I call you Joan?' Anne finally asked. 'I'd be pleased if you called me Anne.'

Anne's familiar tone seemed to surprise yet please the woman. She ventured a smile.

'I know your husband's story,' Anne said. 'He didn't cause the shipwreck in 1782, nor did he kill anyone.'

Joan nodded. 'He's a good man, entangled in circumstances beyond his control. I had so hoped that we could leave this country tomorrow. We came so close.'

'How much did you know about your husband's predicament?'

'He told my mother and me everything – I think. He survived the shipwreck, hid with us at the White Gull for a few days, and then sailed to Charleston on a naval ship. The war with the French was still raging at sea. We thought we'd never see him again. But after the war he came back in disguise and with a new name, Groves. We renewed our friendship. He couldn't stay in England. He knew too much; Judd would kill him. He said he had good prospects in America and would take me there one day. I had no future in Bristol, so I've waited.'

Her voice failed, overcome by emotion. 'Our wedding in the church was simple but so beautiful, the high point of my life. Then this . . . I feel like I've fallen off a cliff. What will happen to us? We're trapped in a black box with no air to breathe.'

Anne leaned forward and held Joan's hand. 'I see rays of hope in your situation – if your husband chooses to cooperate in a prosecution of Seth Judd at the Admiralty in London. What do you think?'

'I don't understand how the court operates. What shall we do in the weeks or months while the court prepares for the trial? On the morning before our wedding, a sailor with a cropped ear confronted my mother at the White Gull and warned that the police were after Judd. If Isaac were to help them, bad things would happen to me. Suppose Isaac co-operates with the court, will it protect him and me from Judd and his men?'

'You will live in a secure home in London under the court's supervision.'

Joan looked sceptical. 'Why should the court be so kind to us?'

'The court puts a very high value on Isaac's testimony. Judd is such a dangerous and clever criminal that he must be removed from society. To secure Isaac's testimony the court will go to unusual lengths to protect him.'

Joan frowned. 'This sounds too good to be true. Suppose Isaac refuses to cooperate. You can't force him – I know that much about English law. What will you do?'

'It's not up to me. But this much I do know. The law can use harsh methods of persuasion on reluctant witnesses to crime. The Church Court might hold him for months and fine him for using a false name in your marriage. The Admiralty could charge him as Judd's accomplice in the murder of the Parkers, and hold him for trial in London's Newgate prison, a dreadful place. I can't predict how the court would rule. After all, Isaac *did* leave the *Mercury* with ten pieces of the murdered man's gold. He may still have them. I'm not a betting person, but I think it's in Isaac's interests to do all that he can to put Judd in prison for the rest of his life.'

Joan muttered, 'Or hang him. That's what he deserves.'

Encouraged by this remark, Anne went on, 'Judge Williams and the Bow Street officer Dick Burton *really* want to convict Judd. Your husband's testimony is crucial. He could bargain with them for good security, for release from any and all criminal charges, and for possibly even a reward.'

Joan seemed intrigued. 'So what am I supposed to do?'

'Persuade him to cooperate with Williams and Burton.'

She took a deep breath and sighed. 'Then I'll try.'

Anne heard Judge Williams' voice in the hallway outside the mayor's office. 'You should soon have the opportunity. By the way, what did Isaac do with the pieces of gold?'

'He bought a busy grog shop in Charleston – and he paid for our wedding.'

Anne was taken aback. In an artless moment, she had expected to hear that Isaac had given the 'blood money' to charity. What would the Admiralty think?

Peter and the constable had taken Grimes to a different ante-room to await questioning in the mayor's office. Judge Williams and Dick Burton had been told to arrive in the late afternoon. While waiting for them, Peter's first task was to make Grimes sober. Strong coffee was tried and worked well enough for an informal, preliminary interrogation to begin.

But it proved impossible to disarm Grimes' truculence. He insisted that he'd done nothing wrong. Groves was now his name, despite what the Church of England might say. He had no part in the shipwreck and murders of 1782, and he didn't witness any crime. No one could force him to testify against Judd. He demanded to see a lawyer who would persuade a magistrate to order his release. He and his bride intended to leave Bristol tomorrow on the ship to Charleston.

Since it was pointless to argue with the man, Peter decided to wait for Judge Williams and the Bow Street detective who would soon arrive. He turned the conversation to conditions in Charleston and Grimes' home there and other less contentious issues.

'Who'll care for your mother when you're back in America?'

Grimes answered the question spontaneously as her son. 'I've hired an honest lawyer to look after her affairs and to see that she'll be decently buried.' He scowled. 'The Infirmary surgeons have no respect for the dead and want to cut them up and show the pieces to their students. They're a bunch of butchers.'

At four o'clock Williams and Burton finally arrived. Anne met them at the door to the anteroom and showed them into the mayor's office. The judge was bubbling with excitement, convinced that he was at the climax of his long investigation. The Bow Street officer was pale and drawn with pain and his expression was more guarded. He used to say to Anne that hopes were often dashed. It was best not to raise them too high.

The mayor sat at his writing table and they declared themselves an unofficial court of inquiry. Peter left Grimes in the custody of a constable and joined them. He and Anne reported what they had learned from Grimes and his wife.

Then Peter fetched Grimes and sat him in a chair facing the court. Anne brought in his wife, and they sat off to one side. Dick Burton nodded to Anne. She was to take notes.

Burton began the discussion. 'Mr Grimes, if you will tell us what you witnessed on the night of the twenty-first of June 1782, on the sloop *Mercury,* we'll ask you to sign a written deposition and confirm your testimony before the Admiralty a few months from now. In the meantime we'll provide you and your wife with comfortable lodging, protection, and a generous reward at the end so that you and your wife can get on with your life together.'

Grimes sneered. 'All I can tell you is that the ship hit a rock. I got in the dinghy and made for shore. I didn't see what happened on board. If Seth committed any crimes, I didn't witness them.' Grimes fell silent and looked down at his hands clasped tightly before him.

Burton nodded to Williams who continued, 'This is an extraordinary offer, and costly to us. We recognize how difficult this testimony is for you, but we're convinced that there's no other way to convict Captain Judd of the despicable crimes he committed on the *Mercury.* We also must prevent him from committing any more. Recently, he has twice attempted to assassinate a young deaf woman, Janice Parker.'

Grimes glanced up. 'That must be Oliver Parker's daughter. She was a bright, pretty child when I left.' For a moment he seemed lost in thought. Then he stared at the judge. 'You don't need me. If you know so much, why don't you arrest him?'

'He hires others for his crimes, like the man with the cropped ear who spied on your wedding celebration today, the same man who threatened you at the White Gull a few hours before your wedding.'

Grimes made an unconvincing dismissive gesture.

Judge Williams gazed sternly at him. 'Young man, you don't seem to understand your situation. You're not free to leave tomorrow. If you refuse to agree to tell the truth to the Admiralty, I'll conclude that you were in fact a willing accomplice in Judd's crimes on the *Mercury*. After all, you never reported him to the police. You took ten of the gold pieces that he stole from Oliver Parker and spent them on yourself. So, tomorrow, instead of sailing like a free spirit to Charleston, you'll ride in irons to Newgate.'

The judge leaned back, crossed his arms over his chest. For a long moment, the room was silent. Isaac searched the stern faces of the men before him. Anne gave him no comfort either.

Then Joan spoke. 'Think, Isaac, with you in prison for months, perhaps years, what's to become of us? I'll live in terror at the mercy of Judd's men. Tell the truth. Judd's a villain. Let them hang him. Then he'll no longer be able to threaten us; we'll be free.'

Grimes watched her with mouth agape, his eyes wide. When she finished, he breathed heavily, shaking his head. His eyes began to glisten. Finally, he met the judge's unflinching gaze and said softly, 'I accept your offer, God save us.'

Peter and the constable took Isaac and Joan Grimes to rooms in the Mint. When their meager possessions were retrieved, they would be moved to a secure residence in London. Constables were searching Bristol for Captain Judd as well as for the sailor with the cropped ear. The mayor set a watch in the harbour in the event that Judd, with or without Amelia, might try to escape by sea. He had failed to silence Grimes, and Nate Taylor was securely in custody. Both men could give damaging testimony against him.

His arrest would be no easy task. He was an elusive as well as a clever and dangerous man. Dick Burton had kept track of him while he was supposed to be living at the York Hotel. He came to Bath for a day or two according to no discernible plan. Burton's informants in the hotel couldn't say where he went.

Two days ago, Anne and Burton had found him together with Amelia at Thomas Parker's house in the Circus. As of last night when Burton visited the Assembly Rooms, no one had seen Judd, and he had checked out of his room at the hotel. Amelia had also apparently left the city.

Burton suggested to Anne that they ride back to the inn together and continue their discussion of Seth Judd.

'Where are the ships that Judd owns?' Anne asked, as they got under way.

Burton shook his head. 'The excise officers might know. I'll ask them. He's likely to keep one of the ships nearby in case he has to leave Bristol in a hurry. But he might decide to stay and defend himself in the Admiralty rather than flee. The testimony of our witnesses could be challenged. Neither Taylor nor Grimes actually *saw* the murder of the Parkers; they heard a shot and saw the captain with a bloody knife. Taylor entered the cabin and saw the Parkers' bodies.'

'Both seamen did see Captain Judd shoot the mate and throw him overboard.'

'True, but the mate was disobeying the captain's orders. Granted, Judd's defence would sound implausible to us. But the Admiralty is inclined to give a ship's captain the benefit of any doubt.'

Anne agreed. 'That's what happened at the inquiry in 1782 when the court ruled that the shipwreck was an accident.' She paused, reflecting. 'I wonder where Judd keeps his diary and other personal papers. And where has he hidden his money? That's where I think he might be right now.'

'Do you have an idea?'

She nodded. 'Tomorrow, I'd like to search Morland Court, the Parker estate in Somerset. His mother still lives there.'

TO TRAP A SEAFOX

Morland Court, Tuesday, 17 November

At dawn, André and Anne rode out of Bristol westward into Somersetshire towards the Parker estate, an hour's journey by coach. Last night André had joined Anne at the White Gull and stayed overnight. Burton also spent the night there to prepare for tomorrow's large and complicated attempt to apprehend Captain Judd and his men and seize his papers. Bristol constables were enlisted as well as a cutter of the excise service.

This morning, unfortunately, Burton's arthritis flared up and prevented him from making the trip. He deputized André and equipped him and Anne with instructions, letters of recommendation and a search warrant to be used if necessary.

Solicitor Barnstaple had also sent Anne permission to inspect the estate. She had earlier informed him of Thomas Parker's death and asked what was to be done.

'How much can we expect to accomplish here in a day?' asked André, as the coach rolled past broad, gleaned wheat fields to the left and right of the road.

Anne replied, 'Mr Barnstaple's request that we inspect conditions is mostly a pretext for gaining entrance. It shouldn't take much time to find out if Captain Judd is now at the estate and has hidden his secret papers in one of its buildings. We must contact Lieutenant Howe at ten o'clock. We have a few hours.'

André reflected, 'An illegal business as diverse and widespread as Judd's requires extensive records. Morland Court would be a convenient place to keep them: it's close to Bristol, where he conducts much of his business and has bribed most of the excise and customs officers. It's also a highly respectable and privileged place, and unlikely to arouse any suspicion of illegal activity.'

Anne added, 'And it's where his mother lives and can protect his papers.'

'We should be cautious,' said André. 'Judd may be armed and have insinuated some of his men into the staff or have bought support among the household servants.'

For that reason, Burton had stressed the element of surprise and had warned of danger. The coachman and the guard were Bristol constables, armed and in disguise. Other mounted constables would patrol the roads leading to the estate. Both Anne and her grandfather carried hidden pistols.

At the gate to the manor house Anne showed the porter her permission to visit the estate, then asked if Captain Seth Judd might be there. She added casually, 'We've made his acquaintance this season in Bath.'

The porter replied that Captain Judd occasionally passed

through the gate on his way to visit his mother, but the porter hadn't seen him recently. Anne remarked softly to her grandfather, 'Judd could come and go unobserved by boat from the Bristol Channel. We'll keep looking.'

From the gate they drove on slowly towards the manor house. Anne had noticed a lively, bright young boy pass through the gate while they were speaking with the porter. 'That was Benjamin,' the porter had said. Now the boy was walking on the edge of the road ahead of them.

'Stop for the boy,' she called out to the coachman. She beckoned Benjamin to the coach. 'Could you help us, young man?' She held out a sixpence. At the sight of the shining silver coin his eyes opened wide. He nodded. 'You know Captain Judd, don't you, Benjamin?' The boy nodded again. 'Is he here today?'

'Yes. I saw him leave the manor house an hour after sunrise and walk to his mother's cottage.'

'Thank you, Benjamin. Where's the steward's office?' As the executor of Oliver Parker's will, and in charge of the trust that administered Janice's properties, Barnstaple hired stewards to manage them. Since 1782, Mr Amos Jones was in charge of the Somerset property; his wife was the housekeeper. Their work appeared to be satisfactory and returned an annual profit.

'It's there.' The boy pointed to a plain, single-storey, stone building off to one side of the manor house.

'You've been helpful. Here's your reward.' She handed him the coin. 'Keep it secret, don't tell *anybody*. They would be jealous and take it from you.'

'I know,' he said in a tone that was worldly-wise beyond his years.

Amos Jones' office reflected the character of its occupant: dull, well organized. File boxes stood at attention in ordered ranks on shelves from floor to ceiling. On his writing table lay a few neat stacks of paper. The man himself was short, narrow-shouldered, and middle-aged. His eyes had a nervous tic, but his manner was otherwise cool and efficient – and now a little wary.

Anne showed her papers and explained that she was acting on behalf of Janice Parker, the young owner of the estate.

'Mr André Cartier, my grandfather, has come along to help. We hope to report to Mr Barnstaple that everything is in good order.' She paused for an afterthought. 'By the way, have you seen Captain Seth Judd? We'd like to have a word with him. He might be visiting his mother.'

The steward replied rather too quickly. 'He's not here now.' Anne hoped that her scepticism didn't show on her face, or on André's. She wondered why the steward would lie.

'Several days ago,' Jones continued, 'the captain arrived with his friend, Miss Swan. She boasted that she was Thomas Parker's heir. Captain Judd was going to show her around.'

'How did he react?'

'Difficult to tell. He seemed surprised and annoyed. Whether at me or at his friend, I can't say. Perhaps he felt embarrassed.'

'We'll meet the captain another time,' Anne said. 'By the way, does anyone occupy the manor house? We'd like to visit it.'

'The estate's trustee lets it out. There have been several tenants.'

'And who lives there now?' Anne resented having to pull information from this man.

'Since two years ago Captain Judd has held the lease. He actually lives there infrequently.'

'Thank you. Now we'll be about our business.' She explained that she was familiar with the estate and would show it to André.

'May I have my papers back – and the keys?'

The steward carefully examined the papers a second time, reluctance all over his face. 'Really, I should accompany you,' he murmured.

Anne glared at him. 'That won't be necessary. As I said, I've known Morland since my youth and don't need a guide – just the keys and my papers.' Though his offer was reasonable on the face of it, she had grown suspicious of him. She held out her hand.

He hesitated, pressed his lips together tightly, then gave her the papers, reached into a drawer for a ring of keys, and gave it to her.

André spoke up. 'Our coachman and the guard will take the coach to the stable, then wait for us in the servants' quarters.'

Anne and André left the steward and set out for the manor

house. The steward's wife, the housekeeper, came to the door
with a mixture of surprise and suspicion. Anne offered her
usual explanation, showed her papers, and asked to see Captain
Judd's rooms. A look of horror came over the housekeeper's
face. 'I dare not. He'll be terribly angry. He has threatened
anyone who enters without permission with the most dreadful
consequences.'

'Good,' Anne whispered to her grandfather. 'Then he's
hiding something important in there.'

'He can vent his anger at us,' Anne said to the housekeeper.

André showed her the search warrant. 'Lead us to his apartment.'

Judd occupied a suite of rooms on the first floor in the
north-east, oldest part of the building. They climbed the stairs
and entered a large, square room that served as a parlour. Near
the fireplace were two upholstered chairs and a tea table. A
few nautical maps hung on the walls that were otherwise bare.
In the next room was a sleeping alcove, an armoire, and little
else.

Anne asked the housekeeper, 'How does the captain pass
his time when he's in this building?'

'He's very secretive and wants to be by himself. He tells
me what he wants to eat. I bring it to him on a tray. In the
evening, he frequently asks me to fetch a girl for his bed.
They come from certain families in the village who work for
him.'

Anne lifted an eyebrow; she sensed anger welling up. 'I
assume they smuggle or deal in smuggled goods. Do they
dare to refuse the captain?'

The housekeeper shrugged. 'The girls come gladly enough.
He treats them no worse than most men and pays them well.'

Finally, they came to the thick oak door of the tower.
From her visits years ago, Anne recalled the tall, four-storey,
rectangular stone building attached to the north-east corner
of the manor house. The upper two storeys with their narrow
slit windows still reflected its original military purpose. The
ground floor and the first floor had been converted to more
peaceful use, and modern windows had been cut through
the thick walls.

'The captain calls this his study,' said the housekeeper. She
had begun to speak in a low voice and glanced over her shoulder

as if Judd were creeping up on her, trying to hear what she was saying. 'I don't have the key. He opens it for me on the few occasions when I'm supposed to clean the room.'

The housekeeper stepped aside while Anne examined the lock. It was about two years old, installed at the time that Judd first leased the manor house. 'It's cheap, a simple mechanism,' she said, taking the tools from her bag. She opened the door in a couple of minutes.

Inside, the room reminded Anne of a dungeon – the stone walls were rough-hewn; the wooden beam ceiling was lofty. Stone tiles covered the floor. A large Turkish carpet lay under Judd's writing table that stood beneath a three-bay window. The only other source of natural light was a pair of high, narrow windows. Several brass sconces hung on the empty walls. In a corner to the left of the table was a fireplace. To the right of the table was a small cabinet. The table was bare except for a tray of writing materials. It had a single drawer.

In a few words, the room's atmosphere was gloomy, conducive to morose thinking. This wasn't a business office. That would be elsewhere, probably in his mother's cottage. Here the captain would write entries in his diary. Perhaps he sat by the fire and conjured up daring schemes and weighed their cost against their reward.

While the housekeeper stood in the open doorway, wringing her hands, fearing that the captain would suddenly surprise them, Anne and André studied the room for hiding places. The stone tiles were firmly cemented to the floor. The walls were solid stone. The drawer in the writing table was the most likely place. Anne started towards it, drawing the tools from her bag. She was certain that Judd would have locked the drawer. The diary was probably inside.

Before she could set to work, André caught her arm and pulled her away. 'Stay clear of the table.'

'What's the matter?' Irritation crept into her voice. The housekeeper stared at the scene with alarm.

André's face was tense; his neck was taut. 'I must study the table first.' He lowered himself to the floor and slid on his back under the table. For a few minutes he gingerly searched behind the drawer. 'I found it. Watch.' He pulled a lever. A sharp report shook the table. An instant later, a thin steel dart was imbedded in a piece of firewood on a pile opposite the drawer.

André rose from the floor and stood pale and trembling by the table. 'Can you imagine if you were up close there, working with your tools?' He pointed with a shaking finger to the lock. 'Judd has concealed a crossbow between the drawer and the top of the table. If he's going to be away from the apartment for any length of time, he sets the mechanism to go off whenever the drawer is pulled or even moved slightly. The dart passes through a small hole above the lock.'

'How did you suspect this trap?'

'Besides guns and sword canes, I've made several cross-bows. They've become fashionable in recent years at archery contests. And having come to know the mind of the Sea Fox, I guessed that this is how he might protect his diary.'

Anne took deep breaths to calm her nerves, then hesi-tantly picked the lock and pulled open the drawer. There lay a book, Judd's diary. On its black cover was embossed a heraldic shield. A man and a woman, black, naked, and in chains, stood facing each other against a blue sea. A large, upright barrel of rum was between them. A brig sailed behind them. Below the shield was the motto, 'I shall prevail'.

André glanced at Anne, puzzled. 'What's it mean?'

'I recognize the shield. Sir Abraham Parker designed it when he purchased the baronet's title from the king. Parker had a wry sense of humour. The money for that purchase came from his trade in slaves and rum.'

'And the motto?'

'Seth Judd must have chosen it to express his determin-ation to become the lord of Morland Court.'

It was midmorning when Anne and André left the tower with Judd's diary in her bag. Scanning it, they discovered that it was written entirely in a shorthand or code. 'We'll figure it out later,' André said.

Anne agreed. 'Our next step is to see whether the excise men are ready. The tide should be right for them about now. We'll take the view from the Observatory. It's my favourite place at Morland Court, and perhaps Judd's as well. From there we can survey the entire estate and its harbour on the

Bristol Channel. We'll also gain a good view of his mother's cottage where the boy Benjamin last saw him.'

From the manor house they walked on a path up a gentle slope through a sparse, low growth of bushes and stunted trees. They came to an octagonal stone building on the rocky outcrop. A narrow stone terrace around the building offered a view in every direction. To the west was the Bristol Channel with Wales on the opposite shore a dozen miles away.

A sheep pasture extended from the Observatory's terrace down to the water. A cove formed a small harbour. A jetty gave extra protection to a dock, where one of Judd's cutters was moored ready to sail. Nearby was a stone building that could be used for storage and seamen's lodging. Two men were scraping the hull of an overturned boat. Fishing nets and sails were hung out to dry. A few small boats lay on the shore.

'There are probably more men in the building,' Anne remarked with growing concern.

'And we should assume that they have weapons nearby,' André added. 'At night they turn into the captain's smugglers. We'll leave them to the excise officers.'

The channel teemed with ships of all types. André peered through a pocket telescope. 'A ship is slowly sailing near us, the excise cutter, the *Endeavor,* that Burton promised. It's flying the red ensign instead of the blue, pretending to be a merchant coastal vessel waiting for high tide at ten o'clock. The men on board are disguised as common seamen. An officer is holding a telescope to his eye and sees us. Now he's signaling that he'll draw closer and await word from us. High tide is the moment for the attack. I trust that our disguised Bristol constables will guard the stables and the mounted constables on the Bristol road will advance on the manor house from the east.'

'I'm relieved,' Anne said. 'Burton's plan is working well thus far. The excise men will block any attempt by Judd to escape by sea and capture his men in the dock area.' She pointed to a covered platform on the Observatory's flat roof. 'When I was last at Morland seven years ago, a powerful telescope was mounted there.'

She produced a key from the steward's ring and opened the door. 'Seth must have his own key. Let's hope that he doesn't surprise us. He or one of his men probably comes here from time to time to survey the area, more frequently if they have any reason to fear a visit from the Excise. If he has heard of the Excise's new leadership in Bristol, he might be worried and could be up there now. We'll take the risk.'

They entered cautiously, pistols drawn and cocked. But the interior was empty. They breathed sighs of relief and holstered their weapons. They climbed a narrow, iron, circular stairway up to the telescope's platform.

André sneezed. 'Anne, someone has been here this morning. My nose detects tobacco. And now I see some pipe ashes.'

'I noticed them, too. The tobacco smells familiar, rather sweet, like the one Thomas Parker smoked that set off Janice's asthma. Its strong scent was also on Judd's clothes when Burton and I interrogated him last Saturday at Parker's house in the Circus. Of course, he's probably not the only person in the Bristol area to smoke this tobacco. But it's a remarkable coincidence.'

André pulled aside the heavy canvas cover that protected the instrument. The telescope had been lowered and was pointing towards the road to Bristol. 'Judd might have seen us coming.'

'Yes, he could observe the entire estate and much of the countryside as far as Bristol.'

They figured out how to manipulate the instrument. Anne pointed it towards a large two-storey cottage situated between the manor house and the nearest village to the south. She told André to take a look. 'That's where Judd's mother lives. Is there any sign of him or her?'

'A woman is throwing a bucket of slops to pigs in a pen. But she's too young to be his mother.'

'She must be a maid,' Anne surmised. 'I want to talk to her.'

'A man is just now approaching the cottage, in great haste.' André paused, staring into the instrument. 'I do believe that he's Jones, the steward.'

'He'll announce our arrival, probably to Judd, certainly to his mother,' Anne said. 'We must go down to the cottage. But now it's ten o'clock and time to signal for the excise men to come.'

André turned the instrument towards the *Endeavor*. The officer in charge was staring expectantly at the Observatory.

André went to the balustrade and gave the pre-arranged hand signals. Anne took over the telescope and followed the sequel. The cutter immediately lowered a long boat filled with excise men. They rowed rapidly into the harbour, pulled up to the dock, and leaped from the boat.

By this time, Judd's men working outside had become alarmed and ran into the large stone building. Moments later, they emerged followed by several others, carrying cutlasses and pikes, ready to do battle. The excise men, armed with pistols and muskets, fired a volley. Several smugglers fell; the others threw down their weapons. They were quickly shackled, while several excise men dashed across the pasture up towards the ridge.

Anne turned the telescope towards the cottage just as a man with a pistol in each hand emerged. 'It's Judd,' Anne said, and beckoned her grandfather to take a look. 'He's coming towards us,' exclaimed André and drew his pistol.

When Judd reached the crest of the ridge a few feet from the Observatory, he saw excise men in the pasture running towards him. For a moment, he hesitated and glanced at the Observatory. Anne and André had ducked down and were concealed by the balustrade on top of the building.

He looked back. Bristol constables came out of the manor house and blocked his retreat. Desperate, he tried the Observatory's door and slipped in.

'Good morning, Captain. Put down your pistols.' André had descended the stairs and hidden behind the door. His pistol pointed at the captain's head. From above Anne also aimed a pistol at him. For an instant Judd may have thought he could fight his way out of the trap. But his situation was impossible and his better judgement prevailed. He carefully uncocked his pistols and laid them on a nearby table.

'Congratulations, Monsieur and Madame Cartier, you are the first enemy in ten years to outwit me.'

Moments later, two excise men came through the door, followed by Lieutenant Howe, their commander. 'Gentlemen,' said André, 'this is Captain Seth Judd, wanted for smuggling and murder. Take him away.' For a moment the excise men stared at the scene, eyes wide in amazement. Then they shackled Judd and, without further ceremony, led him back down the pasture towards their cutter.

Anne and André left the Observatory and stood on the terrace, together with Howe who had remained behind. His face was flushed with the excitement of capturing a major smugglers' nest. For a few minutes, they quietly watched Judd and his captors until they reached the dock and climbed into the long boat. Meanwhile other agents arrived at the terrace.

Anne introduced her grandfather and showed the officer her papers from Burton.

'Lieutenant Howe at your service, Madame,' the young officer said with a bow. He scanned the papers, glancing up at Anne with a bemused expression. She sensed that he was a brash, cocky young man but trying to be polite out of respect for Burton.

'Mr Burton told me that we would meet you, his female agent. You would be familiar with the estate and could lead us to Captain Judd. So far, Burton has been right. We found contraband tobacco and silk down there.' The officer pointed to the large stone building by the dock. 'And now we have Judd.'

They walked around the Observatory, taking in the view.

'This is a vast estate,' exclaimed the lieutenant. 'How can we best secure it?'

André replied, 'Two of our Bristol constables are guarding the stables. Other constables have occupied the manor house. You and a few of your men should go to the steward's office and find his records – especially the secret ones. Mr Jones is involved in the smugglers' ring and may be tempted to destroy incriminating evidence.'

Howe immediately sent off two of his men, saying that he would soon follow them.

Anne told the officer, 'Now we'll search Madame Judd's cottage and try to find her son's papers. He was staying there. Mr Burton has asked me to interrogate Judd's mother. She won't tell me anything that might incriminate her son, but she might inadvertently reveal where we might find his papers.'

'The papers would be a great prize and seal his fate,' the officer remarked.

'Would you order a couple of your men to go with us and stand by in case we need help?'

'Gladly,' he replied.

A TROVE OF EVIDENCE

Morland Court and Bristol, Tuesday, 17 November

Madame Judd lived in a spacious, rustic building that reminded Anne of Marie-Antoinette's regal 'cottage' at Versailles. A pear espalier spread over the entire south wall. Its leaves had turned an autumnal russet colour. The building was much larger, better built, and more pleasing to the eye than the hovels of the estate's tenants in the nearby village. Abraham Parker had intended his cottage to be an idyllic setting for the hours of pleasure that he enjoyed with his mistress.

Anne approached the cottage with a mixture of heightened anticipation and trepidation, even though André and two excise agents were behind her. What kind of woman had produced such a daunting man as Captain Seth Judd, the Sea Fox? As Anne racked her memory, an image of Catherine Judd surfaced from the past, at first faintly, then in sharper focus. A domestic servant, a beautiful woman, and Abraham Parker's favourite, then shunted aside and turned bitter. She would now be close to seventy.

Anne tried to think back seven years. Oliver and his wife had just died, leaving their ten-year-old daughter Janice alone at the estate, confused and grieving. Anne had accompanied her cousin, Beverly, to comfort the girl and make arrangements for her care. Thomas Parker was to be her guardian. But early on, he had told Beverly that Janice was *her* responsibility.

On that visit, Anne had met Madame Judd, who was temporarily helping Mildred Fox, Janice's nanny. In the course of that meeting, Anne grew to dislike and distrust Madame Judd. Her sympathy for the unfortunate girl appeared false. She seemed mostly curious about the Parker family's wealth and who would manage it on the girl's behalf. Anne granted that her antipathy towards Seth Judd influenced her opinion of his mother.

Anne signaled André to come forward and the excise agents to hide near the cottage. Then she knocked. The maid opened the door, the same young woman that Anne had seen through the telescope. Apprehension flashed across the maid's face when she saw the two strangers. André asked for Madame Judd. Her voice trembling, the maid said that madame was indisposed and not seeing anyone today.

'Ask her whom she would rather speak to, André and Anne Cartier or the excise officers. That's her choice.'

The maid disappeared for a few moments, then returned and beckoned them in. She led them through a small entrance hall into a warm, comfortable parlour. A spinet stood in a far corner. Shelves lined one wall, their books bound in gilded red leather. African spears and shields decorated the opposite wall, attesting to Captain Judd's part in the slave trade. Fine porcelain vases were gracefully arranged on the mantelpiece.

Wearing a silk house dress, Madame Judd sat in a richly upholstered chair by the fire. Her beauty had faded but not vanished. The white silk bonnet concealing her grey hair framed the noble structure of her face. She glared at them as they entered.

'What do you want?' She didn't invite them to sit down.

Unabashed, Anne and André pulled up chairs and sat facing her. André said, 'First, you may summon the steward. We know that he's hiding here.'

Madame Judd nodded to the maid still standing inside by the door. A few moments later she came back with the trembling steward. 'Return to your office, sir,' said André. 'You will find it occupied by excise men. If you have any sense of what's good for you, you will assist their investigation.'

The steward cringed, his face turned pale, and he seemed frozen to the spot.

'Go, man!' André shouted at him. He scampered out like a frightened rabbit.

'You say excise officers?' asked Madame Judd, apprehension creeping into her tone.

'Yes,' André replied. 'They have taken over the estate and have arrested your son, Seth. They have found contraband tobacco and silk in the large building by the dock.'

'How can they prove that he's involved?'

'The dock workers will implicate him. The officers will see to that.'

'Neither you nor the officers can force me to betray him.' She cocked her head and studied Anne with a gimlet eye. 'I know you, the London singer and dancer who used to please Old Parker. Are you now a spy for the excise service?'

'Since the death of Thomas Parker five days ago, I've been in charge of his ward, Janice Parker. On her behalf – and with Solicitor Barnstaple's permission – my grandfather and I have come to inspect the estate. Things here are not as they should be.'

André leaned over to Anne and whispered in her ear, 'I'll continue to question her. You take the maid and search the building.'

Anne understood André's mind. Madame Judd would never reveal her son's secret papers. The maid, however, might know where they were and be tricked or persuaded into revealing them.

Anne went immediately to the maid who still stood near the door. 'Come with me,' Anne commanded. The young woman threw a desperate glance towards her mistress who gave her a warning look. Anne seized her at the elbow and half-shoved her through a dining room into the kitchen. 'We'll have a talk here.' Anne pointed to a large wooden table in the middle of the room. A pot of tea stood on the iron stove. 'Pour each of us a cup,' Anne said.

At this familiar task the maid began to relax. 'Tell me about yourself,' Anne asked gently. The maid took a sip of tea and hesitantly began to speak. She was Mary, the steward's niece, and had worked two years for Madame Judd, mostly tending to her grooming and other personal needs. Girls from the village came in for most of the cooking and cleaning.

Mary's speech revealed that she was intelligent, had received some elementary education, and could probably read and write. Even in a servant's simple woolen costume, she appeared quite presentable. She could easily find work as a lady's maid or companion or move to the city and clerk in a millinery shop. So why did her uncle place her here? Perhaps to spy?

'How does madame treat you?' Anne asked.

Mary shrugged. 'She doesn't beat me.' Her tone expressed no fondness for her mistress.

'We know that her son, Seth, comes here often. Where does he stay?' Anne finished her cup of tea.

The maid hesitated.

'Show me.' Anne put a little steel into her voice.

Mary led Anne up a narrow flight of stairs into an upper level. At the door she remarked, 'I've been told that he has lived here since he was a child.'

She showed Anne into a large room with a low ceiling and white plaster walls. A fine brown mahogany writing table stood by one of several windows. A sleeping alcove and a wardrobe occupied the far wall. On the other walls hung a brace of pistols, a cutlass, and several nautical maps. Anne browsed in a few books – mostly having to do with commerce and navigation. Above the mantelpiece hung the portrait of a beautiful young woman. On closer inspection Anne recognized her as Madame Judd when she was Abraham Parker's mistress. The work of an expert hand, the painting accurately insinuated the woman's pride and intelligence.

'Mary,' Anne began, 'you must realize that you are deeply involved in Seth Judd's large smuggling enterprise, as is your uncle the steward. If you cooperate with me, I can help you escape the dire consequences. If you prove stubborn, you will go down with Seth Judd and his associates. The excise officers are pitiless. They will arrest you, imprison you in Newgate in London, and bring you before an Admiralty court, charged with aiding and abetting Seth's smuggling. So the first thing you can do to save yourself is to tell me where Seth keeps his secret papers.'

The maid couldn't speak, just shook her head. Finally she croaked, 'I'm just a maid in this house. The captain and his mother never confide in me or allow me to listen to their conversations.'

'When your uncle gave you this job, you were supposed to spy on Captain Judd. To protect himself, your uncle had to know what Judd was up to. I want to know what you learned.'

The maid drew a deep breath, then spoke in a strained voice. 'I've seen papers on his table while he was writing, but I haven't watched him take them out or put them away. Last night, however, I noticed that the portrait of his mother was hanging at an odd angle. I haven't had an opportunity to examine it.'

'By the way, why were you here last night?'

The maid blushed with embarrassment, chewed on her lower lip. 'It's hard to refuse the captain anything.'

'I understand,' Anne said quickly. 'Let's see what's behind the portrait.'

They removed it from the wall and found a locked cabinet. Anne opened it with her tools. Inside was a strongbox, also locked. Anne shook it and heard the sound of coins, but she couldn't master its unusual, probably foreign mechanism.

She heard steps on the stairs. An excise officer entered the room. 'We found these keys in Judd's pocket and thought you might need them.'

'You came just in time,' Anne said. One of the keys opened the box. It was nearly full of Spanish gold coins. Anne's heart leaped. This box matched Nate Taylor's description of the one that Oliver Parker carried on board the *Mercury* seven years ago. The coins could probably be traced to the Spanish ship captured by Judd's privateer. That should strengthen the case against him at the Admiralty.

Still, where were Judd's papers? Most likely in this room, Anne thought. Surveying the walls, her eyes stopped at the locked wardrobe to the left of the sleeping alcove. Another of Judd's keys opened a shallow space filled with clothing hung on hooks from above. She pushed them apart and tapped the back wall. It sounded hollow. Eventually, she found a hidden lever and opened the wall to deep shelves loaded with file boxes of old account books, diaries, and other records and papers.

She called to the excise officer. 'All this evidence must eventually go to the Admiralty in London for Captain Judd's trial. But take it first to the mayor's office in Bristol, where Judge William Williams and the Bow Street officer, Dick Burton, will examine it.'

The excise officer studied the shelves and said, 'I'll get men and wagons to move this to Bristol.' As he was leaving, he glanced sharply at the maid. 'We're putting the prisoners on our cutter. Shall I take her, too?'

Anne shook her head. 'It would be better to keep her separate from the others, especially from Captain Judd. He could intimidate her, and she would refuse to give evidence. My grandfather and I and the Bristol constables shall be responsible for her.'

The officer nodded in agreement. 'Then, you may as well take charge of Madame Judd until the judge can hear her story, also free from her son's influence.'

'We'll take her and the maid to Bristol by coach, but first we must go downstairs and find out what my grandfather has learned from her; then we'll speak to the steward.'

They found André sitting at Madame Judd's writing table, an account book opened before him. From her chair by the fire she glowered at him. An excise agent stood alert at her shoulder.

When Anne expressed surprise, André threw a glance at Madame Judd. 'She's had quite a temper tantrum, even drew a small pistol from her sleeve. So I disarmed her and asked the agent for assistance.'

He lifted the account book. 'I found her record of the captain's transactions with smuggled goods. It appears careful and thorough. She's been doing it for years and kept it hidden behind the hearth.'

To the excise officer André remarked, 'All Judd's customers are here, as well as excise officers and other officials whom he bribed. You'll want to pay them a visit.'

Anne and André hastened to the steward's building. Pale and drawn, wringing his hands, Jones stood in a corner of his little office. Lieutenant Howe and a pair of other excise officers sat around the writing table, going through the estate's files for more evidence of Judd's smuggling operations.

'Have you found anything of use?' asked André.

'Nothing,' replied Howe. He stared balefully at the steward. 'The files indicate that Captain Judd paid rent for the upstairs apartment in the manor house and a dockage fee to the estate for the past two years. That's all. We've concluded that Mr Jones must have kept a separate account of his secret dealings with the smugglers. We'll have to beat the truth out of him. It would strengthen our case against the captain.'

The hapless steward cringed. His secret account would also implicate him in the captain's illegal enterprise. Without the steward's complicity the scheme couldn't have worked in a place so close to Bristol.

Anne warned the officer, 'Mr Jones is a frail man and might not survive harsh interrogation. Treat him leniently and you might gain his secret accounts and another witness against the captain.'

Howe leaned back in his chair, stroking his chin, then nodded. 'We'll follow your suggestion.' He gave her a conde-scending smile. 'Go ahead, Madame, question him yourself. He might talk to a woman.'

Anne swallowed a sharp retort about arrogant males. She turned to the shaking steward and asked gently, 'Where can we talk?'

He pointed to a door and said, 'Follow me.' André joined them.

They entered a small parlour and sat facing each other. Anne leaned forward and looked Jones in the eye. 'I deeply sympathize with you, sir, for you are in an appalling situ-ation. You face personal disgrace, heavy fines, and years in a prison or the hangman's noose. The law may pursue your wife as well. She must have known what was going on.'

Anne paused for this dreadful prospect to sink into the steward's imagination. She heard a stirring in the next room and sensed that Mrs Jones was listening at the door.

'I feel,' Anne went on, 'that circumstances have unfortu-nately combined against you. In most respects you have been an exemplary steward. I can honestly say to Mr Barnstaple that the estate appears to be in excellent condition. So, tell me how you fell into this predicament.'

'At the beginning it all seemed harmless,' he replied. Under further questioning he admitted receiving money from Judd for small favors, then for allowing him to moor his cutter at the dock and to store certain goods for his coastal trade. But Jones grew suspicious that Judd was bringing contraband into the estate and distributing it in Bristol and Bath. That was too risky. The excise service would eventually find out. The outcome would be dire.

So he ordered his niece Mary – she was also his ward – to go to work for Madame Judd and find out for sure what her son was up to. Madame Judd was suspicious, but as her health deteri-orated she needed help. In a trial period, Mary proved much more pleasant and able than any of Madame Judd's previous maids. Moreover, Seth Judd took a liking to her. At a cost to her virtue, she eventually confirmed her uncle's worst fears: the captain was doing a brisk illegal business from the Parker dock.

Then it was too late. Jones was too deep into the smuggling scheme. If he tried to back out, the excise officers would mock his excuses. Now, to save his skin, he had to help conceal the smugglers. Otherwise, he could expect the worst.

Anne gave Jones a sympathetic smile. 'You are caught between Captain Seth Judd and the excise service, the devil and the deep blue sea. So, now we must find a way to prevent your destruction.'

For the first time, Jones looked to her with a glimmer of hope.

'In a manner of speaking,' she went on, 'the excise service is willing to bargain. If you open your accounts and testify against Seth Judd, they will tell the Admiralty that your illegal actions were performed under duress, greatly mitigating your guilt.'

Jones protested, 'But even from prison Judd will pursue me. He has many friends in the smuggling fraternity, even in the excise service. They will seek revenge on his behalf.'

Anne shook her head. 'He's bluffing. His network is coming apart. Don't worry; you won't be alone giving testimony in court. Many of his associates will join you. Together you will make his conviction certain. He will hang and no longer be a threat to you or anyone else.'

Jones stared at his shoes, agonizing over his choices.

Anne leaned back, crossed her arms over her chest, and waited. Finally, she asked, 'Where have you hidden your papers?'

He let out a sigh and replied, 'Under my writing table.'

Anne ordered the steward back into the office and recovered the papers. They recorded the captain's movements on the estate, the arrival and departure of his cutter, and summaries of conversations between the steward and the captain. Especially damning were the steward's misleading or false statements in reply to excise agent's inquiries about the captain's activities.

After reading the papers, Lieutenant Howe exclaimed, 'This man should go to the gallows with the captain.' Still in the office, Jones grew deathly pale. Anne thought he was about to faint.

She spoke softly to André in French. 'We must take responsibility for Jones. Otherwise he may refuse to testify. Or, be unable to. I also believe that the estate needs him until Barnstaple can find another steward.'

André nodded, then addressed Lieutenant Howe, 'Sir, as a deputy of the Bow Street magistrate, I wish to hold Jones here on the estate for a few days. There's no danger that he might run away. I'll keep an eye on him.'

The officer looked askance.

'I'll stay with him,' André explained. 'I know something about managing a business. This investigation has turned the steward's office and its files into a huge mess. I'll help Jones put everything back in order for the next steward. In a few days, when I'm finished, I'll bring Jones to Bristol or Bath, or wherever Judge Williams and Dick Burton wish to question him.'

Howe thought for a moment. 'You may have him. I trust that he'll be ready to testify before the Admiralty in a couple of months.' He threw a parting malevolent glance at the steward and left.

Anne turned to her grandfather. 'One of the constables will stay with you. The other will go with me to Bristol with Mary Jones and Madame Judd. Judge Williams and Dick Burton will be anxious to question them and to hear our story.'

Early in the evening Anne brought Madame Judd and Mary Jones to a room next to the mayor's office and took notes while Williams and Burton questioned them. Though her voice nearly failed her, Miss Jones described spying for her uncle. On several occasions, she had overheard Seth speaking to his men or his mother concerning names, goods, and dates of smuggling at Morland Court. Her words had the ring of truth.

'You have been helpful,' said the judge as he released her. 'But we might need to speak to you again, so remain in Bristol until I say you are free to leave.'

After the hearing, Anne asked the young woman about her situation. She appeared relieved to be free and said that she would stay with a relative.

In contrast, Madame Judd refused to cooperate. 'I have nothing to say to you,' she told Judge Williams, glaring at him with an expression akin to contempt.

'In that case,' said the judge in a huff, 'you'll stew in the city's house of correction, the Bridewell, until you come to a better frame of mind.' A constable led her away.

Anne was about to leave the mayor's office when Peter walked in, his face flushed with excitement.

'Stay,' he said to Anne. 'You'll want to hear this.'

He addressed Dick Burton. 'My spy has found a seaman with a cropped ear, together with a man who might have been his partner in the attack on Janice in Crescent Fields. Without doubt they would deny the accusation and could produce alibis from other seamen. Unfortunately, there are dozens of seamen in Bristol with cropped ears. I can't distinguish one from another. I saw the villains we are seeking only briefly during Grimes' wedding party.'

Burton asked Anne, 'Could you identify them for us, Madame Cartier?'

'Where are they?' she asked.

Peter replied, 'My spy followed them to a brothel near the quay. I've posted a watchman outside to keep track of them.'

'How shall I confront them?' Anne was beginning to feel uneasy. The dramatic events at Morland Court had tired her. Another adventure was unappealing.

'The watchman and I will bring them to his post in the harbour. You can identify them there.'

She recalled the villains. Then images from that evening in Crescent Fields surged up in her mind. A knife's steel blade flashed again before her inner eye. A sailor's face leered at her. She shook off a growing reluctance and said, 'I'll do it.'

It was dark when Anne and Peter reached the watchman's post. 'Wait here,' said Peter, his voice rising with excitement. 'I must entice the men away from the brothel. If I were to take them by force, I would provoke a riot. Seamen stick together, especially when they've been carousing.'

Situated on the ground floor of a decrepit building, the watch room was small and filthy. Paint peeled from its cracked plaster walls. Anne distrusted its chairs and the table so she stood facing the door, leaning on her cane, fingering the release lever. She had also brought her pistol.

She shivered. Was it from fear or the cold, clammy air? A glowing charcoal brazier struggled vainly to chase November's chill from the room. An oil lamp hanging from the low ceiling shed just enough light for her purpose. If he were the man, she would recognize him.

Outside were the noises of the street – the wheels of a cart, indistinct voices of passers-by. Then louder voices near the door. 'Why here?' a man shouted. The door burst open. Peter and a constable struggled into the room, holding up a man. Head down, he staggered towards Anne.

She saw the cropped ear. Then the man raised his head and stared at her. Their eyes met in an instant of mutual recognition. 'That's the man,' she told Peter and stepped back.

'Bitch,' the man shouted, suddenly sober and wild. He shook his captors loose and lurched at her. She stuck her cane between his legs and raised it with all her strength.

He gasped, bent over double, let out a mighty groan. Anne stepped aside as he crashed into the table and lay writhing on the floor.

With difficulty the constable shackled him. Seconds later, watchmen appeared at the door, dragged the man out and threw him into a cart. His partner stood in the street, stupefied. The constable shackled him too, lifted him also into the cart, and drove away. The entire incident lasted no more than five minutes.

With a mixture of embarrassment and concern, Peter asked Anne, 'Are you all right? The villain wasn't as drunk as we thought.'

She nodded. 'That was more than I bargained for. But I'm glad we caught them. That's one less threat to the life of Janice Parker.'

'In the morning,' Peter said, 'I'll take the two villains to Bath. A magistrate will charge them for their assault on Jacob and Janice.'

They returned to the White Gull to spend the night. Anne was weary but relieved. Janice's safety was almost secure.

A SMUGGLER'S DEFENSE

Anne spent the morning writing a detailed report for Dick Burton on yesterday's dramatic events at Morland Court. After a quick lunch, she hastened to the Bristol mayor's office. When she arrived, Burton, Judge Williams, and Lieutenant Howe were already at the writing table. Anne took a seat off to one side and prepared to take notes.

While they waited for Peter to come with the cropped-ear sailor, Burton reported on the secret financial records kept by Madame Judd at the estate. According to a letter to his mother, Judd worried that the government was making significant inroads into smuggling. His business was becoming riskier and less profitable. Burton and Williams would soon put together a strong case against him and might bring him to trial at the Admiralty. So Judd recently made quick sales to merchants and other customers from Bristol to London. In a day or two he intended to sell the rest of his contraband at a deep discount and leave Britain for America.

'He had purchased passage to New York for two – no doubt Amelia Swan would sail with him.'

'Which ship?' Anne asked. 'Perhaps we can intercept her. She must be hiding in this area and plans to arrive at the quay shortly prior to sailing.'

'The *Jupiter*. Its overhaul has just been completed.'

At that moment, Peter Cartier entered the room. 'I've brought with me the cropped ear sailor. He looks like he has wrestled with an angry bear, but he's willing and able to talk.'

Anne had told Dick Burton about her role in subduing the sailor but asked that he refrain from informing Judge Williams. 'He would think I was a coarse savage.'

'The judge doesn't have to know,' Burton said, smiling. 'I'm proud of you.'

The sailor shuffled into the room, shackled. His left cheek

was black and blue, his nose swollen. He recognized Anne immediately and groaned as he recalled the pain and humiliation she had inflicted.

Judge Williams gave him a withering look, then asked, 'Who hired you to attack Janice Parker and Jacob Woodhouse in Crescent Fields?'

The sailor glanced at Peter, who nodded.

'Captain Judd, your Honour.'

Burton asked, 'Will you repeat your testimony at the Admiralty?'

'Oh yes, sir.' The man nearly groveled as he spoke.

The judge nodded to the constable who led the sailor away. Burton asked Peter, 'Why was the sailor so forthcoming?'

'Word is out that the captain is arrested, his power broken. Among his smugglers, it's now every man for himself. The sailor hopes that his testimony will save him from being hanged.'

Captain Judd was brought into the room in drab prison garb and shackled. He held his head high and defiant. But his eyes had a new, hunted look that Anne hadn't noticed before. The fox was trapped in a corner.

Burton and Williams took turns questioning him. Since he didn't know yet that his records had been discovered, he claimed that he didn't engage in smuggling and knew only what he heard in taverns and coffee shops.

Dick Burton reached into his portfolio and pulled out Judd's diary. 'Do you recognize this?' He held it up for all to see, stroked the cover's heraldic crest, and fanned the pages.

Anne knew that Burton could not yet read the shorthand. He was bluffing.

But he said to Judd, 'You may as well tell the truth. We have Nate Taylor's account books, plus all the account books and other personal papers that were hidden in your mother's cottage. In addition, we have Jones' hidden records.'

The captain stared at the diary and appeared shaken. Finally, he nodded. 'If it pleases you, I'll admit to smuggling, an ancient and common practice in England.'

'A hanging offence, nonetheless,' Burton remarked.

Judd blinked.

It was now Judge Williams' turn. 'You will recall that we

met seven years ago in an Admiralty inquiry into the sinking of the sloop, *Mercury*. At the time I wasn't satisfied that the deaths of Oliver Parker and his wife and the mate were accidental. Since you've set your mind on telling the truth, tell me now what actually happened.'

'I acted in self-defense,' Judd began. 'In the course of a quarrel over shares of a prize, Oliver drew a pistol. I shot first. Then his wife attacked me, and I stabbed her.'

'What was the quarrel about? The particulars, please.'

'As we were leaving Waterford in Ireland, I learned that Oliver had carried contraband gold on board, the undeclared prize from a Spanish ship that I had recently captured. I had found it in the captain's cabin and concealed it. When my ship docked in Waterford and cleared the Prize Court, I handed the gold over to Oliver and said that we should share the treasure equally. He had already received a major share of the legal, declared prize. Instead of accepting my proposal, he kept the entire treasure. If I were to object, he would prevent me from ever commanding another ship. Under the circumstances I had to give in to him, but I waited for an opportunity to recover my rightful share.'

Burton raised a hand and asked, 'What about the mate? What had he done to deserve death?'

'He disobeyed my orders to stay at the wheel and caused the ship to run aground.'

'And our witnesses against you, who are nameless for the time being?'

'They are self-serving liars.'

Burton had prudently withheld key pieces of evidence. For even in prison Judd could arrange for his associates in the smuggling trade to intimidate witnesses and destroy incriminating papers.

Judge Williams declared the interrogation over. Judd was led from the room.

'What do you want me to do with him?' asked Lieutenant Howe, who had custody of the captain.

'Move him to Bath,' Williams replied. 'We'll hold him in prison while we study his diary and papers again and question the other smugglers whom you captured yesterday. Judd's also one of several suspects in our continuing investigation into the poisoning of Thomas Parker. When we've finished

with him, we'll send him on to London to await trial at the
Admiralty.'

It was Madame Judd's turn next. A constable led her into
the room, shackled like her son. She had agreed to an interrogation. A night in the house of correction had apparently
chastened her.

She wore a rough, heavy, brown woolen gown, girded at
the waist by a plain rope. Her hair was grey and hadn't been
groomed. Still, she was a strong, attractive woman. Her
complexion had turned pale but was free of blemish or wrinkles. Anne couldn't detect any fear or anxiety in her eyes. She
stood erect before the writing table.

'Madame,' began Judge Williams, 'you are accused of
assisting your son, Captain Judd, in the crime of smuggling
over a period of several years. What do you say in your
defence?'

'You have my account books and my personal papers. They
speak for me. Yes, I assisted my son in every way that I could.'
She paused, then hesitantly asked, 'What has happened to
him?'

Judge Williams seemed about to dismiss her question. But
Burton broke in, 'I'll answer her.' He gave the woman a brief,
straightforward account of the captain's arrest and the
discovery of their papers, as well as the steward's. 'They reveal
his smuggling enterprise in precise detail.'

'This evidence,' Williams added, 'together with the testimony of at least three credible witnesses, should ensure his
conviction.'

'And execution,' Madame Judd said softly, without emotion.

'I don't know what the Admiralty will do with him,' Burton
said.

She gave Burton a nod of appreciation. 'To speak in my
defence, or Seth's, would be a waste of words. I never believed
that smuggling was wrong,' she said, her voice gathering
strength. 'Illegal, but not wrong. Certainly not as bad as trading
in slaves, like Old Parker and so many leading citizens of
Bristol have done and still do. Seth sold smuggled goods of
high quality to some of the kingdom's most respectable people.
Of course, the government complained of the lost revenue.
Hypocrites. They would only have wasted it on warships and

cannons or on feathering their own nests. So, with a clear conscience I helped Seth – ran errands for him, received payments, distributed bribes, and so on.'

She began to cough. 'Asthma,' she muttered. 'The Bridewell is cold, damp, and mouldy, unfit for a human being.' She struggled to speak.

Anne rose from her chair. 'I believe there's hot tea in the next room. I'll get some for you.'

In a minute Anne was back and served Madame Judd a cup. Anne glanced a question at Burton. He nodded.

Anne waited a few moments until she seemed to have recovered her voice. 'Did the captain ever comment to you on the wreck of the *Mercury*?'

She lowered her cup and looked Anne in the eye. 'Seth's a good man.'

'Really? But he killed his brother and sister-in-law and the ship's mate.'

'They quarreled over money. Oliver was greedy. They fought. Seth won. Seth's always had to fight for what should be his. The mate was a fool. He should have obeyed orders.' She fell into a reverie. 'Seth was a kind and generous son. That's how I'll always remember him.' Her voice trailed off. She stared into her cup of tea. She seemed to think of her son as already dead.

'That's enough. We'll leave now,' said Burton.

'What should be done with Madame Judd?' Anne asked Burton, as they reached the exit from the Council Building. 'She's unrepentant.'

Burton grimaced while he eased himself down the steps with his cane. Once on the pavement he turned to Anne. 'We'll send her, like her son, to Newgate in London to await trial before the Admiralty Court. She'll be charged as his accomplice in the smuggling.'

'Then, have you completed your business in Bristol?'

'Yes.' He pointed with his cane to a coach waiting in the street. 'I'll return to Bath now.'

'May I return with you?'

'My pleasure, Madame. We'll share the coach with the papers and the diary that we seized. Some of them are still in code and need to be deciphered.'

Anne was encouraged. 'Perhaps they'll shed light on the mystery of Thomas Parker's death.'

Late in the evening, Anne picked up Janice at the Woodhouse home. She had spent three nights and three days with the family. On the way back to the apartment on Queen Square, the young woman signed with unusual abandon. Happiness radiated from her face.

'Madame Woodhouse and I read London newspapers together, selecting stories to insert in the Woodhouse paper. I learned so much that I wrote a few small pieces myself.'

'I'm happy for you, Janice. You may have found a worthwhile path to pursue in life.'

Preparing for bed, the two women brushed each other's hair. Their conversation turned to the events in Bristol and Morland Court.

Anne remarked, 'Seth and his men are arrested and in prison, including the sailor with the cropped ear who attacked you and Jacob in Crescent Fields, You needn't worry any more.'

Janice stiffened. 'Where's Amelia? She's still at large and could arrange for my death.'

'It's true,' Anne admitted. 'No one has seen her since Sunday. Despite Burton's orders, she might have left Bath and is hiding in the area. We may catch her if she attempts to board a ship to America.'

Janice shivered. 'She might instead be hiding in Bath or, more likely, in London, where she has roots. It could be months before she's caught or reappears. I won't feel safe until she's in prison.'

MYSTERY UNRAVELLED

Bath, Thursday, 19 November–Monday, 23 November

After breakfast, Anne walked to Beverly's apartment. The maid showed her into the parlour. 'My mistress is still in bed, but I'll announce your arrival.'
While waiting, Anne wondered what her cousin had done

since they met last Saturday. Burton had questioned her again on Sunday, called her a suspect, and told her to remain in Bath until the investigation concluded. That could not have pleased her.

By this time, she was probably bored, irritated, and impatient. Still, she might draw consolation from the fact that her estranged husband was dead. She was now legally free to marry Jack Grimshaw and lead a conventional life. Nothing held her in Bath, or in England, except the investigation.

After a lengthy wait, Anne was called into Beverly's room. She sat at a tea table in a silk robe, a grumpy expression on her face. Breakfast was about to be served. She asked Anne to join her.

'This apartment has become a prison for me. I can't bear going out and meeting people. I imagine that they're talking behind my back. Everybody thinks I must have poisoned Thomas's drink. I had the opportunity to do it, and I had publicly declared that I hated him and wanted to be free of him.'

Anne understood her cousin's predicament but couldn't honestly think of any consoling or reassuring words to offer. Dick Burton wasn't finished with Beverly. Her future was problematic.

Nonetheless, Anne asked, 'What will you do when the investigation ends?'

'I'll return to London for a few days to confer with Barnstaple about my property. I need to know if my dowry is separate from my husband's estate. Or, could his creditors claim my money? When that's settled, I'll leave for Nice and Jack Grimshaw.'

Anne noticed that there was no place for Janice in Beverly's plans.

The weekend passed in the usual routine at the Pump Room, the Abbey Church, and the Assembly Rooms. Then, Monday morning, Burton called Anne to his office. His experts had produced a clean copy of the shorthand in Captain Judd's diary. He greeted Anne with a grim expression.

'Madame Cartier, read this passage in Judd's hand.'

The page was dated 12 November, the night of Thomas Parker's death.

Something went wrong tonight. As planned, Amelia put a strong dose of laudanum in Janice Parker's punch to cause a fatal asthmatic seizure. Her uncle died instead. 'What happened?' I asked Amelia afterwards. She said that Beverly must have switched the glass to Parker's place on the waiter's tray. She was at the drinks counter at the time and the only one near the tray. She must have seen what Amelia had done and seized the opportunity to get rid of her husband. Fortunately, Amelia was quick-witted. When she saw Parker die, she cried out that Beverly had poisoned him.

Burton gazed at Anne. 'So, who killed Thomas Parker?'

Anne replied, 'I doubt that Judd would lie to his diary. He and Amelia clearly conspired to kill Janice.'

'But,' Burton quickly added, 'their scheme misfired and they unwittingly enabled Madame Parker to kill her husband.'

Anne frowned. 'You draw too much from the diary. Amelia didn't say that she actually saw Beverly move the glasses.'

'True, but Beverly Parker alone was in a position to do so. Granted, the case against her isn't as strong as I would like. But it's sufficient to go to trial. No other potential suspect – neither Seth Judd nor Amelia – has nearly as strong a motive to kill Thomas Parker as his estranged wife has, nor as good an opportunity. I'll order constables to bring her to the Bath prison today. Then in a day or two, she'll be transferred to Taunton for trial.'

Burton had made up his mind. Further discussion was pointless. Anne left his office deeply distressed but not surprised. Burton usually judged correctly. Beverly *could* have done the deed, but Anne wasn't convinced that she had.

At noon, Anne returned to her apartment on Queen Square. Janice joined her a few minutes later. She had spent the morning observing Mr Woodhouse at work in the printing room. In the past few days she had learned enough to be helpful. Woodhouse had her lay out a brief advertisement and do a few other simple tasks.

Harriet's maid had prepared a meal for the two women – potato and leek soup and salad. She served it and left. That gave Anne an opportunity to repeat to Janice the gist of Dick Burton's argument for putting Beverly on trial. As she spoke, she studied Janice closely. Brow furrowed, eyes cast down, Janice seemed to grow troubled.

'Do you really think that Mr Burton will send her to prison?' Janice asked.

'Yes, though I doubt that he wants to, and he still appears uncertain. But the evidence against her seems strong enough to present to a court. Judd's diary was the last straw. It revealed that neither he nor Amelia wanted Parker dead. As your heir, he was key to their scheme to get your money. Also, Amelia placed Beverly alone in a position to switch glasses on the waiter's tray. In brief, according to Burton, Beverly is the only person with sufficient motive and opportunity to kill your uncle.'

'Should you warn her?'

'On the way home I stopped at her apartment. Her maid said that Beverly had left at midmorning and had not yet returned. I wrote a note alerting her.'

They had finished their meal and were about to leave the table when someone hammered on the front door. Anne went downstairs and found Beverly's maid, wild-eyed, her bonnet askew. She spoke between gasps for breath.

'The constables have come to take Mistress Beverly to prison. I'm supposed to bring her things there. They wouldn't say what she'd done, but they must think she killed her husband.' The maid curtsied and dashed off.

Anne rushed up the stairs. Janice had opened the door to the apartment and watched Anne from the landing.

'She's been arrested?' Janice signed.

'Yes,' Anne replied. 'Let's see what's happening.'

They ran the short distance to Milsom Street and arrived just as two sturdy constables brought Beverly out of the building. In the open doorway her maid wept. On the street dozens of passers-by stopped to gape.

A dazed expression on her face, Beverly looked straight ahead. Her elegant silk gown was nearly torn off her back – she must have resisted the officers. And she had lost her bonnet. Her wrists and feet were shackled. Pushed forward by the men, she could only shuffle towards the waiting coach.

Anne was aghast. 'Sir!' she said to the older of the officers, 'Must you manhandle this lady like a convicted felon? She's not guilty until an English jury says she is.'

'M'am,' he replied brusquely, 'she's charged with murder and put up a fight when we arrived. We'll take no chances with her.' Then he and his companion shoved Beverly into the coach and jumped in after her. At the crack of a whip, the coach lurched forward and rattled down the street.

For a long moment Anne and Janice stood in the street, bewildered. Then Anne said, 'We can do nothing here.'

They returned to the house on Queen Square and to their apartment. Numbed by seeing Beverly, humiliated and in despair, they sat at the table and stared at each other. Janice began to sign. 'I can't allow this to go on. You know how much I dislike Beverly. She has been a bad mother to me. I'm deaf because of her. But now I must admit that she could not have killed Thomas Parker.'

'If not her,' Anne asked, 'then who?'

Janice met Anne's eye and didn't flinch. 'I switched glasses with Parker when he was drunk and wasn't looking. At the time I didn't know that Amelia had poisoned mine, but I was afraid.'

'Why didn't you tell Mr Burton? Now he's made a serious, embarrassing mistake and given Beverly a dreadful shock.' Anne paused, gazing at Janice with reproach.

'I know that I should have told him, but I couldn't bring myself to do it. I suppose he's a good man but I feel that I can't trust him. Like everyone else I know, he's not concerned about me but about the law, or his reputation, or something else.'

'You could at least have told me.'

Tears came to the young woman's eyes. She reached across the table and took Anne's hand. 'You're the only person close to me whom I can trust. But in this case you were working with Mr Burton and Judge Williams, so I wasn't sure what to do. I thought if I did nothing the problem would just go away. No one would be arrested. Who would care? No one loved Parker or would miss him, least of all Amelia. She only wanted his money and prestige.'

Anne gave Janice a reassuring smile and a handkerchief to dry her tears. They sat still for a long minute.

Finally, Anne said, 'We'll have to speak to Mr Burton. That may be painful.'

At three in the afternoon, Burton's door was open. He was in his office, writing at his table. A pile of papers lay before him. His cane hung from a hook on the wall behind him. A thin autumnal light from the window bathed his pale, scarred face. He looked old and tired. Anne felt pity for him.

The arrival of Anne and Janice seemed to catch him by surprise. Disturbed in his work, he frowned momentarily, and then smiled a welcome. He gestured for them to sit. 'Give me a minute to check these documents. They will accompany Madame Beverly Parker to the court at Taunton. The charges against her must be correct as to the facts and clearly stated.'

This was a very awkward moment for Anne, and surely for Janice as well. Anne could only guess how Burton would react to the news they were bringing. At the least, he would feel as if he had been made a fool, sending the wrong person to trial. To reverse course would be hard for his professional pride.

'Well, that's it,' he said, putting the documents in a folder and sealing it. He looked up at the two women. 'What can I do for you?' His face reflected the satisfaction that he felt, having completed the tasks that the government and fate had set before him. He had put down a major smuggling oper- ation and had solved a murder – all within a few weeks.

Struggling to control her voice, Anne replied, 'We've come to tell you about a new development in the Parker case.'

Instantly, Burton sat up, alert and wary. 'What could that possibly be?'

Janice signed to Anne, who spoke for her. 'Janice switched glasses with Thomas Parker. Beverly is innocent.' Anne added, 'Janice is signing because her asthma makes it too difficult for her to speak. She is under great stress.'

Burton leaned back, stroking the scar on his cheek. His eyes were inscrutable. Finally, he asked Janice through tight lips, 'Why have you waited until now to tell me? I'll look like an idiot.'

'I was afraid to implicate myself until now, when an inno- cent person is about to be punished.'

Burton tilted his head and studied her silently. 'Tell me exactly what happened.'

Janice retold the story she had told Anne. The glass that Amelia had poisoned had reached Janice; Beverly had not diverted it to her estranged husband.

'Were you aware at the time that the punch in your glass was poisoned?'

'No, I thought only that it might be, so I was afraid to drink it. Someone had tried twice to kill me; the latest attempt was last Saturday. I was sure he would try again.'

'Why didn't you tell Parker that the drink might be poisoned?'

'My asthma bothered me so much that I could hardly breathe and couldn't speak. It acts up when I'm nervous or under pressure. Besides, neither Parker nor Amelia understood my signing. So what was the point of telling them? Even if they had understood, they would have thought that I was crazy and insisted that I drink the punch. I could prove that it was poisoned only if I drank and it killed me.'

For a minute, Burton gazed at the files on the writing table, occasionally shaking his head. Finally, he said to Anne, 'The story Janice has just told me is consistent with the passage in Judd's journal where Amelia says she had put poison in Janice's glass. As you reminded me, Amelia didn't actually see Madame Parker switch glasses. So, Janice's confession exculpates her. My next question is, does Janice incur any responsibility for her uncle's death?'

'I don't think so,' argued Anne. 'She couldn't know that the drink was poisoned.'

Burton addressed Janice. 'I too want to believe that you are innocent of murder. But two facts stand in the way: first, you didn't *have* to pass the glass to Parker; no one forced you to do it. You could have simply done nothing with the glass. Second, you passed the drink to Parker furtively. Why didn't you want him to know?'

'They were insisting that I drink the punch. Amelia claimed that since Parker had paid for it, I was ungrateful. So you see they left me with no other recourse but to deceive them.'

Burton appeared to hesitate. 'Our magistrates are supposed to avoid speculation. In this case, they might focus simply on the fact that Miss Parker furtively gave Parker a drink that proved to be poisoned. That would make her an accomplice to Amelia's crime.'

Anne raised a hand to caution him. 'It seems to me that Janice should be considered as no more than an accidental accomplice, like a coachman who happens to drive a murderer to or from the scene of his crime.'

'But suppose the coachman noticed a bulge in his passenger's pocket and a grim expression on his face . . .'

Burton sighed. 'I quibble, Madame. I believe you are correct. Janice is no longer a suspect. Now I must order Madame Parker to be released with an apology. She will be relieved, of course, but furious with me for the indignity of her arrest, the hours she spent in jail, and the shackles she wore. The constables treated her as a dangerous felon.'

Anne glanced towards Janice, 'She should be grateful to you for coming forward. Hopefully, you and she will put aside past differences.'

'Madame, I now see the irony in this case. Amelia un-intentionally killed her lover while attempting to kill Janice so that he could inherit her wealth.'

A courier entered the room. 'I've come from Bristol's mayor,' he said, handing over an envelope.

Burton glanced at the seal, broke it, and scanned the message. He smiled, then read aloud,

Late this morning one of our constables arrested Amelia Swan as she attempted to board a brig about to sail to New York. She had disguised herself as a middle-aged woman, wearing a wig and plain clothing. But our man has social ambitions and frequents the Pump Room in Bath. He recognized her exotic perfume. So she left for London and Newgate prison instead of America. Yours etc.

Burton turned to Janice. 'That's good news. The last serious threat to your life is on her way to prison. You may breathe easier and enjoy the rest of the season in Bath without fear.'

EPILOGUE

Paris, Monday, 1 March 1790

L ate in the afternoon, rain beat against the windows of the provost's residence on Rue St Honoré. Anne Cartier received a letter from Dick Burton, dated Saturday, 20 February, and dictated to a scribe. He reported that the Admiralty's court, ten days earlier, had convicted Captain Judd and Amelia Swan of murder and conspiracy to murder as well as aggravated smuggling. The court sentenced them to be hanged.

> The sentence was carried out a week later. As I dictate these lines, I've been told that Madame Judd has hanged herself in Newgate prison. Nate Taylor received clemency in consideration of his testimony against Judd. The court sent him and the cropped-eared sailor and his companion to Botany Bay for life. The steward, Amos Jones, received seven years there. This new prison colony lies on the other side of the globe in south-eastern Australia. We are now sending hundreds of convicts there every year. Isaac Grimes was cleared of complicity in Judd's crime, and received a reward for helping to convict him. He was present when his mother died in the Bristol Infirmary. She has been decently buried. Grimes and his wife will soon sail to Charleston in the United States. I thank you, Madame Cartier, for your part in bringing justice to the West Country. You made my work there enjoyable as well as successful.
>
> Gratefully yours,
> Burton

Anne laid the letter on the table. To her surprise she felt sad that Seth and Amelia were hanged. Their talents could have been put to good use in Australia.

She glanced at Burton's letter. Other episodes from Bath now came to mind. In December, Beverly Parker had stopped in Paris for a couple of days en route to Nice and Jack Grimshaw. Anne noticed that her cousin seemed intent on learning from her mistakes, especially in regard to Janice. The young woman's confession to Burton had deeply touched her and stirred up regrets for her past failures in raising her.

Janice Parker remained in Bath with the Woodhouse family. David Woodhouse became her guardian. Harriet Ware moved to London to sing in Covent Garden and to be near Peter Cartier. André Cartier was back at work in his Hampstead shop, rejuvenated by his adventure in Bath.

AUTHOR'S NOTE

The Parker estate, Morland Court, is a lightly fictionalized version of Clevedon Court, a 700-year-old manor house near Bristol. It is today a property of the National Trust. I've situated Morland Court a few miles closer to the Bristol Channel.

The full title of the Assembly Rooms in Bath is the Upper or New Assembly Rooms. At the time of this story there was also a Lower or Old Assembly Rooms located behind the Abbey Church.

For the condition of English women in the early modern period, read Anne Laurence, *Women in England, 1500–1760: A Social History* (New York, 1994). See pp. 227–235 for women and their property rights, or the lack thereof. There was little change in either law or custom by 1789.

Madge Dresser, *Slavery Obscured: The Social History of the Slave Trade in an English Provincial Port [Bristol]* (London, 2001) is a readable account of that evil trade and the efforts of the Quakers and other reformers to abolish it.

For a general survey of smuggling in Britain, read Neville Williams, *Contraband Cargoes: Seven Centuries of Smuggling* (London, 1959). Richard Platt's *Smuggling in the British Isles: A History* (Stroud, UK, Tempus, 2006) is a popular description of smugglers and their associates. For the government's fight against smuggling, see E.K. Chatterton, *King's Cutters and Smugglers, 1700–1855* (New York, 1971).

The suppression of smuggling was chiefly the responsibility of the Board of Excise and the Board of Customs, two departments of the British government's Exchequer or Treasury. Customs officers attempted to stop the smugglers at sea and on the coast. Excise officers tried to suppress the inland trade in smuggled or unlicensed goods. Their duties overlapped and both services used cutters.

These revenue services were loathed and feared in eighteenth-century Britain as threats to individual liberty. Their officers brought serious criminal cases, not to local authorities but to the Admiralty in London, which administered a body of law distinct from the Common Law. Admiralty magistrates followed authoritarian principles and procedures drawn from ancient Roman law. For example, the magistrates heard criminal cases, such as the fictitious murders of Oliver Parker and his wife, without juries.

362638

BLAYNEY		
CANOW.		
COWRA		
FORBES		
MANILDRA		
ORANGE	7/09	
MOLONG		